THE HIDDEN WARRIOR

# DRAGON RISING

M. LYNN

Cover by Covers by Combs
Editing by Melissa A. Craven

*For the authors who keep me writing.*

# NOTE FROM THE AUTHOR

Mulan is one of the greatest stories that has been told since long before Disney wrote catchy tunes. It stems from a culture that is rich and beautiful in its history, a culture many know little about. I've never had as much fun researching for a book as I did this one, and I'm still not perfect in my knowledge. I doubt I ever will be.

This is one of the many reasons Dragon Rising is set in the fictional world of Piao rather than a reimagined China. The culture woven through this book is largely Chinese as are the names and some of the terms, but other parts have been altered in order to fit the story and help it make more sense to a vast majority of readers.

If you have experience with the Chinese language, you will notice the naming structures in this book have been changed and a few of the consonants existing in certain words I have written are not part of the language.

Please forgive the adaptations as multiple cultures and mindsets meld to create a Piao that I hope is half as rich in culture as China.

Also, please forgive the addition of live dragons. Those did not exist in ancient China. At least, I don't think they did <;

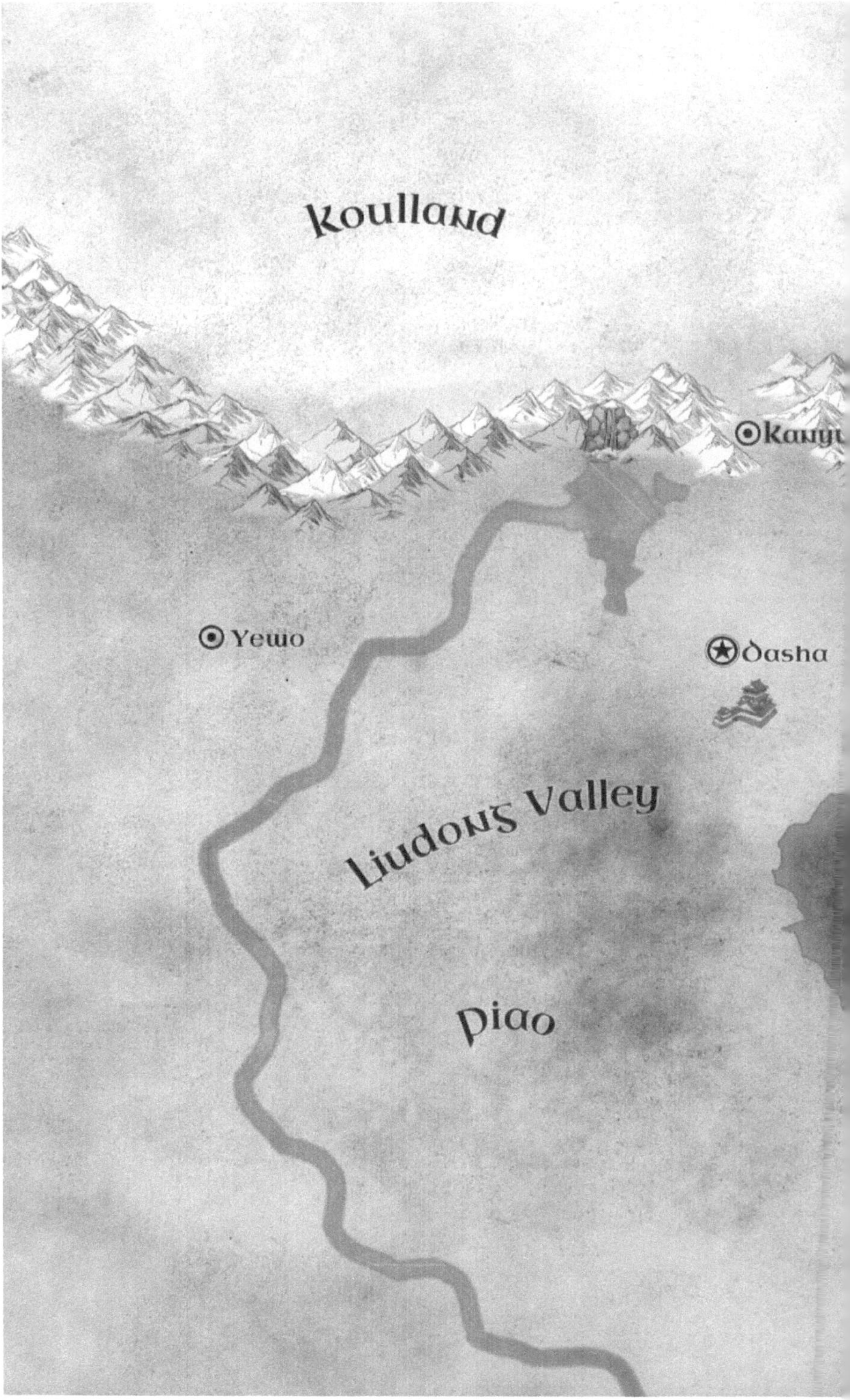

Koulland

Yewo

Dasha

Liudong Valley

Piao

Lóng bǎolěi
Zhouchang

# CHAPTER 1

Hua

Hua Minglan didn't fear death.

At least not hers.

What scared her was watching the people she loved suffer for nothing more than the history in their blood. Because as descendants of the last Dragon Lords of Piao, the Minglans had dragon blood.

The capitol city wasn't a welcome place for anyone suspected of harboring the ancient power inside them. No dragon had been seen in Piao in a hundred years, yet the legends called their blood royal. It was said those with dragon blood were fit to sit on the emperor's gilded throne.

It was also a death sentence. The Wei dynasty had ruled Piao for many generations, and it was the emperor's duty to hunt down any threat to his power.

Which brought them to the festival of the dragon, a celebration that hadn't existed in more than five years —not since the last round of executions took place under the stars with paper dragons dancing through the square.

Her father tightened his grip on her arm as they entered the city on foot and dropped his voice. "You must be prepared, Hua. It is never a good thing for anyone to be called to the dragon festival." After receiving a summons from the emperor, her father packed Hua and her mother up and the three of them made the five-day journey from Zhouchang to Dasha, leaving her little brother and grandmother behind.

Running a hand down her side, Hua felt for the dagger her father insisted she hide beneath the folds of her silk robe. The feel of the curved hilt gave her some sense of calm, of peace.

Hua Minglan wasn't like normal girls. Most girls her age spent their time painting their faces and dreaming of the husbands their fathers would choose for them.

Hua preferred traipsing through the woods with a bow on her back. She'd trained in weapons since she was young because her father wanted her to be able to protect herself no matter who came for her.

Unlike her older sister, Luna, who'd refused to be anything other than the perfect Piao woman. When the new emperor chose her for one of his consorts, she'd basked in the honor. Their mother gushed about the opportunity.

Only Hua and her father knew what it could mean.

Only they wondered if the emperor somehow knew of the history of their family. That they'd changed their family name to separate themselves from any knowledge of dragon blood after her grandfather was executed long before she was born.

"Hua." Gen Minglan wasn't a man to be ignored. He'd been a general during the civil war, fighting for the same man who killed his father. "I want you to find your sister."

"You mean..." She looked up at him. "I can go off by myself?"

"You can take care of yourself."

"No," her mother cut in. "It isn't proper for a young lady to be unaccompanied."

"Fa." Her father sighed. "Hua is capable. She can bring Luna into the open where we may be allowed to speak with her. We may not be able to get close to Luna otherwise, especially if suspicion has fallen onto us. I just need to know." Thickness coated his words. "We've had no word of Luna since she was taken from us. This is our first chance. I just want Hua to find out if our daughter is okay."

Her mother's shoulders dropped, and Hua knew she'd argue no more. Her father pressed a dagger into her palm, smaller than the one she had on her, but no less deadly. "Be safe, Hua. We will meet you near the market side of the square." He kissed her forehead.

Hua walked across the dark square in front of the

royal palace, lit only by a large fire in the center of the square, and the lanterns strung between the two-story buildings.

When Luna was chosen as consort, the emperor claimed it was in recognition of Gen Minglan's military service. He'd risen from nothing to lead the emperor's men.

Hua knew so little of the new emperor. He was the younger son of one of the old emperor's lesser consorts—not the empress. Did he mistreat her sister? Did he accuse her of having the dragon blood?

Very few people in Piao even knew what it meant to have the blood anymore. No dragon had risen in so long, the people forgot. They saw it as a curse worthy of execution more than a blessing. Hua couldn't say she disagreed with them about the curse part.

Glancing back at her parents, she saw her father speaking to a younger man, a strained smile on his face. She wondered if his limp bothered him or if it was the company of the man he spoke to.

Now that Luna was a part of the emperor's court, the family's status improved, making Hua a desirable match. She knew she couldn't avoid it forever. Her father wanted to keep her close, to protect her, but he wouldn't be around forever.

She folded her arms across the long silk emerald robe she wore. Gold threading showed her rise in desirability, but it also made her uncomfortable.

Her long, shimmering black hair hung loose, announcing her marriage eligibility to each person she passed. That by tying themselves to her, they too could enjoy status.

Hua sighed, feeling too many eyes on her. Before her father left for war six years ago, they'd been simple farmers living in Zhouchang, a province east of the Liudong River.

He'd returned a bit broken but honored as well. Then he'd gone back to his simple ways and allowed Luna to leave them.

Hua didn't want to hate the emperor for taking her sister, for being a constant threat to their family. She didn't want to feel anything about it at all. But she missed her best friend.

A throat cleared, and Hua jerked her head up, realizing she hadn't taken notice of where she was walking and almost collided with the man himself.

Emperor Bo Xu Wei stood with a bemused expression on his handsome face and a retinue of guards and servants following behind him.

Hua's cheeks flamed. She hid the dagger behind her back. Showing it in the emperor's presence would mean instant death. Her eyes flicked to the daos carried by the guards. "Uh, your Imperial Majesty." She curtsied the way her father taught her before lifting her eyes to his.

Emperor Bo Xu was a young man a little older than Hua's eighteen years. He'd been the supreme ruler of Piao for only two years.

Intense mahogany eyes stared back at her. "Are you okay?" He tilted his head to the side.

The noises from the crowd pushed in at Hua, suffocating her, drowning her. It was too much. The shy girl from the small village wasn't meant to be around people. She missed her dog, Chichi, and the quiet lands stretching in the distance behind her home.

"I'm…" She couldn't breathe. Embarrassment fought with panic as she tried to claw her way to the surface of her emotions. How could she break down in front of the emperor? His people stared at her as if she were nothing more than a serf with no business talking to such a great man.

And that was exactly how she felt.

Heat burned up her skin, cooling instantly as a hand gripped her elbow. Hua turned her head to find Luna standing at her side. She didn't know when her sister arrived, but she didn't care.

"Luna," she choked out.

"Breathe, Hua. Just breathe." She turned to the emperor and dropped into a much more graceful curtsy than Hua's. "I am deeply sorry, your Imperial Majesty. My sister has a mental deficiency."

Hua choked on a protest, wanting to refute her sister's false words, but Luna elbowed her.

Sympathy entered the emperor's gaze. "I am sorry to hear that, Luna. Please send my best wishes to your family." He turned without another word and led his long train of followers to accost some other unsuspecting citizens.

Hua's breathing calmed, and she took the chance to notice the people hanging back, watching them. As consort, Luna was afforded a host of servants—women and eunuchs only. Luna seemed to forget they were there as she gripped Hua's arm tighter and dragged her away.

"Ow," Hua hissed. "I don't have a mental deficiency."

Luna pulled her between two buildings where the shadows hid them. "If you embarrass me in front of the emperor again, you'll have physical deficiencies."

"That's not the way a lady of the court should speak." Hua rubbed her arm.

Both girls stood silent for only a moment longer before Luna threw her arms around Hua. "I've been searching for you since the festival began."

Hua sank into her sister's embrace. She hadn't seen her in more than a year. "I missed you."

Luna pulled back, sparing a quick glance for her servants who stood nearby and dropped her voice so they couldn't hear. "You shouldn't have wandered away from Father. It isn't safe for you here in Dasha."

"We were summoned," she hissed. "The emperor probably has people seeking Father to arrest him now."

A laugh burst free of Luna, and she covered her mouth. "I'm sorry. I didn't think. I never considered what the summons would mean to Father. The emperor didn't request your presence. I did."

"But he signed it."

"As a favor to me. I'm a consort, Hua. I'm supposed to cut ties to my family. He saw how much I missed you and offered to help."

"Wha-why would he do that?"

She leveled Hua with a stare. "He isn't his father.

There hasn't been a single execution of the blooded since he came to power."

"It's only a matter of time. I know our histories, Luna. The emperors always seek out those they see as threats to their power."

"Yes, but just because someone has dragon blood does not mean they are a threat. The dragons abandoned Piao long ago."

She was right, of course. Having the blood meant one was susceptible to a dragon living inside them. It didn't mean the dragon was already there.

She blew out a breath and collapsed back against the wall. "Father says I need to marry. For protection."

Luna's lips drew down. "Hua." Her sigh sounded so much like their mother's it had Hua drawing back. "It's time. You know that."

Most of the girls Hua knew in the village at home chattered with non-stop excitement about moving away from their homes to create families of their own.

But Hua wasn't like them. She didn't want to leave her parents or her younger brother. She wanted Luna to return, but nothing remained the same no matter how hard she held on.

"Come on." Luna took her hand. "Would you like to meet some of the princes and princesses?"

Hua wanted to say no. The royal family held no interest for her, especially knowing they'd want her dead if they knew the truth.

The emperor's father once had twelve consorts. Ten of them bore children, some more than one. Bo Xu Wei was not the eldest or even the son of the empress, but he was the one his father chose to succeed him.

Unlike his father, Bo Xu Wei only selected four consorts and had yet to hold a ceremony to choose the empress.

Luna introduced Hua to so many people she would never remember all their names. Their eyes did not alight in interest as the emperor's had. When they looked at her, she wondered if they compared her to her elegant sister beside her. Luna's hair, even longer than Hua's, was parted in the middle and wrapped in a knot at the nape of her neck.

Her deep purple robe spoke of wealth and status with its long, square sleeves, and elaborate belt. She spoke with confidence and moved with grace.

Hua never realized just how much her sister would fit the role she was chosen for. She found herself tuning out the conversations and listening to the soft music nearby instead. Two flutists played a sweet melody, punctuated by the light ringing of the bells hanging from their instruments. The steady beat of the hide-covered drums echoed the rhythm of Hua's heartbeat.

The warm air of an autumn night had sweat dotting across her brow. She should have been worried about the state of the crushed pearl powder her mother applied to her face, but that would have required energy.

"Hua." Her mother's bark snapped her out of the daze.

She turned to find her parents crossing the square

toward them. Fa Minglan was a small woman engulfed by her yellow robe. She wore her hair like Luna's, but a less kind expression flashed across her face.

"You found your sister." Her mother crossed her arms.

Finishing her conversation and wishing the people well, Luna turned to her parents with a smile. "Mama." She rushed into their mother's arms before hugging their father as well.

"Why didn't you bring Ru?" Luna asked, her lips forming a pout. "I'd have liked to see my brother."

Their father smiled indulgently. "It was a five-day journey for us to reach Dasha. Ru is only four years old. We had to leave him with my mother."

Luna's shoulders slumped.

Their mother eyed her servants lingering next to them. "I am glad you're happy, Luna." She didn't bother to actually ask if Luna was happy. She only assumed.

"Are you safe?" their father asked.

From the smile spreading across Luna's face, Hua knew the answer to that. "This is… more than I could have imagined." She reached for Hua's hand and squeezed.

A uniformed man approached, and all Hua could do was stare. Clear eyes found her, and a smile lit up the stranger's beautiful face. He ran a hand down the front of his pressed military uniform, pushing any lingering wrinkles from the fabric, before turning to her father and bowing. "Gen Minglan."

Hua's father stared for a moment before recognition lit in his eyes. "Luca Kai. I haven't seen you since you were a teenager."

He laughed. "I've done some growing up since then."

"Your father told me you earned yourself a military rank."

"I imagine he told you a lot about me." He turned his smile on Hua's mother. "Taitai Minglan. It is a pleasure."

"General." She smiled.

Luna and Hua exchanged a suspicious look. Calling their mother taitai was a sign of respect, but also a way to earn her favor, and it wasn't often their mother softened her countenance.

Hua's father put a hand on her back and pulled her forward. "Hua, this is General Luca Kai. His father and I are old friends."

Luca bowed. "You are as beautiful as I've been led to believe, Hua Minglan."

She couldn't stop the scowl from forming on her face. "Why would you need to be told of my looks?"

Her mother clucked her tongue in disapproval, but Luca's grin widened. "I look forward to knowing you."

"Too bad you won't get the chance." She crossed her arms over her chest.

"Hua," her father snapped, leaning close. "Luca's father and I have spoken of arrangements."

"Arrangements?" She didn't like the sound of that.

"He is a suitable suitor who can provide certain... protections."

Hua froze. Suitor? Her gaze slid over the man before her. Tall. Lean muscles. Smug grin.

"He has a good position in the emperor's army, and I trust his family."

Luca nodded. "Second in command to General Li himself."

General Li? Hua knew the stories of the young general who'd already made a name for himself. They spoke of him in the villages in hushed tones. He was said to have an unrivaled ruthlessness.

But she refused to fear this man her father wanted to tie her to. Lifting her chin, she met his eyes. "No matter what my parents decide, I will marry you if I deem you are worthy."

Her mother gasped, but to her relief, Luca laughed. "As you wish. In the coming weeks, I will leave with General Li on a march to the border. May I write to you while I'm away?"

"You may."

He shook her father's hand once more and bowed to her before sauntering away. Hua watched him for a moment before turning hard eyes on her parents. They met her gaze. It was well within their rights to ambush her this way and negotiate her future with anyone they pleased.

That didn't mean she'd make it easy on them.

Luna, ever the peacemaker, stepped in. "Can Hua spend the rest of the festival with me? I promise she'll be safe." She gestured to two of her eunuchs and the daos that hung at their waists.

Fa opened her mouth to say something, but Gen

cut her off. "Yes. We have some business to attend to in the meantime."

Their father couldn't go anywhere without trying to make deals for the yields of their crops, even when a threat hung over his head. Everyone within a week's journey of Dasha was at the festival. It was the best place for negotiations and provided Hua the escape she needed.

Luna pulled Hua away from their parents and giggled like a girl much younger than her twenty years. "Come with me."

She led her weaving through the crowd toward a row of columns near the enormous palace steps. The palace sat on a raised platform faced with dark stone. Almost black wooden walls rose toward a sloped tile roof. Balconies spanned the upper floors. Hua had never seen an emperor's speech before, but she could imagine the young emperor standing high above the crowd, his enchanting eyes peering over them.

Luna directed Hua through an open plaza to the side of the steps where two stone pillars sat, dragons snaking up their sides as if they could protect the city.

Luna's servants gave them a bit of space but stayed within eyesight. Luna sat with her back against the pillar and her body shielded from view. Hua followed suit. Someone would have to know they were there in order to find them.

"I can't believe they let me walk into that." Hua groaned.

"Walk into what?" Luna lifted her face, settling her

eyes on the stars above as her voice took on a wistful tone. "That man was perfect."

"For you, maybe."

"Hua, when will you start to take your future seriously? You cannot live with Mother and Father your entire life. When next spring comes, you'll be of age to leave home. And did you even see that Luca man? If I wasn't pledged to the emperor, I'd be insanely jealous. And a soldier! Is there anything more attractive?"

Hua covered her face with her hands so her sister couldn't see her burning cheeks. "He was okay." In truth, men were a mystery to her. Even before becoming a consort, her sister knew how to speak to them, how to make them fall in love with her, a skill Hua could never hope to master.

"If father trusts him, then so do I. Our lives will never be peaceful, Hua. Not with the threat of discovery hanging over us."

"Can we talk about something else?" She lowered her hands. "Please?"

Luna smiled, her white teeth flashing in the night. "I love festivals."

Hua snorted. For reasons of safety, she'd never been to a festival or even visited the capital before. And now that she had, all she wanted was to go home to her wide-open fields. She smoothed her robe around her legs, concealing the pants underneath.

Luna's lips tipped up into a smile. "Rest easy, Hua. You're not in danger here. I know father has trained you your entire life to look over your shoulder for enemies, but maybe it's time you tried to be normal." She laughed. "Then you can be happy too."

Sometimes her sister was ridiculous. What was normal? Falling all over yourself to look perfect and act like everyone else?

"I think I'm in love with the emperor." Luna's voice was so soft Hua, thought she'd misheard her.

"You're not," Hua scoffed.

"What would you know?" she snapped. "I'm his favored consort."

"Luna, don't be ridiculous. The emperor will choose an empress soon, and it'll be someone with a much higher status than the daughter of the Minglans of Zhouchang, a family with little history because we didn't exist before father created the name." Luna was the only consort whose father held no title. Sure, there would be a ceremony and a competition to choose the empress, but the daughter of an army general turned farmer would never be allowed to win.

Luna huffed. "It isn't up to the emperor to choose. I will carve my golden statue and prove that I have heaven's mandate to be the empress just as Bo Xu has it to be the emperor. He wasn't the oldest nor the strongest of the old emperor's children, yet his father recognized heaven choosing him."

Hua hadn't seen her sister in so long and didn't want to make her mad on their one night together. She wasn't a fighter and wouldn't win an argument with Luna. "I hope you're right."

Luna leaned her head on Hua's shoulder. "Can I tell you a secret?"

Hua nodded. "You've always been able to."

"I'm pregnant." Her smile widened. "I will have the first of the emperor's children."

A child of the emperor with dragon blood? Hua wanted to be happy for her sister. She didn't want to be the girl who questioned everything. But what kind of life would Luna have when she had to keep such a secret from the people she supposedly loved? If she told the emperor of their child's blood, he'd know about the rest of the Minglans and have no choice but to hunt them down just like the emperors before him. Dragon blood was a direct threat to their power. It was said to be royal, giving a person the right to rule.

Hua wanted better for the sister she loved more than life itself.

But honesty wasn't what her sister needed in that moment. Hua brushed a hand over Luna's soft hair. "I love you, Jiejie." She smiled at the old term for older sister.

Her joyful laugh filled the night around them. "And I love you, Meimei." Little sister. They'd been calling each other by those terms since they knew how to talk, and there was a comfort in the familiarity.

They sat in silence for a long while, just enjoying being around each other again. They were young, and that night felt like the beginning of their lives. Luna would be a mother to a prince, and who knew where Hua was headed? Into a marriage with the handsome general?

The sisters weren't ready to be separated yet.

It wasn't until shouting from the square reached

their sanctuary that Luna sat up. Her servants ran toward them. The two men had their daos drawn.

"Madam," one of the women yelled. "There has been an attack."

"An attack?" Luna shot to her feet.

"It's the Kou."

The name sent a chill through Hua. Nomads to the north of Piao, the Kou had been terrorizing the border for a decade, forcing a mass migration of people to the central cities.

And now they'd come to Dasha. Luna and Hua huddled together as they rounded the pillars, searching for any sign of the attack. Shadows ran the lengths of the buildings towering over the square where only moments before, the people of Piao had been celebrating.

Now, the citizens scrambled for cover as arrows rained down from above.

"We need to make it up the palace steps," one of the eunuchs said. "We have no choice but to run."

"But Hua…" Luna's panicked eyes met hers. Those not of the court could not enter the palace.

"She will have to find her own way to safety." The man kept his eyes trained on the archers. "Consort Luna is my only concern."

Luna shook her head violently, and Hua gripped her hands. "I can't leave you."

"Yes, you can." Hua tried to infuse acceptance into her gaze. All she wanted was her sister to be safe. The only place for that was the palace. A tear leaked from Hua's eyes. "I need to find Mama and Ba. I also need you to be safe. Promise me as soon as you start running, you won't look back."

When Luna didn't say anything, Hua gripped her tighter. "Promise me!"

Tears streamed down Luna's face. "Yes." She squeezed her eyes tight. "I promise."

Hua released her. "Go." She looked to the eunuchs and serving girls. "Get her to that palace."

Footsteps sounded against the stone as the crowd continued to run, ducking into buildings that would be no use as the Kou came down from their perches on high to slaughter them all. Hua's hands shook as she watched Luna's people form up around her. With one final glance, Luna started to run.

She took the steps two at a time, holding the ends of her robe up to prevent herself from tripping. Her ebony hair broke free of her knot and flew about her face.

Hua couldn't move from her place until Luna was safe inside the palace. She watched her grow smaller and smaller as she neared the palace entryway.

It happened in slow motion. A crossbow bolt sailed through the air, ripping through Hua's life, as it reached its intended target.

Luna's body jerked back, frozen in time for only a moment, before slamming into the stone, her chin bouncing off a step.

Her servants scrambled to check on her, to see if she still lived.

But Hua knew the moment her sister's heart

stopped beating because it matched the stillness within her own chest.

An arrow flew through the air near Hua as she sprinted up the steps. Luna's servants left her, running for their own lives.

Hua couldn't blame them for their self-preservation, but she also couldn't leave her sister. Luna was her everything, her best friend. She collapsed to the ground next to her body, knowing when she felt for a pulse, there would be no beat against her finger.

Tears didn't come because it wasn't real. It couldn't be.

Luna was larger than life. She was the joy of an everyday existence, happy and free. She loved and didn't hold back. Not like Hua.

Luna deserved to live.

Hua couldn't focus on anything other than the chasm opening inside her as she cradled her sister's head in her lap. People ran by, taking no notice of the girl frozen in grief or the blood dripping down the steps.

A roar sounded in the distant spaces of her mind as warriors clad in lacquered leather armor cut through the crowd.

The emperor's forces ran out to meet them, daos crashing against halberds. Steal glinted in the silver moonlight, reflecting it back into the sky as if this kind of world deserved no light. A world without Luna. A world where even the center of Piao was vulnerable to a brutal attack.

"No."

Hua recognized the voice of the emperor as his guards tried to force him up the steps.

"We need to get you to safety," one of them yelled back over the din of battle.

Hua lifted her face, wanting to see the man her sister claimed to love. Did he even love her? He'd had a claim on her in life, but in death, she didn't deserve anyone who wouldn't trade places with her.

He froze, catching sight of her, his eyes drifting to Luna. A cry broke free of his lips, and the young man, the most powerful in Piao, did what Hua could not. He wept.

"My Luna," he cried.

Did he know she'd carried his child? Had she told him?

Hua used her body to shield Luna from the man who'd done this to her. He'd brought her here. He'd chosen her. She should have married a simple man and been safe in the village not far from her family. Instead, she'd abandoned them for the prestige promised to her.

Was death prestige enough, she wondered. Did it mean Luna earned her place?

Hua narrowed her eyes as the emperor continued his tortured wailing. His guards forced him up the steps and managed to get to the palace safely.

A woman's cry broke Hua out of her daze. "Mama." She knew it wasn't her mother, but somewhere out there, her parents ran from the same danger. "Ba." She jumped to her feet just as a body collided with hers, sending her rolling down the final steps.

A volley of arrows sailed toward the spot she'd been only moments before. The man, her savior, landed next to her with a thud.

She wanted to thank him, but the words sat cold in her throat.

As arrows fell down around her, one flew right for her chest. It struck her right above her heart but did not pierce her skin. She cried out, expecting to feel it tear through her flesh. Instead, it clattered to the ground. Her entire body froze as she stared down at the tiny hole in her robe, a hole made by an arrowhead.

It wasn't possible.

The man who'd tackled her glanced back at her. Did he see that, or was she hallucinating in her grief? He pushed his muscled frame up to his feet. "Come." He grabbed her arm and pulled her behind the pillars. It was the same place she'd watched her sister fall.

Tears hung in her lashes, not daring to fall. How was any of this possible? She shouldn't be standing there. The arrow should have sent her into the next life to join Luna.

"Are you trying to get yourself killed?" the man asked, his voice unkind as he peered around the pillars. His dao hung in a scabbard at his waist. The single-edged sword was a warrior's weapon.

But he wore no uniform. Instead, his robe hung to his knees with trousers appearing underneath.

What would he say if he'd seen that arrow?

"I have to find my baba and mama." She breathed heavily, trying to stop the images of her death flying toward her through the sky.

The man threw a scowl over his shoulder. "You need to stay here and let Piao's warriors handle this fight. I should be out there, but my brother would be disappointed if I left some... girl... to fend for herself."

Hua didn't ask who his brother was. She didn't ask his name. None of that mattered. Nothing mattered. Not anymore.

The festival of dragons had turned into a bloody affair, and she wasn't sure Piao would ever be the same.

She sure wouldn't.

Maybe she'd imagined it in her grief over losing Luna. That was the only explanation.

A Kou warrior dropped to the ground in front of their hiding place, a halberd stuck in the back of his head. One of the emperor's men pulled the battle ax free without so much as a second glance at the hulking brute he'd felled.

The Kou were unlike any foe of Piao's. Brutal and strong, they hacked their way through countries. They'd been trying to take everything Piao had for a decade. They didn't want to settle among the Piao folk, only conquer them and control the trading routes along the Liudong River to the sea.

Hua didn't know when the fear left her. Maybe it was about the time she wished she could join her sister and stay with her forever. Maybe it was when she faced her own end. But the fight didn't scare her.

A Kou man caught sight of them and ran their way. Hua's savior—as she called him—prepared to meet the charge, and Hua took the opportunity to run past them both, dodging out of the way of the attacker's long spear.

Neither of them could follow her as they fought each other. Out in the square, chaos reigned supreme. Dead bodies littered the ground, blood coating the stones. Dasha would never be free of these memories. No matter what happened this night, the blood would never wash away.

She twisted out of the way of another attacker and darted through the crowd of swarming warriors intent on killing each other. The soldier she met briefly with her father—Luca-- ran past her, throwing himself against the enemies, trying to break them. Hua kept running.

Ordinary citizens had already either found places to hide, or they were dead.

She refused to believe her parents left her too.

"Hua," someone called to her.

Hua turned on her heel. A man waved her forward. She recognized him as a friend of her father's but couldn't recall his name. Sprinting toward him, she didn't wait until she reached him to speak. "Have you seen them?"

He didn't get a chance to answer her because her father appeared at the window, and she ran into the shop, launching herself into his arms. "Ba."

He squeezed her as if he'd never thought he'd see her again. "My dear girl."

"Where's Mama?" she asked.

He pulled her farther into the shop to get out of sight. "She's here. We're both okay."

None of them were okay. Their central city was attacked. People died. Yes, the emperor's forces would fight them off. They were the best-trained army in the world, and the Kou didn't stand a chance.

But still, it would never be okay again.

She followed her father down a staircase into the back, where more people than she could count huddled together, flinching at every sound. Her mama jumped up when she saw them, climbing over people to reach her daughter.

She put a hand on each shoulder, checking her over.

Hua should have told her she wasn't injured, that her body was fine. But how could her body be fine when her insides felt hollow? How could it be fine when she'd felt the sharp point of an arrow against her skin?

"Luna's dead." She spoke so quietly at first no one heard her.

Her Ba's brow creased.

Hua cleared her throat, knowing how empty her voice sounded. "Luna… she's… she died."

It took a moment for the realization to sink into her parents. Their eldest daughter would never smile at them again. She'd never dance or laugh until her sides hurt.

Their faces fell, slowly at first, and then it was as if they collapsed in on themselves. She'd never seen her mother cry before and couldn't take her eyes from the moisture coating her cheeks. Her father gathered them both to him, only releasing them when a loud bang sounded above.

For the first time, Hua looked out over the faces in the room. These people were witnesses to the Minglans' grief, to their heart-wrenching agony.

Hua broke away from her parents and found a spot in the far corner to curl in on herself and pretend there was something, anything, she could do to fix her family.

# CHAPTER 2

Jian

Jian Li was many things. Brother to a powerful man. Unmatched warrior. And loyal general.

General Altan of the Kou was few of those things. Talented with the dao, he had loyalty to no one but himself.

When Jian saw him enter the bloody square, stepping over bodies of the people who'd be alive if it wasn't for the Kou, he could see little else. For some unknown reason, he'd been searching for the girl who ran from his protection. A girl he could have sworn took an arrow to the chest. But that wasn't possible. In the chaos, his eyes played tricks on him.

The girl cared little for herself as she bent over the fallen woman Jian recognized as one of the emperor's consorts. Then he saved her, got her to a place she could hide from the foreign attack, and she'd run.

He shook his head, waiting for his opening. His warriors pushed the invaders back to the perimeter of the square away from the palace. That was the goal. Protect the emperor at all costs, no matter who else they couldn't save.

But Jian knew Emperor Bo Xu Wei, and Bo wouldn't have approved of the strategy that left the citizens of Dasha vulnerable.

Fire rose toward the sky, angry red flames dancing as they ravaged buildings full of those who'd hidden in them.

Something had to be done.

General Altan was a large man with wide, hulking shoulders hunched forward. A prominent brow jutted out above dark eyes. He rubbed his pointed chin as he surveyed the remaining Kou soldiers atop the houses with bows and crossbows aimed down below.

Jian found a discarded shield on the ground near a fallen warrior. Crossbow bolts could still pierce the metal, but they wouldn't reach his skin.

He leapt over a mass of bodies, his feet landing in a puddle of blood that splashed up his robes. He should have known better than to think he could take a night away from his scaled armor.

Dao raised in one hand, he charged, prepared to meet the full might of Altan as he had many times before.

He was halfway across the square when he heard it. A horn. The Kou's signal to retreat. Altan finally saw him, his lips curving up into a wicked grin for just a moment before running forward, ignoring the signal to retreat.

"Jian Li." His lip curled. "I was hoping to see you here."

The accented words fell on Jian, reminding him of a time when he'd spoke to Batukhan Altan every day. They'd been friends almost… if you discounted the fact that Jian was a spy lying to everyone he knew in Koulland.

Except for her… Altan's sister. She'd known exactly who he was and loved him enough to leave with him. At least she had tried.

There was no time for remembering the past.

"Are you going to fight me?" Jian gripped his dao, preparing for an attack. In another life, the man before him would have been on his side. They both mourned the same woman. But they blamed each other for her death.

Altan flicked his eyes to his retreating men. "Not today, Li. This attack was a warning. The Kou grow in strength. Soon, Piao will not be able to stand against us. We are coming for you." His voice dropped. "And I will make you pay for what you did to her."

If his country wasn't in danger, Jian would let him. Maybe he deserved punishment. She was dead, and here he stood, still unable to save her.

Was that why he'd saved the girl?

Altan gave him one final long look before making

for the nearest horse and launching himself into the saddle.

Jian breathed heavily as the Kou slipped back into the darkness from which they'd come, shadows in the night.

"One day," he promised General Altan's retreating form. "One day, you and I will finish this."

He surveyed the damage, sadness growing inside him as he watched his warriors go from fighting the Kou to pulling people from burning buildings. They arrived back in the square, coughing and choking on the billowing smoke.

It would be a long time before they had numbers of the dead, but Jian already knew it would be more than Piao could bear. These scars would never heal.

The attack lasted only hours, yet it felt like years had passed. Jian's eyes found the girl he'd saved, the one who shouldn't still be standing, as she stumbled from a building to his left, clutching two others who looked like her parents.

Tension released inside him for only a moment before it snapped back into place as he realized the night wasn't over. He needed to make sure Bo was okay, to see to it that Piao still had their emperor and that he hadn't lost one of the last people in this life he cared for.

He ignored the protest from his legs and sprinted toward the steps that would take him to the platform where the palace sat above the square. He'd counted the steps once as a child with Bo and their childhood companion, Luca. Forty-Three. A random number, but one that seemed almost insurmountable to three small boys.

No guards stood outside the palace, so Jian burst into the entryway, throwing himself into the chaos. Soldiers, servants, consorts, and all those who were part of the court stared at him as he broke through their ranks.

If Bo's advisers had their way, Jian wouldn't be considered a member of the court and therefore not allowed into the palace. But Bo insisted on infuriating them by making his own decisions.

Jian pushed his way through to a crowd of advisors. "Where's the emperor?"

Chen Wang, personal servant to the emperor, had the audacity to look affronted. "He is mourning his city and not to be disturbed by the likes of you."

Jian had been practicing his restraint and refused to punch the man as he wanted to. He clenched his fists at his side. "You tell me where Bo is right this instant, or I'll see to it you're thrown from the palace."

"He would never—"

"Are you so sure about that?" It was no secret Bo trusted Jian more than the sycophants vying for his attention.

Chen shrank back. "He's in the temple."

Jian didn't spare him a final look as he thundered through the maze of halls. The temple was an ornate building behind the main palace. A narrow courtyard connected the two with high walls on either side. Outside the entrance, a massive stone statue of Buddha greeted all visitors and directed them toward the gold-plated double doors, where ancient carvings of dragons adorned the structures.

Inside spoke of the prosperity of Piao under Bo's father and now him. Golden statues were spaced throughout the room. Red jade pillars lined the marble walkway, ending at a sheer curtain. No one dared interrupt Bo while he prayed—except for Jian. Beyond the curtain, the emperor of Piao, the newest ruler in the Wei dynasty, kneeled in front of a golden dragon statue and wept.

Jian approached him and kneeled beside him. Bo didn't bother drying his eyes as he raised his face to the statue. "Bother, have you come to tell me my city is lost?"

Jian cleared his throat. "The Kou have retreated. Your army is currently putting out the fires and taking care of your people."

Bo's shoulders shook. "I tried to go back out there. I wanted to help my people, but my guards physically restrained me. They sent me here to the temple and told me I wasn't to leave."

Jian hated when people tried to control Bo and dictate his actions as emperor, but he couldn't fault it this time. "If General Altan had seen you, you wouldn't have survived."

Bo snapped his gaze to Jian's. "He was with them?"

Jian nodded. "I was going to face him before they sounded the retreat."

Bo reached for Jian's hand. "I'm glad you didn't. He is a dangerous man, Jian."

"So am I."

Bo didn't drop his hand. They hadn't grown up knowing they were brothers, but they'd been friends anyway. Jian was raised as an orphan, told his father was a friend of the emperor's who'd died in battle. It wasn't really a lie. Jian's mother—and Bo's—had been a consort of the emperor who'd fallen in love with a soldier. She'd gotten pregnant with Jian when Bo was less than a year old. The court knew right away it wasn't the emperor's child.

Jian sometimes tried to picture her scared and alone. The soldier faced execution immediately, but she was forced to wait for her death, knowing it was coming as soon as she gave birth. The story remained a secret until Empress Yanyu revealed it before the emperor's death, hoping it would mean her son, Dequan, would become emperor once everyone knew how impure Bo's mother was.

It hadn't. The old emperor chose one of his younger sons to succeed him, claiming he had the mandate of heaven.

"Maybe he was wrong." Bo's voice was so quiet Jian had to strain to hear him.

"Who was wrong?"

"Ba. Maybe he chose the wrong son. Heaven does not smile upon me. The dragons have abandoned me." The ancestors of the Wei dynasty were said to live in the world as dragon spirits, bringing protection and luck down upon those they favored.

Jian sighed, a weariness raced through him that went straight to the bone. "Bo, you need to hear me now. This is not your fault, and Piao will need a strong ruler now more than ever. Who is it that tells me your elder brothers are nothing but brutes?"

"Maybe Piao needs a brute right now."

"No." Jian pushed to his feet, unable to look at his brother any longer. He'd never known Bo to be weak. Walking toward the statue, he examined the ornate bronze gong beside it. The priests would preach something about this suffering being meant to be. Life is suffering, they'd say. It didn't end until one reached Nirvana.

But Jian rejected those teachings. He didn't want to spend every moment in this life in pain. He wouldn't accept that nights like these had to happen, that there was a cause. No, the attack was senseless, cruel.

He turned back to his brother. "Piao doesn't need a brutish emperor because you have me. I am your strength, your dao."

Bo wiped the tears from his face. He'd never let anyone else see the stoic emperor that way. "We must protect my people the way I couldn't protect Luna. We must be the dragons."

Jian's shoulders deflated. He didn't need to ask who Luna was. Bo cared for his consorts, though probably not in the way they wanted. Yes, he performed his duties, attempting to produce heirs, but he wasn't in love with them.

Jian always felt great sympathy for his brother. He'd never be able to show the kingdom who he was. An emperor was a symbol of power surrounded by his harem. He wasn't supposed to have thoughts about other men.

Bo's voice broke Jian out of his own thoughts. "Luna was truly good." He smiled sadly. "While most of the court was conniving and scheming, she just lived. Pure sunshine, that was what she was. Meili." Beautiful. He stood, flattening the creases in his ornate robe and tying the belt tighter.

Jian put a hand on his shoulder. The court would be aghast to see anyone—even family—treat the emperor so familiarly.

Bo gave him a grateful smile and straightened his shoulders. "Take me to see the damage."

With a short nod, Jian led him from the temple and back into the palace. As soon as they entered the front hall, all noise ceased.

Jian stopped and turned to his brother, watching the anguish fade from his eyes, masked behind the quiet strength the kingdom knew him for. Bo may have been young when he became emperor, but he would not allow them to respect him less for it.

His guards approached, and Bo began to speak. "The people outside these walls need our help. I want cookfires started. Bring stores from the army's supply held in western Dasha." One of the guards began to object, but one look from Bo shut him up. "And I will go out among my people tonight."

That drew more than a few protests. Chen couldn't hide the scowl on his face. "You will be vulnerable."

"Not any more so than I was during the festival. This time I will be even more protected because General Li will walk with me."

Chen's scowl deepened, and he muttered under his breath but didn't respond.

Bo walked to where his consorts huddled together. There were only three left with Luna gone. Lihua, the youngest, had a delicate kind of beauty with her porcelain skin and tiny eyes. Alix was the fiercest of the group, but she'd been Luna's most common companion and tears now streaked her once perfect makeup. Holea, the eldest, stood farthest back from the other two, always alone. Yet, Bo loved them all. They were his family.

He kissed each of their hands, saying, "I am pleased you are whole."

Yanyu Mei approached, and Jian's defenses went up. Beside her was prince Duyi, the youngest of Bo's brothers. She'd never recovered from her husband choosing Bo as his successor instead of one of her five sons. She had been the empress after all.

Bo greeted her courteously as he always did.

She curtsied, but there was a stiffness about her.

"Have you come to give me your condolences about my dear Luna?" Bo asked as if it wasn't a ridiculous question. Yanyu resented each member of Bo's harem because as soon as they bore children, her sons would fall further from the seat of power she thought was theirs.

She held out her hand for him to take. When he did, she gave one squeeze and walked away. Duyi stayed behind, shuffling his feet. Jian could tell the teenager was trying not to cry. Bo relaxed and wrapped an arm around Duyi's shoulders. He loved all his brothers despite their constant conniving for power.

"I'm glad you're safe," Bo whispered.

"You too." Duyi sniffled.

"Do you want to come with me?"

Duyi lifted his face to Bo as if surprised to be included. He nodded but stopped when his mother yelled for him. His shoulders dropped. "I-I can't."

Bo squeezed him to his side once more before releasing him. "Okay, didi."

Duyi smiled at the affectionate way the emperor called him little brother.

Bo jerked his head toward Jian and marched to the massive doors that would lead them to the aftermath of the battle.

Guards formed up around the two brothers as they pushed out into the open air. Bo sucked in a breath, but Jian had already seen the damage. Gray smoke swirled through the night air, curling toward the sky.

Bo's eyes fixed on where Luna's body had been, but someone had already removed it. It impressed Jian how quickly the people of Piao could recover from a night such as this. Attacks from the Kou weren't anything new, but they usually only occurred in the border cities. Dasha sat in the center of the kingdom, far away from Koulland to the north.

For most of the night, Bo oversaw the feeding of his people. The flute players from the festival struck up a haunting melody, fitting in the ghostly atmosphere. The guards complained of exhaustion, yet Bo and Jian refused to sleep.

They sat in front of one of the many fires that burned across the city, silent for a long while.

The guards let a man past their ranks, and he dropped into the seat next to Bo's with an exaggerated sigh. Luca Kai, Jian's second in command and best friend was like no other man he'd ever known. Even after the horrors of battle, there was a lightness to him most others envied.

Bo handed him his own copper mug of tea. "You look exhausted."

Luca took it. "Yes, your Imperial Majesty." Normally, he only used the title in jest, but there was no mocking in his tone this night. "It's been a long night."

Jian gestured to a streak of blood on Luca's uniform.

"Not mine." Luca took a sip of tea. The three men grew up together. Luca's father was one of the old emperor's most trusted generals. Luca and Bo were the only people Jian truly trusted in this world.

Luca drained the mug and set it aside. "One moment, I'm meeting my intended, and the next, I'm fighting for my life. Tonight has been something, all right."

Bo choked on his own tongue. "Did you say intended?" He shifted his eyes away, refusing to look at Luca.

Jian constantly wondered where things stood between the two men. They'd always cared about each other, but the impossibility of their situation had to weigh on them.

Scrubbing a hand across his face, Luca sighed. "She's very spirited. Our courtship was going to be delayed because of the border checks, but now I imagine we will be doing much more than examining the battlements in the mountain passes."

Bo, dao laid across his lap, leaned forward. "We're going to have to respond to this."

Jian sighed. He'd known Piao couldn't stand by doing nothing any longer. They'd satisfied themselves with stationing army units in the border villages to protect them against attack, but it had been a long time since they'd led an offensive strike.

"We will." Jian set his mug aside, eyeing the guards to make sure they weren't overheard as he dropped his voice. "That's what General Altan wanted. He's been antagonizing us for too long, trying to goad us into a war we aren't ready for."

Bo rubbed his eyes. "When you were in Koulland, the settlements you found spoke more of their goals than any actions here. As time marches on, they're laying down their nomadic lifestyle."

Jian nodded. "And what is the most valuable thing in the Eastern kingdoms?"

"Trade routes." Luca cursed. "Ports. Ships. Roads. Access to faraway kingdoms."

Bo jumped to his feet and paced away from the fire, his ever-present guards shadowing each movement. He returned seconds later, unable to stand still. "Why now?"

Jian knew the answer without even thinking about it. "Altan has been given command of their forces." Batukhan Altan was not a man satisfied with standing still. War was his life, and he was good at it.

Luca sighed. "So, what we're saying is this wasn't an isolated attack? That they haven't just been crossing into the border villages to pillage? Are we going to war with the Kou?"

Bo looked to the sky as if the stars could give him any answer he searched for. "I'm saying we don't have a choice."

"You do realize the Kou are born warriors, right?" Luca looked from Jian to Bo. "They train to fight from the time they can first hold a sword. Our army is depleted from years of peace. We have let the numbers dwindle. Do you really want to go against the clans of the Kou with farmers and merchant boys holding daos for the first time in their lives?"

Bo met Jian's gaze. "There's one thing I have that they don't."

"What's that?" Jian held the look.

"I have Jian Li. And he will command my armies."

Jian shot to his feet. "You can't be serious, Bo. Your commanders will never accept that decree."

"They will obey their emperor. As will you, Commander Li." His tone softened. "I don't trust anyone else to protect my people. Be my dragon. Please."

It wouldn't be easy. *Be my dragon.* He didn't know where to start with that. What Bo asked of him bordered on the impossible. He'd have to increase the size of their army, training any boy or man in Piao who was willing, and then lead them to their probable deaths.

Their kingdom would never be the same.

*Be my dragon.*

Jian's eyes caught on the profile of a familiar girl. The one who'd run into the danger. Yes, for people like her, they'd fight, they'd die.

"I accept the command." Jian bowed his head in respect to his brother. Bo's trust in him would give him the strength he'd need in the coming days.

Bo rested a hand on the crown of Jian's head in a familiar blessing and dropped his voice. "You'll be safe, won't you?"

Bo knew nothing of war. Sure, he was trained in tactics and how to plan ahead, but he'd never felt the bite of steel in his flesh or seen the light leave an opponent's eyes. In a way, the emperor was innocent, pure. There was no blood on his hands. Jian didn't want to be the one to tell him there was no safety in war. Anything could happen, but it didn't make the battle any less worthy of a fight.

Lifting his head, Jian met his eyes. "I will try."

It was all he could promise.

"And you, Luca?" Bo's sad eyes turned on Luca.

This was why he was a beloved emperor in Piao. He cared. And he had Jian to prevent his heart from being blackened by the things that would need to be done.

Luca swallowed, looking from Jian to Bo. "You know me, Bo. I'll do what is necessary. But I will be at

Jian's side every step of the way. We will look out for each other."

"That is all I can ask." Bo turned away from them and straightened his shoulders, becoming the emperor once more. As his guards led him back toward the palace, Jian couldn't help but wonder if Bo's men would truly look after him.

# CHAPTER 3

Hua

How could Zhouchang look untouched when Dasha had been forever changed? Hua searched the village for familiar faces as the traveling party broke off, going their different ways. The journey from Dasha had been a somber one full of memories of the people who'd never return home.

Hua followed her parents away from the others they'd joined on the road. The five-day journey wore on them. They had only one horse—her father's war beast, Heima—and took turns riding her.

When the small home at the edge of the patchwork fields came into view, rolling hills stretching behind it,

Hua's entire body relaxed. This was where she belonged.

Where she never wanted to leave.

The dark walls grew larger as they neared. A wooden swing hung from the large privet tree sitting outside their front door. Hua fixed her gaze on it remembering two little girls who'd spent hours at a time pushing each other, seeing just how high they could fly above the ground.

Every part of their farm held memories of Luna.

She averted her eyes, instead focusing on the low stone wall skirting the edges of the yard. Her sister wasn't coming back. She'd never race across the fields or climb the trees surrounding their property. She wouldn't sit atop the waist-high wall, her feet dangling off as her body shook with laughter.

A bark snapped her from her thoughts, and she started running, needing the comfort only her best friend could give her.

"Chichi!" She reached him and fell to the ground, throwing her arms around his hulking brindle frame. He tackled her to the grass, licking her face. A sob shook through her, and still, she held back the tears. "It's all wrong, Chichi. It's all wrong. She should be here. We should never have let her go to Dasha."

He pressed his paws to her chest, keeping her from rising as he stared down with understanding brown eyes. She knew it was silly. Her dog didn't know what she'd said, he didn't truly see inside her heart, but sometimes she thought he was more than a simple animal.

Another body collided with Chichi, throwing him to the side as Hua's little brother jumped on them.

"Hua! You're back."

She sniffled, pulling the boy flat against her and never wanting to let go. "Ru, I missed you."

"You have to tell me everything." His excited eyes tore through her heart. Ru didn't know Luna. He'd been too young when she left to remember her. Hua told him stories of their eldest sister, her best friend, but stories weren't the real thing.

At least he'd be spared the grief that now lived in their parents' eyes, the emptiness inside her.

He rolled off her and sprinted toward their parents cresting the hill. "Mama! Ba!"

Their father dropped his cane and lowered himself to his knees, holding out his arms. Ru ran into them as another shadow fell over Hua. She lifted her eyes to her grandmother. "Nainai."

Her grandmother held a hand down, and Hua gripped it, accepting the help to stand. The gray-haired woman wrapped her arms around Hua. "I'm glad you're home and safe. I've been so worried."

"Me too." She buried her face in her grandmother's shoulder, inhaling the familiar scent of cherries. She spent a lot of time picking the fruit from the trees at the side of their house, humming while she did.

Hua's parents reached them, Ru now in their mother's arms. Chichi ran excited circles around the family. He never liked when they weren't whole.

Would they ever be whole again?

"Mama." Hua's father kissed his mother's cheek.

"Come inside," her grandmother said, gesturing toward the house. "We expected you to stay in Dasha a few more days, but I will fix us a meal."

Hua didn't listen as her parents explained their early return. She didn't watch as her grandmother received the news that she still couldn't believe herself. Instead, she entered the house and climbed the wooden staircase to the loft she'd once shared with Luna. As she climbed out the window onto the low roof, the sun sank low on the horizon. Below, Chichi sat outside the front door, barking for entrance. Chatter from the house drifted out to her sanctuary, but she couldn't be around them.

She sat with her legs hanging over the edge of the flat roof. Luna yelled at her many times over the years for sitting so near the edge. She'd been afraid of death, of pain.

Hua was different. She didn't fear the end. Some called it courage—the way she always skirted danger, balancing on the edge of a knife. Only Hua knew it for what it was. Cowardice.

No, death didn't scare her. She gave pain no mind.

Life itself held the darkness. Sometimes Hua thought her family were the only people she could feel connected to. She'd never wanted to know more about the boys and girls she met in her studies. Her best friend was a dog. It was something Luca Kai would soon learn.

As darkness let the stars shine through up above, someone climbed out the window behind her, and she didn't need to turn to see who it was.

There was only one other person who didn't fear the roof.

"Nainai." She shook her head. "Should have known it wouldn't take long for you to find me." She turned to see her grandmother. Jie Ming Minglan saw more than anyone realized. She took great pleasure in being underestimated due to her advanced age, because she constantly proved everyone wrong.

Except Hua. She'd always known her grandmother wasn't the frail woman she appeared to be.

"Hua." She slid to the edge and sat just as Hua did. One moment of misplaced balance, and she could tumble off the roof. Part of Hua imagined her doing some elaborate move, rolling as she landed and popping back up as if nothing was wrong.

The image almost made Hua want to laugh. Almost.

Her grandmother put a hand on her back, rubbing in circles. "Luna was too good for the world of consorts and palace deceptions."

Hua didn't know what to say to that. She'd always thought the same, but in Piao, it was such an honor to be chosen by the emperor, most people never considered what it took from the women. Yet, Luna seemed happy.

Hua sniffed. "Nainai, I'm trying really hard not to blame the emperor for Luna's death." She clamped her shaking hands arounds the edge of the roof. "I know the attack wasn't his fault, but none of us would have been there if his eyes hadn't fallen on our family, if we hadn't won favor. We'd still be poor farmers under threat because of our blood, but at least we'd be whole."

"It does us no good to live in alternate realities, Hua. You can miss Luna—we all will—but don't for one second claim you aren't whole because she's gone. What's inside you has nothing to do with anyone but yourself. I don't want to see you lost in grief and anger."

"She was my sister."

"No one claimed this life was an easy one. Luna was a bright soul, but her loss doesn't make the sky any darker."

Hua's shoulders shook, and her grandmother wrapped an arm around her. "Cry for her now, Hua. And then be the kind of person she would have wanted you to be. You are the strength in this house, and your family will need you."

She didn't know how her grandmother could say that. Hua had never been her family's strength. Her father, Luna, and even her mother were stronger than her. She laid back, lifting her eyes to the stars above in the cloudless sky.

Directly above her, stars connected into an image of a dragon, but the constellation had no name she was aware of. Her father used to show her the stars, but he never once mentioned a dragon protecting them from the sky.

"What's it called, Nainai?"

Her grandmother leaned back next to Hua. "What are you talking of, Hua?"

She lifted one finger to trace the lines of the great beast. "The dragon."

"Dragon?"

"In the sky. The stars connect each night to form a dragon. It looks down from above as if protecting us from the dangers of the world." She released a sigh.

"Hua, I see no dragon."

"But it's right there." She pointed straight up. "It has been since I was a child." Hua turned to look at her grandmother. "Can you tell me one of the stories like you used to?"

"Which stories are these?"

"Of the dragons. They were Luna's favorites."

Her grandmother smiled. "The Minglans of Zhouchang are an illusion. The family is a combination of two dragon bloodlines hidden from the crown. When I married your grandfather, our shared name was Guimo. My husband was a brilliant man. He didn't need a dragon inside him because he had his own brand of fire. Yet, it didn't save him from the emperor's executions." She closed her eyes as if trying to remember.

"The dragons of Piao were said to bring luck, but that wasn't their true purpose. They were serpentine creatures roaming the skies to protect the kingdom. Only those born of the dragon families could call them back. Some people claimed the dragons were descended from the human families themselves, that the dragon lived inside the chosen until called forth."

"I learned that in my studies. The people were

dragons." Hua loved the stories because they could distract her from real life.

"No, child. The dragons were separate entities. The humans were merely their hosts. Together, they were called the Nagi. A long time ago, one person from every generation was chosen by one of these magnificent creatures. But now, it has been many centuries since anyone has shown the signs. Now, all we have are the stories."

"Sometimes stories are just as powerful as the real thing."

"No, Hua. Piao is going to travel down a dark road, and stories cannot save us. But then, neither can the dragons if they do not return. Come, we should go inside."

"No, wait. Did you know?" she whispered. "That they were planning to send me away?"

Her grandmother sighed. "This is the way of life. You cannot stay young forever. Your parents do not wish to send you away any more than you wish to leave, but you are of an age where it is time to create a life and a family separate from ours."

"Family." Hua shook her head, tears building in her eyes. "Luna was pregnant. She was going to have her own family." One that didn't include Hua. Yet, she'd seen the happiness in her sister. The child brought her joy. But it, along with her, was extinguished with a single Kou crossbow bolt. No dragon could change that now.

Her grandmother smoothed her hair away from

her face. "I fear there will be many more tragedies in the coming months."

"They need to pay." Hua's jaw hardened as anger seared through her heart. "The Kou took Luna and so many other people. I hope they feel every bit of loss we've experienced."

"Vengeance is a great destroyer, Hua. It provides none of the solace you seek."

Hua didn't respond to that because in that moment, she wanted no solace. She needed to feel every bit of grief and anger. She wanted a dragon to rain down chaos on her enemies.

Her mother's voice called from inside that supper was ready. Hua followed her grandmother back through the window. With one final glance at the dragon constellation above, she joined her family.

Who would Luna have wanted her to be? A simple girl who married the man her family told her to and lived happily ever after?

Was it a betrayal of her sister to be anything else?

*I'm in love with the emperor.* Luna's words ran on a loop in her mind. She'd looked so happy with that light in her eyes. What would it be like to feel that joy?

Turning to look at her father, Hua studied him, wishing he'd find her someone she could love like her sister had, wishing she were capable of believing in the feeling. Even if the anger didn't threaten to shred her from the inside out, she knew she wasn't meant for a simple life.

"Are you okay?" her father handed her a bowl of stew as she sat down.

She shook her head as the tears she'd refused to cry finally broke through, trailing down her cheeks unchecked. Her entire body quivered as reality crashed in around her.

It was real. She believed it now. Luna was never coming back. She'd never sit around this table with them again.

Ru walked around the table and pulled himself into her lap, resting his head on her collarbone as she wound her arms around him. "Please don't cry, Hua."

Resting her cheek against his soft curls, she got control of her breathing. Her family watched as if they too wished they could fall apart.

But that wasn't the Minglan way. As children of a revered general, they'd been taught to strengthen themselves against emotion.

Hua counted backwards in her head as her father once bade her. By the time she reached one, the tears stopped flowing. Ru reached up and wiped away the tears shining on her face. "Why are you so sad?"

She met his eyes, soaking in the innocence. He didn't know what this pain was like, not yet. She smiled and brushed his hair back out of his eyes. "I'm just tired, Ru-Ru. It was a long journey."

He slid from her lap and sat in the chair next to her. "Okay, but I'm sleeping with you tonight so I can make sure you don't cry anymore."

As if her tears provided some clarity, Hua sat straighter, realizing no one was going to give her the strength her grandmother claimed she had. It had to come from within.

No one else could repair her heart or allow her to move past this into a future she no longer recognized.

She was a Minglan, every bit her father's daughter.

As she lay in bed that night, Luna's smiling face floated in the spaces of her mind. They hadn't expected the Kou to attack the festival, and didn't know what came next, but Hua wouldn't let foreign invaders break her family.

"I'll protect them, Luna." Hua whispered the promise as she curled her body around Ru's sleeping form. "Whatever happens, I'll keep them safe."

# CHAPTER 4

Hua

The days grew colder and with each setting of the sun, Hua felt as if she'd slipped further and further away from her sister. Nothing changed in Zhouchang in the months following the attack. News of the Piao troop movements reached the village, spawning rumors of battles in the mountain passes at the northern part of the kingdom.

The Kou were a fierce enemy, driving the army back into their own kingdom.

To Hua, it sounded as if Piao would never win.

She charged across the open field on light feet, tracking the bear her father spoke of at breakfast. He said it killed two cows in the northern fields in the night. His plan was to take a hunting party to find the predator around the noon hour, but Hua couldn't wait that long. She could practically hear the things he'd say once he found out she planned to find it herself.

But it wasn't the first time she'd chased predators away from their farm.

Carrying a simple wooden bow in one hand, she passed into the trees, stopping to examine the animal tracks on the muddy ground.

From a young age, her grandmother taught her to shoot a bow—much to the consternation of her mother. While Luna excelled in all manner of schooling, musical instruments, and even intricate sewing, Hua had different skills.

Shooting with deadly accuracy and tracking a target were two. She'd also learned to fight from her father. If the emperor's men came for the Minglans, no amount of skill could protect them, but being prepared gave them a bit more peace of mind.

It also made her an excellent hunter. The women of the village looked down on her for her activities, but she didn't mind. She'd never needed friends.

Rustling came from her left, and she stopped, stepping behind a wide tree trunk and peering around the rounded corner. A small brown bear ripped through a bush, shoving the leaves and berries into its mouth.

Hua breathed evenly, willing silence into her every move. Pulling an arrow from the quiver on her back, she nocked the bow and pulled her arm back, letting the string graze the corner of her mouth. Breath in. Breath out. Release.

The arrow sailed toward its target, striking him in the torso.

With a roar, the bear stood tall and charged her hiding place. With fumbling fingers, she yanked another arrow free and barely got it nocked before the bear reached her, lunging with his claws outstretched.

Heat snaked down her arms, and pain seared through her as if something tried to break out from inside her body.

Heart beating rapidly, she released the second arrow, striking the bear right next to the first. It stumbled back before collapsing forward, knocking her to the ground.

Warm blood soaked into her breeches and robe as she squeezed out from under the heavy animal, gasping for breath as she did. The pain subsided, and the heat recoiled as if whatever tried to get out went dormant.

Finally, the weight left her, and she leaned her head back against the ground. Her father was going to kill her, but she wanted to prove she was worth more than sitting inside accomplishing chores meant for girls.

Getting her breathing under control, she pushed herself off the ground and slung the bow across her back with the quiver.

This part of the woods held dense trees that stretched from the edge of her property into the village. She hadn't realized how far she'd tracked the bear until she saw the road leading down into the village. It would be easier to get home from there than to go back through the woods.

Glancing down at her blood-soaked clothes, she sighed. Village it was.

At the far edge of the trees, dirt paths turned to cobblestone streets. Flat-roofed homes with stone walls and square windows lined the way before giving way to larger shops.

A group of young women in silk robes, their faces painted white, eyed her as they spoke to each other in hushed voices.

Old men traced her path with their gazes. The farmer girl with blood on her simple clothing. They didn't know the blood belonged to a bear, and even if they did, would they hate her any less? Did she care?

A wooden post marked where the road forked with a small crowd gathered around it. Hua pushed her way through the throng of young men to find a parchment nailed to the post.

**Men Wanted.**
**The Kou have come to Piao. Now is your chance to do your part and take up your role in this war. Any eligible man who should wish to fight for his country, report to the garrison in Yewo within a fortnight.**

This was it. A call to join the army.

A call to get their vengeance on the Kou warriors who attacked Dasha, the men who killed Luna.

Ignoring the stares, Hua shouldered her way

around the post and took off running down the road away from the village, kicking dust up onto the bottom of her robe. Not for the first time, she hated she'd been born a girl. If she wished to fight, why shouldn't she be able to?

It didn't make any sense. She was as brave as any of those insipid boys her age in the village. A high-pitched yip wiped their excited chatter from her mind as Chichi ran up the path with Ru close on his heels.

"Chichi." Ru gasped for breath as he tried to chase the dog.

Hua slowed, waiting for her brother to see her. Chichi stopped in front of her, panting with his tongue hanging out of his mouth. Bending down, Hua scratched his ears. "You shouldn't run from Ru, buddy."

Ru finally caught up to them, his little legs shaking from the effort. "Hua." His eyes rounded. "You're here."

"What are you doing so far from the house, Ru?"

His shoulders dropped. "Chichi ran off, and there was no one else to catch him."

She put a hand on her brother's head. He didn't yet understand their dog could take care of himself. "Where is everyone else?"

"Out looking for you."

She grimaced, knowing she should have seen that coming. Accompanying her brother back to the house, she scanned the horizon for any sign of her parents.

The door burst open when Hua and Ru arrived home and their mother stood in the doorway with her hands on her hips. She opened her mouth to speak but stopped when she took in the state of Hua's clothing.

"Child, are you okay?"

Hua nodded. "The blood isn't mine. I killed the bear."

Her mother closed her eyes. "I don't know what I did in a previous life to deserve such a disobedient daughter." Snapping her eyes open, she fixed Hua with a stare. "Well, come on. You need to clean up." Her gaze softened when she turned it on Ru. "Run up to the northern pastures to let your father and his men know she's home."

"I'm sorry, Mama," Hua whispered as she passed her to enter the house. "I only wanted to help."

Her mother sighed. "I'll bring you some wash water from the well."

Hua was waiting in the washroom for the water when her grandmother stepped in, worry creasing her forehead. "You gave us all quite the scare, Hua."

"I know, Nainai. I'm sorry."

She cocked her head. "Are you? Hmm... that doesn't seem like the girl I know." She glanced over her shoulder, probably making sure they were still alone. "So, you killed the bear?" Excitement glinted in her bright eyes.

Hua leaned forward. "I tracked it first. Then shot it twice. The second arrow made it fall onto me."

"It was that close?"

She nodded.

"I'm proud of you, girl. Your mother is too. She just worries something will happen to you, especially after—"

"Luna."

Her grandmother nodded.

"I'll be okay, Nainai. I wish she'd see I can take care of myself."

"You never want your mother to stop worrying about you. No matter how strong you are, how capable, those who love you will always fear for you. When your father was away in the war, I prayed every night for his return, terrified we'd never see him again." She touched Hua's cheek. "We love you. That will never end in this life or the next. And neither will the worry." She dropped her hand and winked, leaving seconds before Hua's mother appeared with the buckets of water.

Hua watched the woman who raised her and continued to take care of her. Most people thought her hard. Hua sometimes wondered if she knew how to smile anymore. But her grandmother was right. She never stopped being there.

"Thank you, Mama." She didn't smile. The Minglans were past smiling these days. But the warmth in her voice was enough to cause her mother to take a step back.

"Make sure to clean every bit of blood. I won't have you smelling as if you've been slaughtering animals all day."

"Yes, Mama."

She flicked skeptical eyes to Hua. It wasn't like Hua to acquiesce so easily. After a tense moment, she left Hua to her bath.

Once clean, Hua slipped a woolen robe over her head, tying the end of the square sleeves back to keep them out of her way. Sitting in front of the looking glass, she parted her inky hair and twisted the strands into a bun as her sister had worn hers.

For a moment, she could imagine Luna was sitting there in front of her. They had similar features, but their figures were where those similarities ended. Luna had been thin, and soft from a life of girlish pursuits deemed acceptable for her station.

Hua had muscles where most women did not. She preferred daily runs to evening sewing and forest archery sessions to learning the flute.

Luna developed into a beautiful woman, while most only knew Hua was a girl because of the clothes she wore.

When she climbed down from her loft at suppertime, her father and mother were speaking of messengers and arguing. They stopped talking when they saw Hua.

"What's this about messengers?" she asked, stepping around the table and across the small courtyard into the kitchen.

Her father hesitated for a moment as if trying to decide what to say. Hua couldn't tell if he looked angry about her earlier excursion or not. "General Kai sent a letter for you." She got the distinct impression that wasn't what they'd been discussing, but she let it go, not wanting to do anything to anger her father.

He reached into his pocket and pulled out a folded parchment. Hua took it from him, securing it in her belt. She'd read it later once it didn't feel like her parents were keeping some big secret from her.

Ru's tiny footsteps sounded as he ran in. "What's for dinner?"

Their father pinned Hua with a pointed look, disapproval carved into every line of his face. "Bear."

After supper, Hua retreated to her loft, carrying the handle of a small lantern in her teeth as she ascended the ladder.

Her parents barely spoke to her throughout the entire meal, and she could feel their disappointment in every breath. It wasn't anything new to Hua. Before she left for Dasha, Luna spent her life vying for their acceptance, wanting nothing more than to make them proud.

Hua wanted that too. She longed to see the pride in her mother's eyes or for the long hugs from her father when she did something good. Instead, she got their worry.

Her grandmother claimed that worry equated to love, but it wasn't the kind of love she wanted. If any of her father's farmhands killed the bear picking off their herd, he'd have been lauded with praise, not silence. Why did her father train her if he did not want her using the skills?

Settling onto her stomach on the bed, she set the lantern on the table beside it and pulled the letter from the cinch of her belt. Luca Kai told her he'd write, but she'd never imagined he actually would. What did he want with her? Their fathers were old friends, and the

Minglans held a status as the family of a royal consort —even if she was no longer living.

But Hua? Surely after meeting her at the festival, this man would insist on finding a different wife. He'd want someone who could mend his tunics and prepare edible meals. It was expected. But Hua wanted nothing to do with that kind of life. She longed for adventure.

Glancing down at the parchment in her hands, she shifted closer to the orange circle of light from the lantern. "Will you show me adventure, Luca Kai?"

Hua,

I hope this finds you well. You and I don't know each other, but my father tells me stories of yours. I think you and I are supposed to feel lucky to be forced into this.

Don't show this letter to anyone else. You're not, are you?

I don't want to marry someone I did not choose. I imagine you understand exactly what I mean. I think you're beautiful—is it okay if I say that? But no good relationship is built on beauty alone. I think you're sworn to secrecy as my future wife, so I must tell you that my heart already belongs to another. Though, this person could never return my feelings. Please forgive me for my torn emotions.

I want us to begin with friendship, and I think this letter will help. I'm at a camp near Kanyuan along the border. Commander Li and I are training new recruits and making them into some semblance of a fighting force for the campaign

> against the Kou. This isn't easy, but it is all a grand adventure.

"Adventure," Hua whispered, smoothing her hand across the parchment.

> If you decide to write back, send the message to the garrison in Kanyuan. They will pass it along.
>
> Your friend, hopefully,
>
> Luca

Hua stared at his words a moment longer. If he returned from the war, and she had to marry him, Luca would no doubt regale her with stories. But she didn't want to hear stories, she wanted to live them.

The sounds of a soft argument drifted up the ladder. Hua climbed down slowly, finding her parents in the sitting room. Her father knelt in front of his old armor, cleaning the rust from the shining steel plates.

His wife stood looking down on him with her hands on her hips. "You would leave us? Your family needs you."

His tired eyes lifted to hers before shifting to Hua standing a safe distance away. "My family will be okay."

"Your leg will never hold up to a war campaign. You're injured."

"My leg only hinders me as much as I let it."

She tried a different argument. "You've seen what happens when a man dies with no grown sons. His property becomes Imperial land. Ru is not of an age to inherit, let alone run a farm. If you do not return, we will have nothing." Her knees shook before finally giving out and she fell to the ground in front of him, reaching over the armor to take his hands. "If you do not return, I will have nothing. Who will protect us then?"

Hua couldn't take her eyes from the tears streaming down her mother's face.

"Ba." She stepped closer. "What's happening? Where are you going?"

He closed his eyes, letting a single tear escape. "Our country is facing a war that could destroy us." When he opened them, his eyes held a steely resolve. "The Minglans must fight. It is a sacrifice, my daughter, but we cannot let the Kou destroy us. They've already taken one of my children."

Luna. That was his reason. Hua's even-keeled, calm father wanted revenge for the senseless death of his child. But her mother was right. His leg would get him killed and then what? What would happen to their family?

She thought of the letter in her loft. If she married Luca, her family could have somewhere to go. But would he still want a girl he didn't know if she had nothing? Would he even return from the war?

Her father resumed cleaning his armor as if their arguments wouldn't stop him from leaving them, from fighting for Piao. It was both the most selfless and most selfish thing Hua ever saw her father do.

A cry came from the back room, and she turned to check on Ru. He thrashed about on his bed, in the throes of a nightmare. Crawling into the bed, she pulled his tiny form into her arms.

"I'm going to save our family, Ru-Ru." Even if he'd been awake, he wouldn't know what the words meant.

At the time, neither did Hua.

# CHAPTER 5

Jian

They were going to lose. Jian knew it the moment he led his men into the mountain valley, snow packed underneath their feet.

But Altan was supposed to be there.

"Watch for the target," he yelled to his men.

Where was the Kou camp? Jian's intel said they should be upon it by now, but all he saw was fresh snow stretching out before him. No footprints. No tracks.

He kicked his horse around to survey his cold and tired men, wondering if they should head back to camp. Most of these men had been with him for a long time now. They trusted him, believed in him.

What would they say if they knew how lost their commander felt? That he didn't know how to defeat their greatest enemy?

Silence choked the air for a few heavy beats before an arrow protruded from the chest of the nearest soldier to Jian. Everyone watched as the soldier fell from his horse, his blood staining the snow.

Jian jerked his beast around and lifted his gaze to the ridge where a line of archers appeared.

A trap.

He'd led his men into a trap.

"Retreat!" he yelled. "Retreat!" But it was too late.

Arrows rained down from above, and it all happened in slow motion. Luca leaped from his horse, colliding with Jian and sending him into the snow as their fellow soldiers dropped around them.

An arrow struck the horse he'd been riding only moments before. Luca got up and hauled Jian to his feet.

"I need my bow," Jian yelled over the chaos.

"No." Luca didn't release him. "Jian, the battle is already over."

He looked back over his shoulder to where a few of his men hid in the snow, covering themselves as best they could.

"Jian." Luca jerked him. "Commander."

His title snapped him out of the daze, and his eyes settled on the few horses still standing. "We need to get out of here."

The battle—if it could be called that—lasted no more than a few minutes, and no Piao warrior fired an arrow.

It took no time at all for Jian to lose almost the entire unit under his command.

Jian met Luca's gaze and nodded. "Go." They both took off and pulled themselves onto horses as arrows narrowly missed them.

A few others followed them, not all of them making it far before arrows struck them down.

By the time Jian made it out of range, only Luca and four others accompanied him. The rest of their comrades, their friends, belonged to the mountain.

War killed the spirit and sucked out the soul, but who was Jian kidding? His soul had been shattered years ago.

*Jian wasn't supposed to get involved with the enemy. He knew that. In his mind, he could picture his brother's face. Bo would understand. He knew better than anyone what it was to want someone you couldn't have.*

*But he wouldn't be able to shield Jian from the consequences of compromising his mission. He'd been in Koulland for a year and had been shocked to find settlements. What shocked him more was how much the people reminded him of his own.*

*And then there was her. Qara was the sister of the man Jian was sent to watch. And he'd gotten her killed.*

*General Altan was a ruthless warrior. Jian lifted his*

*head off the dirt floor of the hut they'd kept him in since his attempt to make for the mountain passes into Piao with Qara. As soon as Jian came under suspicion, he'd known it was time to return home. He hadn't asked her to come, to leave everything behind. He hadn't needed to.*

*Qara was everything good in this world. Pure light. She didn't belong among the men surrounding her brother.*

*They didn't know who he was—or who his brother was. He'd be dead if they did. What did they want from him? He hadn't yet been tortured for secrets of his kingdom.*

*Qara's screams as they hauled her away echoed in his ears.*

*It had happened so quickly. Jian would forever remember the thud as her body hit the ground, unconscious. How quickly the light faded from her eyes as they loaded her body onto a horse.*

*And General Altan blamed him.*

*Two Kou soldiers pushed through the wooden door and eyed him with thinly veiled hostility. "Get up," one of them commanded.*

*Jian obeyed, following them out into the warm night air. A full moon hung overhead in a sky littered with bright stars. On any other night, it would have been beautiful.*

*But all Jian could see was the circle of torches at the edge of the village. General Altan stood, surrounded by his people, with grief written across his face. For all his faults, he truly had loved his sister.*

*As soon as he was inside the ring of fire, a hand pushed Jian to his knees.*

*Altan walked forward. He leaned down to look him in the eye. "Jian Li. I know who you are."*

*It was in that moment, Jian realized that was the end. If Altan knew his true identity, he'd never let Jian go. Lifting his face to Piao's greatest enemy, he met his gaze. "Do what you must."*

*He opened his mouth to speak again, but before he could, Altan flicked his wrist so fast Jian didn't see the dao until it was coming for him. Jian rolled to the side, narrowly avoiding the blade.*

*A strangled cry escaped his lips as his breath came out in a gasp. Was it worth fighting for his life if the woman he loved was dead?*

*Ice slithered through Jian's limbs despite the summer heat. Shouting broke out, but he couldn't move.*

*Rage melted the ice as it burned through Jian. He jumped to his feet, knocking away the soldier trying to hold him back.*

*The shouting came closer. The soldier behind him jerked, an arrow protruding from his chest. Soldiers scrambled for cover as arrows rained down around them. A hand gripped Jian's arm, and he prepared to fight them off.*

*"Jian, it's me," a familiar voice yelled.*

*Jian's eyes snapped to his best friend's. Luca pulled on his arm again. "Come on, we have to get out of here."*

*Sparing one final glance for the general who was now locked in a fight, he let the hatred fill his heart.*

Jian snapped his eyes open, his chest heaving. Wiping a hand over his face, he groaned. He'd tried to avoid thoughts of that night, of her, for two years. Until the attack at the festival, he'd only heard Altan's name in reference to the news that he now controlled the Kou armies.

Since then, he'd done everything he could to find the general.

And he had.

Jian had led his men into the northern mountain passes where his source told him Altan was camped with his units. He tried to tell himself it wasn't only about revenge, that his duty overrode his hatred.

But Qara wasn't the only reason he had to hate Altan now. He'd come to Jian's kingdom, attacked his brother's festival, and slaughtered people at will.

A few older generals tried to order Jian to lead his men to Kanyuan, a border town three days from their current position. Jian's forces were needed to help restore the defenses after continuous Kou raids. But they no longer outranked him, something they couldn't seem to understand.

Jian was tired of always defending the kingdom from invaders. It was long past time they went on the offensive.

Only, it had been a trap—a trap Jian hadn't seen until he stepped right into the middle of a mountain pass in winter with snow and arrows rolling down from above.

The unit Jian took into battle was supposed to be the best of the best. He trained his men to anticipate anything, but they hadn't seen General Altan's forces cutting them off at the pass through the northern mountains. They hadn't expected the Kou archers and their deadly accuracy to turn the mountain pass into a one-sided slaughter.

Now, he stood in the camp that had teemed with soldiers only days ago. One remained in the healer's tents, seeing their wounds tended to as they recovered. Others trained aimlessly with no thought to what came next.

Most, though, were gone, and only their ghosts remained.

How had they miscalculated so completely?

It was Jian's fault. He said as much as he penned a letter to the emperor. Bo wouldn't blame him. He never did. But Jian was so blinded by the need to find Altan that he'd led his men to their ends, and he'd never forgive himself for that.

General Yang arrived a week after the battle, his regiment following behind on their large steeds. The air in the camp changed with his presence. Tension replaced grief. No one knew what came next.

Yang commanded the armies until Bo replaced him with Jian. Now, neither man seemed to know what to do with their change in rank.

On one hand, Jian knew he deserved some sort of punishment. He didn't deserve to lead these men any longer, not after he'd made such a mistake. His scouts had warned him of the dangers of the mountain passes, but he'd ignored them.

And his men paid for it.

Yet he couldn't be seen acquiescing to someone of a lesser rank.

Bo would need him as more volunteers joined the

fight. The notices hadn't reached every town yet, but the people in the border villages came in droves.

He waited for an entire day after General Yang's arrival to call on him. He held his head high as he felt the scowls of the men. That hurt the most. He'd lost their loyalty.

General Yang was unlike any of Jian's other old superiors in that he didn't begrudge Jian his relationship with the emperor. He was loyal to Bo in the extreme and once told Jian he didn't see it as his place to determine who the emperor favored. It made Jian respect him all the more for it, but it didn't mean the general had gone any easier on Jian. In fact, he expected more from him. His disappointment cut through Jian like the sharp edge of a dao.

He lifted his eyes from the parchment in front of him to fix Jian with a dark stare before nodding to his guards to give them some privacy.

General Yang gestured to a chair and waited until Jian sat in it to take a seat himself. He steepled his fingers and considered Jian. "You messed up," he began, his voice measured. "Would you like to explain how?"

Jian bristled at that. "You are no longer my commander, General." He emphasized his rank, now lower than it had once been. "I do not answer to you."

General Yang sighed. "That is true, and I trust his Imperial Majesty if he wishes you to lead us into this war. Talk to me, Jian. You were always a bright soldier. How did this happen? Only by discussing it do we make sure it never happens again."

He had a point. Jian rubbed his face. "I underestimated General Altan."

"I'd say." General Yang leaned forward. "I have been warned about this."

"Of what?"

"You can't see past this vendetta you have against Batukhan Altan."

"We should all want him dead." Jian couldn't hold the words in as anger seethed through him.

"Yes, but we don't all make dangerous decisions in hopes that we find him. You of all people should know how smart that man is. He won't fall into one of your traps. You will find him when he wants to be found. We cannot keep searching for him. We must protect Piao. The unit you led was needed in Kanyuan to repair the defenses. The Shan mountains are secondary to that town. You are our leader now. Most of my equals will have trouble accepting that, but I will do what is best for my men, and I believe that is following you. But only if you act with nobility, from a place of logic and strategic planning, not from vengeance or fear."

Jian leaned back in his chair. All he wanted in that moment was to bury his head in his hands as images of the slaughter came back to him. He'd watched the men he'd trained, his friends, fall at the hands of the Kou—just like Qara years before. Now he had to prove he could still lead, or he'd never get the chance to make any of it right.

General Yang sighed. "You're a good soldier, Jian Li. I want to believe in you."

"Some say you just want your command back."

His expression darkened. "No one wants to lead, Jian. No one wants every death to be on their hands, every life to rely on them. We make decisions in our positions that end up costing bloodshed. It is always easier to follow orders than to give them."

"I'm starting to see that for myself."

"You made a choice. You must live with what happened, but you cannot let it keep you from making future decisions. Don't let it instill fear into your heart or Altan will win." He leaned back. "Can I make a suggestion?"

"Of course." Jian nodded.

"Focus your efforts on training the best soldiers. Send your most trusted generals to secure the borders while you build up our forces for an eventual march into Koulland. The army is receiving more untrained soldiers than we can handle. Farmers and shopkeepers are leaving their homes to join us. They are our future, but they must learn to fight."

Jian stood and paced the length of the tent before turning back. He was the commander of the Piao army, and General Yang thought he should train boys?

"I can see your mind working from here." General Yang chuckled. "It's good advice, Jian. These boys and men need to learn what it will take to succeed in this war. That is more important than having the commander building border defenses."

There was merit in that. "Yes, sir. I will follow your orders."

General Yang placed a hand on his shoulder. "They

weren't orders, and I'm not your sir, Commander. In fact, I came here to receive my orders."

Jian swallowed. He didn't trust most of his generals because they didn't trust him. But there was no disdain in Yang's words. "I want you to make camp in the Liudong valley. From there, you are a quick march to Dasha should the emperor have need of you. You're right, we must build up our forces. I will have need of you before the summer ends. Until then, send some of your men to bolster the emperor's guard. Protect him with everything you have."

Bo would be in danger until the Kou were defeated.

General Yang smiled. "Yes, Commander. It would be my honor." He bowed, the grin on his aged face widening. "You sound like a leader, Jian. Sending me to the Liudong valley is the right move." With one final bow, he ended their conversation.

Jian pushed aside the tent flap and stepped into the frigid air. A gust of wind slapped him in the face, but he barely felt it through the crushing weight of his failures.

He avoided his men as he ducked into his own tent, their faces flashing through his mind. He'd never told any of them his true reasoning for going after General Altan so vehemently, that it wasn't only in retaliation for the attack on Dasha.

Two years ago, Jian's mission into Koulland turned into the greatest tragedy of his life. He'd gone there thinking he had nothing to live for. If he died at their hands, at least he would have done some good for his brother first. He'd expected to find a savage land but was instead welcomed into a village of people who thought he was one of them.

Qara was the most beautiful girl Jian had ever seen. It went against every rule of his mission, but he'd been unable to stay away from her. There was something special about her. It only took a few weeks for her to reveal her skill as a seer.

Eventually, she'd introduced him to her brother, General Batukhan Altan.

Batukhan hadn't suspected Jian was anything other than Kou at first and welcomed him into their family. He'd used their connection as his cover while he learned everything he could of them to report to his superiors in Piao.

And he'd made a mistake. He underestimated Altan, not realizing just how far he'd go for his kingdom.

Jian sank onto his cot, burying his head in his hands as he tried to forget the last time he'd seen Qara. She'd had such fear in her eyes. Days later, he'd returned to Piao with his men. It took him a long time to move on from the events in Koulland, but he thought he'd returned to himself. Maybe he wasn't as whole as he'd thought.

Jian released a breath, his entire body shuddering. He'd done it again. He'd gotten people he cared about killed. Maybe Bo's advisers were right. Maybe he didn't deserve the emperor's favor or the prestige within the army. Not when he put his men in danger for nothing more than a vendetta.

He could see them so clearly—the men who now lived only in the memories of those who'd loved them.

How could he be expected to train new soldiers to do the right thing in this war when he wasn't even sure what that was anymore?

He laid back on the cot, closing his eyes and wishing he could return to a time when he didn't know the torment of leadership or the guilt of battle.

Someone entered the tent without asking permission, and Jian knew who it was without opening his eyes.

"Wallowing?" Luca asked, jostling Jian as he sat at the end of the cot. "That isn't like you."

Jian slid his eyes open and shot his friend a scowl. "What do you want?"

He shrugged. "To not be injured." He lifted his bandaged arm. Jian's heart had stopped when an arrow ripped into his friend, his second in command. He'd thought he was dead, and he'd never have been able to forgive himself for that.

"I'm sorry." It was all his fault. "Luca, there's nothing I can do to take any of it back."

"No, you can't." Luca fixed him with a stare. "But we are in the middle of a war, Jian. They'd have us sitting in some border town, waiting for an attack rather than going after the men who want to destroy us. I'm not saying your decision was the right one, but it's time for the army to stop this defensive stance. It's only going to destroy us."

"Look what happens when we go after the Kou. Most of my men are dead."

"That isn't your doing, no matter what anyone else

says. The only person who should shoulder the blame is that bastard Kou general."

There was a time Jian sat with Altan as he did now with Luca, discussing battle tactics and philosophies. They'd been enemies and friends.

"Stop it." Luca frowned.

"Stop what?"

"Thinking of Altan. Your face goes dark every time you do, and it does no one any good. We need you to be better than revenge. If you don't move on from what happened, you'll lose this post and whether you want to believe it or not, you're a good commander. We need you in this fight."

Jian sighed. "I won't be in the fight for a while. I've been reassigned."

Luca's brow scrunched. "You're the commander. How can you be reassigned?"

"General Yang reminded me what will help us win this war. We need numbers."

"I'm not going to like this, am I?"

"Training. That's our new focus."

Luca released a string of curses. "That's just perfect. Are we ever going to see battle again?"

"I can have you assigned to another unit, Luca. You don't have to stay in my service."

"Bullshit." He crossed his arms. "I'm not leaving you. We've been together since before we were eager boys training for a fight we didn't understand. I've known you most of my life. I go where you go."

Jian hadn't realized how much his friend meant to

him until that moment. Other than his brother, Luca Kai was the only person Jian knew he could count on.

He leaned his head back against the pillow, letting his eyes shut once more as he imagined what his future held. He didn't want to prepare men who had no business fighting for war. He didn't want to lead them to their deaths.

But Luca was the most skilled warrior he knew. At least with him by his side, he could try to protect his new men in a way he hadn't protected those he'd failed in the mountain battle.

This war could be the end of Piao, but they wouldn't go down without a fight.

# CHAPTER 6

Hua

Rain drizzled from the gray sky, soaking the world in tears, as if it knew what was coming.

News of the battles along the border of Koulland trickled into Zhouchang over the months since the festival, but the war seemed like a far-off problem that had no effect on life in their central Piao village.

Until it came to their doorstep. Or, to be more accurate, the Minglans' doorstep in the form of her father's announcement that it was finally time for him to leave. The family spent the day in nervous anticipation of the goodbye planned for the next morning.

What could you say to someone you knew you'd probably never see again?

Ru, not understanding any of their sadness, slept curled in a chair. Hua's mother busied herself in the gardens despite the weather, unable to be still.

Hua watched her father dictate instructions to his farm hands for tending to things while he was gone. But only a few hands remained after the others left for the war.

That was the worst part. The waiting.

By evening, the clouds cleared from the sky, but no one in the Minglan house slept save the child who'd be spared memories of anticipation.

Hua climbed through the small window in her loft, finding her balance on the flat roof. Laying back, her gaze drifted to the scattering of stars overhead.

One shone brighter than the others, and she imagined that was Luna looking out for them.

The only sureties in war were death and the grief that followed. Many in Piao would never be the same. Would her family?

The dragon above could offer no true protection, and Hua had begun to think it was nothing more than a trick of her eyes. She'd asked every person in her family, but none of them saw it.

A thunk sounded behind her, and she turned to find her grandmother falling through the window. "It seems this is our spot." She smiled a sad smile that added years to her weathered face. Hua once thought there was no one younger, more capable than the grandmother who taught her to use a bow and to think for herself.

She turned her eyes back to the stars overhead and sighed. "My father can't go to war."

Her grandmother settled in beside her. "Dear, I know you would like me to give you one of my wise—and never wrong—answers to your implied question, but even I have limits." She scooted to the edge of the roof, letting her feet drop over it. "My son is brave. He knows his own challenges and how this will most likely end for him, yet he will not stand back while others fight for Piao, for Luna's memory."

"You don't think he's going to return." Her shoulders dropped.

"I am not a seer. The future has yet to be written."

"Can I ask you a question?"

Her grandmother smirked. "Wasn't that what this entire conversation was about?"

She knew her too well. "Nainai, why is my father the only one with a right to avenge Luna? She was my sister, my other half." Tears built in her eyes. "It should have been me."

Her grandmother's eyes snapped to her. "Never say that, child. One life is not worth more than any other. Luna was not your better, only your equal. Now, to answer your question, the only reason your father has the right is because he was born a man. It's as simple as that. He did nothing to earn his ability to fight—even with an injured leg. If you found some magic to make yourself a man, you could go instead of him." She laughed as if it was the most ridiculous thing she'd ever said.

But the way her eyes shone held some deeper meaning.

Because to Hua, the idea wasn't ridiculous at all.

She could save her father.

She could find the people responsible for Luna's death.

If she died, her family would mourn, but they wouldn't lose everything.

Bravery. That was what it would take. Not skill or experience. Pure, untainted bravery.

A shiver raced down her spine. This war wanted to take everything from the people of Piao, from her. How could the people have courage in the face of that?

And how could she hold on to everything that was slipping away?

By the time Hua was certain her parents were asleep, she only had a few hours until sunrise. There would be no goodbyes for her, no prayers for safety. She brushed a kiss against Ru's forehead before sparing one glance for her parents asleep in their bed across the main floor.

"Please, forgive me," she whispered. "I do this for you."

Her father's armor sat in the sitting room, waiting for him to put it on. Two knives, a dao, and a bow accompanied the steel garment that looked like it was made of fish scales. Taking one of the knives, she entered the washroom and stood in front of the looking glass with her long hair cascading down her back. Holding the knife in her teeth, she used both hands to bunch her hair over one shoulder.

In Piao, a woman's status, her beauty, was in the quality of her hair. As Hua let the ridges of the knife bite into the strands, her own beauty fell down around her.

When all this was done, she would no longer be Hua Minglan, prized daughter of a warrior, sister of one of the emperor's own consorts.

No, she'd be the girl who deceived an entire kingdom, lied to her family, and broke every societal rule.

But her father would live.

She changed into linen breeches with leather knees and a worn white robe with leather shoulders. For the first time, she was grateful she hadn't been blessed with the… assets… her sister had. She wouldn't be able to wear tight clothing without looking like a woman, but the loose clothing and armor would hide her womanly bits. Next, she rummaged in the kitchen for food she could take for the journey to Kanyuan.

She crept back toward the armor with a rucksack full of supplies, trying not to make a sound.

A tunic of chainmail hung to her knees. The red and black scales would protect her chest and arms. She just needed to be able to ride in it, for now.

Footsteps sounded from the back room, and she turned to find her grandmother watching her.

"You knew," Hua whispered.

Her grandmother nodded. “Like I told you before, you were always this family’s strength.” She stepped forward, and it was only then Hua noticed the ink pot and brush she carried. “Can I?” Relief rushed through Hua at the knowledge her grandmother wouldn’t try to stop her. She only wanted to paint a blessing onto her skin.

Hua nodded and took a seat at the table. Her grandmother sat next to her and dipped the brush into the ink. It sent a shiver through Hua when it touched her skin to create swirling symbols she didn’t know the meaning of.

Her grandmother concentrated on the intricate design on the flesh of Hua’s arm. “I give you our family’s blessing, Hua. Strength. Honor. Luck. You will be our protection.” She drew a circle and then traced the lines of a dragon.

Hua watched the image appear. As her grandmother pulled the brush away, the ink forming the dragon started to fade, sinking into her skin. Hua’s eyes widened, and she touched her arm where only seconds before the image lived. All the other symbols remained.

Lifting her eyes to her grandmother, the question sat on the tip of her tongue.

But her grandmother didn’t let her ask it. “There is no time to tell you all you need to know, my dear, Hua. You must leave and not look back. When you are ready, you will understand who you are.” She pressed a hand over Hua’s heart. “Carry us with you, child. For we know you will always protect us.”

She wanted to say she couldn't protect anyone, that she was just one girl leaving to avenge her sister. Instead, she pulled her grandmother into a hug. "I love you. Tell Mama and Baba I'm sorry."

Her grandmother pulled back and cupped her cheek. "You have nothing to be sorry for. They'll see that in time."

Her grandmother stood and walked to the armor before picking up the helmet. "I wish this was all the protection you would need in the coming days."

Hua pulled on the heavy armor, trying to swallow back the emotion rising in her. She slid the helmet over her head, securing the leather strap so it didn't fall down over her eyes.

As soon as she had her weapons secure, she took a step toward the door, almost tilting forward as she did. Regaining her balance, she tried again, this time making it a few more steps.

"May the dragons protect you, Hua."

She looked to her grandmother once more. "And you, Nainai."

Outside, the rain from the day before returned, growing angrier with each passing second. Any other day, Hua wouldn't leave the house in such weather.

But this was no ordinary day.

The raindrops pinged off her steel armor as she stepped into the deluge. No turning back now.

A sharp yip following by a child's cry had her turning back. Ru and Chichi barreled toward her.

"Hua!" Ru's small voice could barely be heard over the rain.

"Go back, Ru." Her voice cracked on his name.

"Where are you going? You can't leave." She stilled for a moment before gathering the courage to turn to her brother. Rain soaked his sleeping gown, and the edge of it dragged in the mud. Chichi stood beside him almost as a guard, looking just as bedraggled.

The dog barked.

Hua couldn't take her eyes from her brother's reddened face. Dark hair stood up wildly.

A cold nose nudged her hand, and she looked down to find Chichi watching her with understanding eyes.

"Do you even know what's happening?" she asked him.

Chichi let out a tiny yip and nudged her once again. She buried her fingers in the bristly hair of his neck, afraid if she let go, everything would be too real.

"Ru." The rain chased away her tears, but they fell relentlessly. "I have to."

His lip quivered. "Will you come back?"

She walked toward him and ran a hand over the top of his head, refusing to lie to him or make promises she didn't know if she could keep. Would she become like Luna? Forgotten in his young mind.

"I love you, didi. Please, don't wake father. I'm trying to save him. Do you understand?"

Ru nodded, sucking his lip between his teeth. "Please, come home."

Nodding once, she released him and turned away. "Take care of him, Chichi."

The walk to the barn felt longer with the heavy load she carried, but she made it without dropping her bag of food and other supplies. Her pulse pounded in her ears as she pulled open the worn wooden door.

Heima watched her, her nostrils flaring in excitement as she neared. Outside, thunder crashed, making the horse rear up.

"Are you sure about this, Hua?" she asked herself.

Could she do it? Could she really protect herself, or was she on a journey to her end?

She knew what it would do to her family to lose her so soon after Luna's death, but it would be nothing compared to the turmoil if her father died.

The beautiful chestnut warhorse calmed as Hua held her palms out in a sign of good will. The horse whinnied.

"It's okay, girl." Hua could barely get the words out as emotionally raw as she was after seeing Ru. She cleared her throat of the tears clogging it. She brushed a hand down Heima's neck and leaned in. "We do not choose our destinies, Heima."

She could hear her grandmother's voice in her head. This is not your destiny. It is a choice.

But a part of her also pictured the pride in Nainai's eyes. She was right. Hua was her family's strength, and she'd fight for them as long as she could. *You will protect us.*

She'd once told her grandmother she believed each choice had already been decided for them. That a person knows deep in their soul what was right. The only choice was whether to listen to that part of you or not.

There was something waiting for her on that

battlefield. She didn't know if it was glory or death or just the simple act of saving her father. This was how she kept her family from breaking apart. "You and I are going on an adventure." Using Luca's word for the war felt right.

She'd claimed that was what she wanted. Something different from a typical life on a farm. Well, she got it.

Saddling Heima was a chore made harder by the crashes of thunder that startled the horse, but Hua managed it before tying the dao and bow to the saddle.

It took all her effort to mount the horse in full armor, and she could only imagine what they'd say of her when she reached the garrison of Kanyuan. Most of the men in her village would head to Yawo for training because it was closer, but Hua needed to find Luca. Something told her he'd be on her side.

As she crossed the rain-soaked hills behind her house, she glanced back one final time.

By the time the first light of the day illuminated the world, she was hours away. Hua lifted her face to the sun rising overhead, wondering if her father hated her when he woke up and found his armor and horse gone.

Whether he hated her or not, he was alive.

She rubbed Heima's neck and bent down. "You and me, girl. We can do this."

Heima only snorted.

She forced a smile onto her face, pushing thoughts of her family to the back of her mind. There was no backing out of this adventure now. Hua Minglan was going to war. Her comrades wouldn't know there was a woman in their midst. She'd lie to everyone she'd meet.

Yet, for the first time since Luna's death, she felt like she could finally breathe again.

# CHAPTER 7

Jian

This was going to go horribly wrong.

That thought rolled through Jian's head as he watched his new unit train. As one of many training camps, men trickled into the area near Kanyuan from central Piao over the weeks, each more ill-prepared than the next. Some were convicts, sent to fight for their freedom. Others were little more than boys who'd probably never seen the sharp edge of a dao.

And then there were the older men, the ones who were probably the least likely to make it out of this. Yet, they'd chosen to come. They should be home working their farms, but the empire was at stake. Too much of Piao's army had already been lost to the Kou. They needed bodies.

And they needed people like Jian to train them. The surviving members of his old unit were with him, here to train these new soldiers. Yet, they didn't trust Jian. Not anymore.

A soldier was nothing but his duty.

Luca jerked his head to let Jian know to follow him. "What are you doing standing apart from everyone?"

Jian folded his hands behind his back. "I am observing."

"You're avoiding."

"You don't know my mind, Luca." He shot his friend a scowl.

Luca sighed and lifted his eyes to the mountains in the distance. They were camped outside the Kanyuan province near the northern Shan ranges—the same mountains that now haunted Jian's dreams. It had been two months since arriving, and there was no hope of leaving anytime soon.

Jian followed Luca's gaze, thankful for the open plains surrounding the camp. He wouldn't have been able to handle being in those valleys. "He's still there."

Luca looked to Jian. "Altan? What makes you think he hasn't retreated to Koulland to prepare for the next wave of attacks?"

"Because I know him."

"But that's the way of the Kou. They don't stay. They don't create settlements in conquered areas of Piao. Instead, they attack, withdraw, and attack again, conserving their strength and playing some game we don't know the rules of yet."

Jian remained expressionless, hoping to avoid showing even his friend how talk of Altan still affected him. "General Altan is unlike any other Kou. His men are supremely loyal to him. He's cunning, and I have no idea what he truly wants. The Kou want our trading routes. That's easy enough to understand. But Altan... there's something else that motivates him."

Luca said the word the moment Jian thought it. "Revenge."

Not for the first time, Jian realized he and Altan might not be so different after all. And he hated himself for it. They both wanted nothing more than to see the other die.

Luca stopped walking as a young recruit led his horse toward them. His inky hair was tied at the back of his head, and he wore ill-fitting armor despite the long journey his tired eyes told Jian he'd been on.

Something sparked in his memory as he watched the young man. Why did the boy look so familiar? He shook his head, realizing they now stood directly in front of him, a look of intimidation on his face.

The boy gave a short bow, his frame much smaller than most of the men who'd reported to camp over the last few weeks. "Hu-Huan Minglan, sir. Reporting to Commander Jian Li," he squeaked in a feminine voice that marked him as too damn young for this fight.

His eyes flicked from Jian to Luca, widening slightly.

Luca jerked to a stop, stepping toward the young man.

Jian, ignoring Luca, nodded. "You've found him." He crossed his arms, having little patience for the formalities that came with his rank. The men who knew him treated him as an equal. Or at least they had before he led them into a trap.

Luca's face reddened, and Jian recognized the expression he got when he held important information back.

Jian studied his newest soldier, unable to stop the thoughts of what could happen to him when they faced the Kou. Altan would slice through the unit of boys and convicts as if they were nothing harder than the snow covering those mountains.

But it was Jian's job to at least try to turn them into capable fighters. He sighed. "You look weary. General Kai, show Minglan where the horses are kept and then take him to fill his belly." He turned his eyes back to Minglan. "Rest tonight. Tomorrow will be the hardest day of your life."

He turned on his heel, leaving him with Luca as he trudged to his own tent. A few men nodded in greeting, but none who'd been under him less than a month ago in the mountain pass.

A female servant who'd been with him for a year smiled as she exited his tent, a bundle of sheets in her arms. "Good day, sir." She lifted the bundle. "Just getting started on the day's washing. You have fresh linens."

"Thank you, May." He'd never get used to the deference shown to him, even by the women surrounding the camp: Cooks as well as those who did the washing and kept camp in order. May left to go about her tasks.

The crash of steel rang in his ears, the sound of boys becoming men, as he went about his evening routine.

He grabbed his dao, running his hand along the blunt edge and stepped back outside. Colors stretched across the horizon as the sun sank behind the tall stone buildings of Kanyuan in the distance.

In the village, he knew all would be quiet by dark. The border towns suffered much in this war and continued to face dangers most in Piao would never understand.

It reminded Jian why he was there, why he did what he did.

Why he allowed boys like Minglan to put themselves within range of the Kou crossbows.

He removed his shirt despite the cool evening air. By the time he got his men into shape, the heatwaves would be upon them.

Throwing his shirt to the ground, he lifted his dao, bringing it down in a slow arc. There were few things he could control in his life, the life of the bastard brother of the emperor. He'd inherited a lot from his father. His temper. His rash decision-making skills.

But each night with a dao in his hands, he was in charge in a way he still didn't feel as commander of the Piao forces. He decided where the blade went. It gave him some sense of peace. His men stayed away while he went through his nightly ritual, making slow, precise movements that required balance and patience.

It wasn't until he was finished, his skin glistening with sweat, he realized he had an audience. The new boy stood across the camp, his eyes fixed on Jian. When Jian lost his unit in the mountain battle, he made the decision not to get close to the new recruits. Maybe then it wouldn't hurt so much when they too died. So, he only learned their family names. When he swept his eyes across the onlookers, most turned away, but not Minglan.

Jian broke his eyes away and bent to retrieve his shirt. Dropping his dao, he pulled it on, letting it drop to his knees. Not bothering to pick up his weapon, he turned and pushed into his tent. He wasn't quite sure why, but he needed to get away from Minglan's unnerving stare.

# CHAPTER 8

Hua

A hand closed around Hua's arm and jerked her toward the side of a tent, hidden from view of lingering soldiers.

She'd known Luca the moment she'd seen him. They'd only met once before, but she saw the recognition returned in his eyes.

"Release me," she growled.

Luca did just that and stepped away. "What game are you playing here, Hua?"

She twisted her fingers in the edge of her sleeves. "I'm not playing a game."

His face reddened. "Really? Because this is war."

"I know that. Your letter said you were training new recruits, so I came. I want to fight."

"You want to fight? But you're..." He sighed, not finishing the sentence. She knew what he wanted to say. She was a woman. She was small, weak. And she would die for it.

"Tell me one good reason why I should have less of a right to fight for my kingdom than any of the boys who've arrived here."

He opened his mouth to speak, but no words came out.

"Do you think I'm weak?"

"I barely know you."

"Answer the question."

"No, but I'm beginning to think you're crazy. Not exactly a quality I was looking for in a wife."

She scowled at that. "I'm not here because our parents have arranged some kind of marriage."

"Then why are you here?"

She dropped her voice, all anger leaving her. "My father was going to come." Her pleading eyes met his. "You know him. He wouldn't last a single battle." As her grandmother told her to, she had to protect her family.

"And you will?"

"Yes." She lifted her chin, daring him to contradict her.

He ran a hand through his hair. "So, what? You want me to just pretend I don't know Huan is a lie? That there is a woman riding with us to war?"

"Exactly. I'm glad you understand."

He sighed. "What if I were to send you home?"

She stepped closer to him. "You'd prevent me from being just as noble as everyone else here, fighting for what they believe in."

"There is nothing noble in death, Hua."

"Then I won't die."

"You say you want to fight for what you believe in. I don't even know what that is."

She let a beat of silence pass between them. "I'm fighting to save my family. And for revenge. They killed my sister, Luca."

His expression fell. "I'm sorry. I'd heard that one of the emperor's consorts fell. I did not know it was Luna." He lifted his eyes to the heavens as if speaking to some greater power. "This could end my career." Blowing out a breath, he lowered his eyes to hers. "I won't tell Commander Li. Whatever happens to you if he finds out is not my doing."

"Why, Luca? You barely know me. Why aren't you turning me in?"

"Because… you remind me of someone. And I have a feeling you'll find a way to join this fight whether I allow it or not. Besides, you were right about one thing. You are of Piao. Who am I to say you have no freedom to fight for our country?" He wrapped an arm around her shoulders. "Be careful, Hua."

She nodded, her respect for the man her father chose grew by the minute. Maybe they could truly be happy together despite his feelings for someone else.

He left her without another word, and she walked into the center of camp, stopping as she caught sight of the commander she'd only met briefly. He stood outside his tent with no tunic covering his torso as he twisted and turned, swinging his dao in controlled arcs.

She'd never seen anyone exude so much power. She'd heard stories of his prowess in battle, never imagining she'd get to see him in person. Silver moonlight reflected off the sweat coating his rippling torso.

Hua watched for a moment, lost in his movements. When his gaze connected with hers, she couldn't look away as recognition set in. She knew him. But from where? After catching her watching, the commander retreated to his tent, and Hua did the same, curling up on her cot as those around her fell asleep.

Pushing up the sleeve of her robe, she traced the faint outline where her grandmother drew the dragon only weeks ago. The ink had disappeared, but in its place were faint red lines. In the dark, she could have sworn the image glowed, as if some kind of light lived inside her. Peering closer, she saw swirling strands of light coming through her pores.

None of it made any sense. Her grandmother letting her go. The arrow that should have pierced her skin. Disappearing ink and translucent light. A crash sounded outside the tent, and she covered her arm quickly.

Maybe it didn't mean anything. Maybe it was only a trick of her mind, scaring her into seeing things that couldn't possibly exist.

Snores sounded throughout the long tent. She

shared the living space with other men she'd only met briefly.

But that wasn't the main reason for her sleeplessness, nor was the strange image on her arm. She'd recognized the commander, the man who'd lead them into battle and she realized why. Her savior's face from the festival was forever burned into her mind. He'd kept her from joining Luna in the next life. She was sure of it.

He'd risked his life for hers. Why? What made a man run into a barrage of arrows to save a girl he didn't know?

*The flap of scaled wings broke through the silence of the night, and a stiff wind blew the hair from Hua's shoulders. She opened her eyes to find the ground far below. A fire raged over the land, destroying everything it its path. Homes, farms, villages... nothing was safe. A child's scream carried on the winds.*

*"I have to save them," Hua whispered to herself. There was no one else, only her. The armies were gone, having locked themselves in battle with one another.*

*She moved closer to the ground and landed with an earth-shaking thud. Running villagers saw her, and she tried to call out to them, but no words came, only a giant roar.*

*She tried to reach the flames to save as many people as she could, but she had no control over her limbs. Instead of helping, a great burst of flame erupted from her mouth, encouraging the fires to grow larger.*

*"No!" she screamed inside her head. "Stop!" But whatever beast held her didn't listen.*

Hua's eyes shot open as a scream clogged in her throat. Sweat coated her brow as she breathed rapidly, her eyes darting around the tent. No fire. No dying villagers.

She rested her head back on the pillow and closed her eyes once more, trying to gain control of her breathing. She flexed her fingers, relief crashed through her when they did as she bade them.

It wasn't real. She focused on the canvas above her head, trying to erase the images from her mind. She'd felt the heat, heard the screams.

Lifting her arm, she stared at the glowing dragon drawn on her skin. Was this her grandmother's doing? Did her blessing call forth the dreams?

"Hua," Luca's sharp call jolted her back to the present, and she sat up, pushing her wool blanket from her legs. She glanced around the tent, seeing not a single other person still sleeping.

"Wo-won't people talk if you're in here with me alone?" She met his gaze.

A smirk spread across his face. "You're a man, Huan." He emphasized her new name. "No one will think anything of it."

"Oh." Her cheeks heated. "Right. Well, then what do you want?"

"Everyone is at breakfast, so I came to see if you'd changed your mind and run off in the night."

"Is that what you were hoping?" She shuffled through the stack of clothes someone had put beside her bed—a black belted robe and shortened pants.

Luca surprised her by laughing. "Maybe a little. Honestly, I'm not sure. It may have been better if you had run off."

She opened her mouth to speak, but he cut her off. "Yet, I find myself curious as to what you can do. Gen Minglan is an interesting man, and I can only assume his daughter has some interesting secrets as well." The way he looked at her made her wonder if he knew of the dragon blood. Had her father told him?

Had he told anyone else?

"I'm not interesting," she scoffed.

His lips widened into a grin. "We'll see about that. Come on." He gestured to her face. "You look like you had a rough night. Let's get some food into you before the commander sets you to training."

"The commander… is he…"

"Terrifying? Yes. Demanding? Absolutely. But he's also the best man I know. Do as he says, and don't listen to any of the rumors about him." He left without another word.

Rumors?

Shaking her head, she got out of bed and made sure no one was coming before changing her clothes quickly.

By the time she approached the cook fires, most of the men were well into their breakfast. She'd met many of them the night before, but their names hadn't stuck.

The commander was the first person she noticed. Images she'd seen from the night before came back to her. Jian Li was pure strength, power. Something about his slow movements, the rippling of his muscles, drew her to him. His deep voice as he'd greeted them matched that of the savior she remembered.

Maybe that power was why men like Luca pledged their loyalty to him.

As she accepted a plate from a young, heavy-set woman with a warm smile, the commander stood to address them.

Commander Jian Li walked back and forth with his hands clasped behind his back. His eyes found Hua joining them, and he froze.

"Minglan. You're late! This is not your mama's house. You are no longer boys. I expect you to be men." His face reddened with each word.

Hua could barely breathe as she felt each word like a punch to the gut. She'd never been yelled at with such force before.

He strode toward her, his large frame looming over her. His eyes bore into hers with a fierceness that turned her blood to ice.

"You are now members of the Imperial Army." His voice lowered, becoming more dangerous somehow. "Piao is counting on us to protect it from the savage Kou. Discipline. Dedication. Daring. The three things I expect from each person in my service. You chose to be here, to fight for the emperor, but I have no problem sending any of you home." His eyes tore from hers and swept over the rest of the eating men. "That goes for each of you. If you're forced to return home before we reach victory, you will leave with nothing but shame. Some of you are seeking freedom from your bonds, others just want to survive the fight. Train hard for me, and I will work hard to make sure you achieve everything you desire. I'm not going to lie to you. The Kou will kill many of us. But I will fight for you. I only ask that you do the same."

He blew out a breath, his eyes drifting to where Luca gave him an approving nod. Hua glanced toward some of the older soldiers, noting how many of them kept their eyes on the ground, not watching the commander with the rapt attention of the others.

"Eat your fill this morning," Commander Li continued. "Trust me, you will need the energy today."

Hua was still shaking as she took an open seat and spooned rice porridge into her mouth.

She sat by herself on a bench, suddenly wishing her grandmother was there. She'd make her feel better as she always did. NaiNai was the wisest person Hua knew. If anyone at home understood why she'd done what she had, it was her grandmother.

Someone sat beside her, and a deep voice spoke. "Minglan, right?" He dug into his food, sticking a full spoon into his mouth.

Hua nodded, lowering her voice. "Huan Minglan." She stuck out her hand.

He peered down at it with a grin as if she was the most amusing thing he'd ever seen. Setting his spoon on his plate, he finally enclosed her hand in his. "Chen Yu." He released her and went back to his food.

A shorter man with wide shoulders sat on her other side knocking Hua into Chen. "You're one of the new boys, right?"

Hua only nodded.

"I'm Yan Sun." He pointed to an impossibly large man with black tattoos snaking up his arms as he sat across from them. "That's Zhao Shi. Don't expect him to say much. He's a convict." He leaned in close to whisper. "Rumor is he used to be a wealthy man. Then he fell in love with one of the emperor's consorts."

Hua sucked in a breath at the mention of the consorts, her mind drifting to Luna.

He chuckled. "Yeah, he's an idiot. But Emperor Bo Xu Wei is not his father. He didn't want the man executed, but his advisors wouldn't let him release him. He's been in prison for three years."

"And the emperor will give him his freedom once this war is over?"

Chen leaned in to join their conversation. "That's what they say. Half the men here are from the prisons. But we all know the truth."

"What's the truth?" Hua looked from Chen to Yan, but it was Zhao who answered.

"They don't expect most of us to survive." His voice was smoother than she'd have expected from such a rough looking man. It spoke of education and breeding.

Before long, Luca ordered them to dump their plates in the designated area. Minglan bowed to the cooks in thanks.

As she walked away, she noticed with relief how

many women surrounded the camp. Cooking. Cleaning. They kept everything in working order so the soldiers could prepare to fight.

The sun beat down on the trainees, keeping away the chill, as they followed Luca to a training course across the open ground to the nearby woods.

Commander Li stood at the front, arms crossed over his chest. "Many times, the difference between winners and losers is endurance. Today, we will see what you can do. I want you to run and run hard. Follow the course. Jump when you have to jump. Crawl when you have to crawl. Do whatever will get you to the end, and then come back to the beginning and do it all over again."

Hua kicked the toe of her boot against the ground, wishing they were better quality for this kind of training. Her family had never been able to afford much better.

A hand landed on her shoulder, and she looked up to see Chen grinning down at her with yellowed teeth. He winked before stepping up to the front, offering to go first. Commander Li gave him an approving nod. "Go."

Chen took off, weaving around barriers with a speed that surprised Hua. He leaped over a low wall as if nothing held him down to the earth. When he disappeared into the trees, the next person took off. Yan's lumbering frame thundered down the path.

"What do you think is in those trees?" someone whispered. Hua couldn't remember his name.

Hua clutched her arms across her chest, wishing

she had a clue what was coming. "I don't know."

The crowd of soldiers cleared out, and by the time Hua stepped up to the starting line, they began trickling back around to begin again. All eyes fell to her as she sucked in a deep breath and tried to decide what to do. She could run a course like this in her sleep, but would that draw unnecessary attention?

Was it better to be seen as capable or overlooked as nothing more than fodder for the crossbows?

The commander's deep voice telling her to go was like a rocket, shooting adrenaline through her bones. She darted away.

The running was easy and made her feel like herself for the first time since leaving home. She reached the first waist-high wall and jumped, her hands trying to propel her off the top of it to land on the other side. Her leg slammed into the brick, her foot catching on the edge, and she fell forward, her arms stretched out to break her fall. It wasn't the most graceful of moves, but she ignored the pain shooting from her shoulder to her skull as her body slammed into the packed dirt ground.

Scrambling forward, she felt a warm trickle of blood winding down her leg. She managed to jump over the next, lower wall, her foot slamming into the ground and causing her to cry out in pain.

She thought of her father and all of his medals from the emperor. Her sister and her love for the powerful man. Minglans didn't give up, so she kept going. She hadn't come this far to let her limitations hold her back. If they'd put a bow or a dao in her hand, they wouldn't laugh at her like she was sure they were doing now.

"This is for you, Ba." Branches whipped her in the face as she entered the woods, following the ribbons marking the way. They led her through a low cave. She slid to her belly and crawled through the tight gap, wondering how the other men managed to fit their bodies through. The walls of the cave closed in on her. She stopped for a moment, her breath ragged.

"It's okay, Hua," she whispered to herself. "You've got this. Don't forget why you're here." Digging her elbows into the dirt, she pulled herself free of the cave and pressed herself even closer to the ground. Twisted wire with what looked like spikes hung overhead. They wanted her to crawl through this? She closed her eyes for a moment, taking a deep breath and letting them flutter open.

With a glance behind her, she realized the next person had almost caught up. She could do this. She could finish.

At the end of the wire, she clenched her jaw and scrambled to her feet, following the path to a massive tree with a base as wide as half a dozen horses standing side by side.

Lifting her eyes to the notches carved into the rough bark, she realized they wanted her to climb it to get to the other side.

"There is nothing to gain by doing something the easy way," she repeated one of her grandmother's favorite phrases. "This life means more when we have to try."

"Well, NaiNai, I'm trying." Blowing out a breath, she gripped one of the notches and stuck her foot into another as a presence appeared behind her.

"Want some help?" Someone asked from behind her, sounding as if he hadn't just run through the course. She threw a look at Zhao over her shoulder. The man convicted just for falling in love held no emotion in his eyes, or any sign of exhaustion on his face.

At that particular moment, she hated him for it. "I've got it."

It took her a moment to pull herself up, but she managed without asking for assistance, and pride snaked through her as she jumped down the other side. Her leg twinged, but it meant nothing compared to the elation of having almost finished.

She ran through the rest of the course with ease, thankful there were no more jumps or climbs. By the time she reached the others, she could barely breathe. A grin stretched across her face.

She bent over, resting her hands on her knees, listening to Commander Li usher the others to start their second run.

As he reached her, she recovered, preparing herself for another embarrassing run of torture. Commander Li studied her, his lips pursing. "You're finished for today, Minglan."

"What?" she sputtered. "I only went once. I can do it again." She could prove herself.

"And if I let you attempt this course again while blood pools in your boot, you may very well kill yourself. Save the self-sacrifice for battle." A scowl marred his features as he glanced at the blood running down the side of her boot. "Get the leg taken care of."

"But—"

"Now!"

His yell was enough to scare birds from trees and rouse the dead, but to her it only sounded like an angry, unhappy man. She made the decision right then that she would not fear the commander. She would not cower. Sure, she'd obey his commands as her superior, but he didn't own her emotions.

Straightening her spine, she met his eyes, refusing to look away as she was sure many did when face to face with this man. "Yes, sir," she bit out, turning on her heel without so much as a bow.

And it felt good. To feel him watching her in surprise. To regain some of the respect for herself she'd lost with his dismissal.

A shock of pain stabbed through her leg, reminding her of the embarrassment she was when faced with anything requiring strength.

She sighed, her body loosening as the indignation she'd felt only moments before faded. Who was she kidding? Of course, Commander Li didn't want her on his course. If it were up to him, she'd probably be sent home.

If he ever found out her true identity, that she was a woman, she wasn't quite sure what he'd do.

And a woman with dragon blood? If that secret came out, she'd be dead before she even saw battle.

The healer sprawled on one of the cots with a leather-bound book in his lap. He didn't look up as he flipped through yellowed pages.

Hua hesitated in the doorway of his tent, waiting for him to notice her. She hadn't wanted to come. If anyone in camp would take notice of her less… manly attributes, it would be a healer.

"Are you going to come in?" His gaze remained on the text in front of him.

"The commander told me to come see you." She winced as she stepped toward him. "Really, I'm okay. I just…" She didn't want him to touch her, to learn her secrets.

He cut off her words by snapping his book shut. "Soldier, do you know the difference between dead men and living men?"

She shook her head.

"The living have working brains in their heads."

"That's not the only…" Her words trailed off as he fixed his eyes on her and jumped to his feet.

"Do you know what people who use their brains do?"

Was it a trick question? She waited for him to answer it.

A smile lit his wizened face. "They admit when they need help." His eyes scanned her, probably looking for injury. "Sit."

She obeyed him and pulled up the end of her robe.

"You may call me Sasha." He pulled over a wooden

stool and sat beside her. "I am possibly the only person in this camp the commander listens to." He winked. "So, if you'd like to continue your training, you will do as I say."

Hua sighed and raised the leg of her pants, revealing a shallow cut. She averted her eyes from the slightly hairy skin, much less hairy than any man's.

Sasha tsked. "Too much blood loss." He reached toward a table to his left where a bowl of water and cloth sat.

Hua sucked in a breath as he cleaned the wound.

"You'll live, I'm afraid."

Her brow scrunched. "You make that sound like a bad thing."

"Well, it means you won't escape your training here." He laughed. "This doesn't need to be stitched up." He set the bowl aside and lifted a small gray stone bowl before rubbing some kind of paste over the cut. "This will help it heal and keep me from having to chop it off. That wouldn't be very much fun at all."

"No." Hua couldn't help the laugh that escaped her. "Please don't do that."

He shot her a wink before cutting a long bandage. "You tell that commander his course causes too much work for me."

"I'm not the only one?"

"Dear no. I've had a constant barrage of injuries to tend to since he set it up. How long have you been in camp?"

"I arrived yesterday."

"Ah." He finished tying off the bandage and sat

back. "That's why you look so weary. Where did you travel from?"

"Zhouchang."

His eyes lit up. "My daughter and her husband lived there for a while. It's a beautiful part of Piao. They ran a smithy in the village."

Hua struggled to suck in a breath. "The smithy? Zhouchang? Are you sure?"

He nodded. "They had to close it when my daughter's son joined the army." His expression fell. "Now, my daughter lives here in the camp along with my wife."

"And her husband?" Hua's voice lowered to a whisper. She'd never traveled to the smithy, but her father was a frequent customer whenever the farm implements broke. After the smithy closed, he had to travel for a day to reach the nearest one.

Sasha carefully lowered her bloodstained pant leg. "We lost him. He rode into battle a few months ago at Commander Li's side. He didn't return."

"I'm sorry." Hua put a hand on his arm and his eyes widened in surprise. He leaned closer, scrutinizing her in a way that made her squirm.

She pulled her hand back and stood, trying to ignore the ache in her leg. "I need to go."

"You won't be allowed back onto the course. I know the commander, and he'll want you to recover further." He stood to follow her to the door and dropped his voice. "You're travel weary, soldier. You need—"

Before he could finish that sentence, a young

woman pushed into the tent, her cheeks flush. "Ba." She smiled kindly.

"May." The corners of his eyes crinkled. "Have you finished your tasks for the day?"

She nodded, her dark braid brushing against her back. "Until this evening. The rest of the ladies are finishing up the washing."

Hua stood frozen on the spot, watching the woman who probably knew her father. She'd seen no others from Zhouchang, much to her relief. Most of the men from the village traveled to the closer training camp at Yewo.

But this woman… she could ruin everything if she knew anything about Gen Minglan or his daughters—and lack of older sons.

Sasha turned to Hua. "I'm sorry, soldier, I do not know your name."

"Huan." She swallowed. "Huan Minglan."

He turned to his daughter. "Soldier Minglan is new to camp. He comes to us from Zhouchang."

Her eyes lit up for only a moment before narrowing. "That's interesting, Ba. Why don't I show Minglan here where the men wash up?" She scanned Hua from head to toe.

Nothing sounded quite so good as a bath. Hua didn't remember the last time she'd been truly clean. Probably when she left home weeks ago. But she didn't want to go anywhere with this woman.

"That's a wonderful idea, May. Thank you. Minglan can't train until tomorrow. Healer's directive. So, he should make the best use of this time." He nodded, dismissing them both.

"Follow me." May exited the tent and took off across the camp. She stopped at a tent. "Wait here." A few moments later, she emerged with a bundle in her arms and started walking without saying a word.

Hua had no choice but to follow her. They entered the trees at the edge of camp and walked until they reached a narrow stream.

"You probably already saw the latrines when you arrived. They're dug into the earth downstream. So, this part of the stream is where the men and women bathe." She threw the bundle she carried to Hua's feet and crossed her arms over her chest.

Hua bent to unwrap the cloth surrounding a bar of soap. It smelled of pine.

"Most of the men don't have access to soaps. Except for the commander and General Kai. But I figured you'd appreciate it."

"Why?" Hua met her gaze.

May's jaw clenched. "The men are idiots."

Hua waited for more explanation.

"They do not see what they do not expect, because they've never had to. Their lives are straightforward and purposeful. Women must scrape and claw for everything we want. It allows us to look for things that shouldn't be there."

"I don't understand."

May unfolded her arms and her gaze softened. "The Minglans of Zhouchang are well-known farmers in the village. Gen Minglan spent a lot of time with my husband." Her face twisted in grief, but it was gone in an instant. "His only son is a child still. Tell me, are you only pretending to be a Minglan?"

She shook her head, finding it hard to breathe.

"That's what I thought. Which one are you? Luna or Hua?"

It should have surprised Hua this woman knew her name. Instead, it only opened the chasm inside her wider. "Luna… she died."

Sadness entered May's gaze. "My husband is in the next life as well, Buddha protect him." She scratched the back of her neck as she studied Hua. "Clean yourself. I will make sure you are not interrupted." She turned her back on Hua.

With shaking fingers, Hua untied her belt and removed her robe. A chilly spring wind blew, but she barely felt it.

Another person knew her secret. How soon would it be before it reached the wrong ears? She looked to May once more before she kicked off her pants and crouched down beside the freezing water, soap and rag in hand.

She was squeezing water from her hair when May came running. "Quick, get dressed."

Alarm flashed through Hua. She pulled her clothes on over her wet body, managing to tie the belt as a stream of women appeared carrying buckets.

Pulling on her boots, Hua joined May as they ran back into the trees to avoid being seen. With each step, Hua's leg ached, but she kept going. By the time she reached camp, wet hair stuck to her face and her breath came out in ragged pants.

May put her hands on her knees and bent over. "That was too close. I didn't think the cooks would come for water so soon."

Hua thought for a moment. "May... why did you help me?"

She straightened and pulled her braid over one shoulder. "You could be any of us, Hua. I want to fight them, I want to defeat the Kou. They killed my husband, and I would ride into battle if it meant making some kind of sense out of it. But I am not a soldier. I don't know if you are, but you have risked everything in coming here. I have to believe there's a reason for that. I need to think all of this war and death has meaning."

"Do you think your Baba knows?" She'd seen the way he looked at her with interest. The old man revealed his thoughts on his face.

May laughed. "Undoubtedly. Baba knows everything. He won't say anything to the commander. He believes all people should choose their own paths in this world."

It amazed Hua there were people like that in Piao. Her parents were traditionalists, wanting her to settle with a husband of their choosing and raise a family. They didn't listen to what she wanted out of life.

Hua sent May a tired smile. It was only day two and already keeping secrets emptied her out. With a sigh, she turned toward the horse pens, needing a piece of home.

# CHAPTER 9

Jian

Jian trudged through camp, exhaustion wearing him down. He'd run the new recruits through the course most of the day before giving them daos and trying to make some sense of their fighting stances.

The truth: they were a mess.

He didn't know how he was ever going to make them battle ready. Most of these men had never held a dao in their lives.

Minglan hadn't returned—not that he'd have let him keep training if he did, nor had he appeared for supper. Jian saw the blood dripping down the young man's leg, but maybe the wound was even worse than he thought. Would he already have to send one of these men home? The boy wasn't the first soldier to get injured on the course, but something in his quiet defiance made Jian want to watch out for him, to make sure he was okay.

Brushing aside the tent flap, his gaze swept the healer's tent, landing on the aged man who'd been with Jian for most of his army career. Healer Sasha lifted a haggard face toward Jian. "What are you doing to these men, Jian? I've had a constant flow of them entering my tent since you finished for the day."

Jian sighed. "They need training, Sasha, not coddling. Where's Minglan?"

Sasha smiled. "Ah, Huan. I like that one. He wandered off with my daughter quite a while ago after I cleaned up his leg." He leveled Jian with an accusing stare.

Jian ignored it. "May knows better than to distract my soldiers." The healer's daughter was a beautiful woman, the kind that made the men in camp want to fight for her. She'd followed her husband into this war, but he'd died alongside most of Jian's men in the mountains. Jian had barely been able to look at her since.

Sasha chuckled. "May knows her place, boy." He was the only man who could get away with using that term for Jian. "She was only being kind to a weary and lost soldier. Something you should do more of. Tell me, Jian, have you distanced yourself from the men so much you don't welcome in the new blood? There was a time you'd have shown that boy around this camp yourself and made sure he wasn't going to keel over from weeks on the road."

"I don't need you criticizing how I run my camp, old man."

Sasha sighed. "I know you carry what happened in the mountains like a noose around your neck, but maybe it's time you start letting go of the past. These men need their commander to care."

"I do care."

Sasha snorted. "You deem a training post as below that of a commander, or you can't look into the faces of your soldiers without seeing those you lost. Whatever your reason is for losing yourself and becoming this..." He looked him up and down. "Angry version of yourself, it's only going to harm you and this unit in the long run."

"I am here to train the best soldiers that I can. It is not a job for a commander, but..."

The healer sighed. "Ah... but you have not been able to bring yourself to command men into war. Despite your title, you leave the running of your army to other men, generals. You're scared, Jian, and it will do no one any good in the end if you cannot lead."

Jian couldn't hear anymore. He'd known Sasha since he was young, but even he could go too far. He turned on his heel and left. Sasha didn't call him back. He'd said everything he'd meant to.

Rubbing his neck, Jian felt the noose of the past tightening, just like Sasha claimed. He'd never be rid of those memories, those failures. The part that hurt the most? None of Sasha's words were false. This camp had proximity to the other training camps, and he'd meant to be more than a commander training a single unit. But then the images of that battle held him back, and he didn't know how to move forward.

He didn't watch where he was going and almost collided with someone in the dark.

"I'm sorry, Commander." May jumped back and stared at the ground, refusing to meet his eyes.

Jian ran a hand through his hair and shifted his eyes away. "Minglan." The word came out harsher than he'd intended. "Do you know where he is?"

Her voice came out quiet. "Y-yes. He's been with the horses since dusk."

Jian issued a short nod and strode away, breathing easier as the distance between them widened.

Stars lit his way as he wound toward the edge of camp where they'd tied the beasts. There'd been a time when Jian believed his men could accomplish anything, but that was before. Before he'd chased after Altan and gotten too many of them killed. Before he'd seen the distrust in the eyes of people who should look to him for leadership. Now, every single member of his unit weighed on his mind. Would they make it out of this war?

To his left, the Shan mountains stood as what should be a barrier between Piao and Koulland. The town of Kanyuan sat near the base of the mountains, only a short ride away. At this hour, people slept in their beds, not knowing when the danger would come from across the passes, hoping the garrison in the city could keep them safe. Jian had to remind himself that was why he was there, to protect those people. It might mean some of his men would die, but the families they protected mattered.

The closest fortification to Kanyuan was Prince Dequan's estate a few hours march away. The valleys between the two had been home to army camps for decades.

As he neared the horses, Minglan's voice reached him from where the soldier sat next to his beast. The other horses whinnied and shied away from Minglan.

"I miss home, Heima." Minglan sighed. "Baba and Mama must be so worried."

Jian knew he was intruding, but he didn't walk away. He'd never had a family other than Bo. No parents to call his own. There wasn't a piece of land in Piao he'd inherit just as those before him had. It sounded like a simple life, but also beautiful. He'd only known war and missions for the emperor. Was it wrong to yearn for a different kind of life?

He'd joined the army as soon as he was old enough to wield a dao, strong enough to fire a crossbow. He was fourteen. Since then, he'd never stayed in one place for long, following his commanders on dangerous missions, telling himself it was all to protect his brother.

In truth, he had very little to lose by fighting in the war.

People like Minglan had everything to lose.

He kept himself out of the circle of light from Minglan's lantern and strained to hear the young man's words.

Minglan sighed. "What do you think Ru is doing, Heima?" Jian could almost hear a smile in his voice. Whoever this Ru was meant something. "I hope he's taking care of Chichi. I don't want them to miss me, girl. Because I know what it's like to miss someone who is never coming home, and if they don't see me again, I want them to forget. I think Ru will. He's young. But not Ba. He'll never forgive himself."

Jian knew he should have backed away. The soldier only meant the words for an animal that couldn't speak back. He tried to push away Minglan's sadness. Jian loved his brother, but they both had duties other than to their family. They were used to being apart for years at a time. He'd never felt sadness over it, just acceptance.

The only time Jian ever regretted being a member of the Piao army was after his identity was discovered in Koulland and Qara died for it.

This life was who he was. Boys like Minglan didn't belong in it. They belonged in their fields and with their families.

Huan dropped his voice, and Jian had to strain to hear it. "I'm scared they'll find out, Heima. If I stand out among these people, they'll suspect me and then everyone back home will be in danger."

What was there to suspect? Jian wanted to hear more, to know if Huan posed a danger to his army, to this war, but the soldier stood and turned away from the horse.

Not wanting to be seen, Jian hurried away.

When he reached his tent, he found Luca sitting inside waiting for him.

"How's Huan doing?" Luca asked.

Jian looked to him in question.

Luca sighed. "You really should learn their given names at some point." He rolled his eyes and lifted his lantern to get a better look at Jian's face.

Jian did know the name of every man who came through his units, though he'd never admit that. He'd never tell Luca he saw their faces as he slept. The need to protect them haunted him.

"Minglan. How is Minglan?"

Jian shrugged. He hadn't gotten the chance to speak to the boy, but his words rolled through Jian's mind. *I'm scared they'll find out.*

"Didn't you go looking for him?"

"Didn't find him." Jian sat across the small table from his friend and rested his elbows on the flat surface.

Luca slid a scroll across to him. "This came today with a messenger."

Jian stared at the rolled parchment for a moment. Messengers rarely brought good news. He unrolled it, and his eyes settled on the words.

Luca waited patiently, not speaking until Jian's dark gaze met his. "They want to move up the timeline."

Jian released the parchment, letting it curl in on itself. "They think I can have these men ready to fight in two months' time?" He was the commander. He shouldn't be getting orders from other officers.

Luca leaned back with a long sigh. "Time's up, Jian.

We can no longer sit back and let the Kou pick off pieces of Piao. You read the entire thing?"

Jian nodded. "My generals want to plan a full assault across the northern pass once the snows melt, the same northern pass Altan trapped us in only months ago."

"But that was only one unit of men. This will be the entire might of the Piao army. We're pushing into Koulland. It's not going to be the same, you know that, right?" Luca dipped his head to force Jian to look at him again. "Altan won't beat us again. These men we're training are not the ones we lost."

"No, they're less skilled, untrained."

"Then I suggest we work hard. If you don't want them to be nothing more than targets for the Kou archers, we have work to do." He stood. "Now is not the time to dwell on the past, Jian. It's not the time to let your hatred of Altan turn to fear because of what happened. We need Commander Jian Li in all his dangerous glory if we're going to have any chance of getting these men out of this alive. The generals are right. It's almost time."

"Dangerous," Jian scoffed.

Luca cocked his head. "Jian, you've always been the most dangerous man I've known. Altan can't take that from you." He gave him one final look before pushing aside the tent flap and leaving Jian with the ghosts of his own mind.

Jian moved to his cot and lay back. Minglan's words came back to him, but not his words of secrets and lies. He'd spoken of his home and in his mind, Jian pictured rolling green hills and a home with a warm hearth, the smell of fresh bread wafting through the door as a little boy ran through with Minglan close behind.

Jian barely knew the young soldier, but the words brought him a sense of peace he hadn't had in a long time. Nightmares of dying men in snowy mountains were replaced with dreams of men working in the fields, whistling as they did. And for the first time in months, he slept through the night.

Jian always rose before the rest of camp. He'd been doing it for years, enjoying the early hours just before the sun rose to light the world. He stepped out of his tent as the first tendrils of white light streaked across the sky, obscuring the stars from view.

He'd run his soldiers hard over the last few days since receiving the message about moving up the battle timeline. He'd had Luca pen a response to General Yang, telling him the men would be ready.

But he wasn't so sure that was possible. They were raw, rough, and he needed a lot more than two months to get them into battle shape.

Breathing in the chilly spring air, he let it wake every part of him. He finished buckling his scabbard around his waist and walked toward the sentries posted at the edge of camp.

"Commander," one of them said, shifting his eyes away to avoid looking at Jian. He was one of the few men in camp who wasn't new, one of the few who had good reason not to trust the commander.

"Sergeant." Jian crossed his arms over his leather armor clad chest. "Anything to report?"

"No," he bit out, adding a late, "sir."

The second sentry, a seasoned soldier, but new to Jian's unit, made his way over. "All quiet out here this morning, Commander. Well, except..."

"Except what?" Jian fixed the man with his darkest scowl. If something was amiss, he had to know.

"One of the new recruits..." The man's brow creased in confusion. "He's been on your course most of the night."

Jian turned without a word. Running the course was too dangerous in the dark. What had the soldier been thinking? He took off at a jog, passing the other tents where the rest of the men would stir within the next couple of hours.

When he reached the start of the course, no one was there. He stopped, huffing out a breath as he scanned the trees for any movement. He started to turn around when he caught a running figure out of the corner of his eye.

Minglan burst from the trees with a speed Jian hadn't seen in the boy since he'd arrive last week. He watched him cross the open land, dirt streaked across his pale cheeks. Minglan's hair, usually tied so neatly into a traditional top-knot, fell loose around his determined face.

He stopped running as soon as he noticed Jian

waiting for him, and his mouth formed a small O as if he'd just been caught doing something wrong.

He approached as one would approach a sleeping tiger, but his eyes found Jian's and held no fear, no intimidation. Minglan wasn't the strongest physically, but he had an inner confidence most of the other men lacked.

Maybe it would save his life.

"Minglan," Jian barked, wincing at his own roughness.

Minglan didn't even flinch. "Morning, Commander." He walked right by him without so much as a bow to grab the water skin on the ground behind him.

Taking a long drink, Minglan wiped the back of his hand across his mouth. "I'm sorry, has it been longer than I thought? I assumed I had more time before reporting for the morning."

Jian watched the boy with confusion. Most of his men rarely strung together more than a 'yes, sir' or 'no, sir' for him.

"When did you wake?" Jian asked.

Minglan shrugged. "Well, waking would mean I actually went to sleep, wouldn't it?"

Jian raised an eyebrow. "You mean to tell me you've been out here all night?"

Red crept into Minglan's cheeks. Buddha, this boy was young. Jian sighed. Young and foolish just as he'd been once upon a time.

Jian's generals would still claim youth was one of his problems, but he'd grown a lot in a few short years and now felt beyond his twenty-four years. Heartbreak and suffering did that to a person.

But Minglan… this boy was an innocent. Had he ever suffered the kind of heart-wrenching agony only the premature death of a loved one could cause?

Minglan set the water skin back in the dirt. "I don't want to die."

Jian took a step back, stunned by the words as much as the bluntness with which they were delivered. "Soldier Minglan, I will do everything in my power to prevent that."

He shook his head, his hair sticking to sweaty cheeks. "That's just it though. You can't hold my hand. This last week has been a shock, Commander, I won't lie and say it wasn't. It showed me just how ill prepared I am. I've spent my life…" He looked down at his hands as if trying to come up with something to complete the sentence. "Ah… working the fields. And one day, I'd really like to go back there, to my family. I will do anything I have to if it means I get to see them again."

Jian couldn't tell Minglan he'd been listening to his conversation with the horse days ago, but even if he hadn't, he'd understand on some level because it was what he'd always wanted. People to come home to.

Minglan had that. He put a hand on Minglan's small shoulder. "We'll get you back to them."

"Promise?" He looked up to Jian with such trust in his eyes it had Jian ripping his hand back. No one should put such faith in him.

Instead of answering him, he turned away. "Your body can only take so much of this course before it needs to rest. Has your leg fully healed from last week?"

Minglan shrugged. "It was just a cut, Commander. Of course, it has."

Considering the boy for a moment, Jian nodded. "Come with me."

He didn't wait for Minglan to follow but sensed his presence close behind as he passed the sentries and stopped near the horse pen where stacks of weapons sat covered by thick canvas to protect them from the weather. It was a crude set up, but it was only meant to be temporary.

Picking two blunted daos out from under the canvas, Jian threw one to Minglan.

The boy caught it mid-air with quick reflexes that surprised Jian.

Jian held his weapon in front of his chest, waiting as Minglan lifted his eyes, once again, not looking away.

Jian cleared his throat. "I haven't yet allowed you to train with a weapon. Let me see how you hold it."

Minglan shifted his weight onto his front foot. A confident smirk appeared on his face.

Jian didn't expect much from the untrained boy, but he respected confidence.

Jian crossed the distance between them, setting one of his large hands over Minglan's on the hilt. "Relax your grip. Have you ever held a dao before? Even most village boys in Piao grow up playing war with blunted weapons."

"My life has not been exactly that of a normal

village boy." Minglan tossed his dao from one hand to the other. "But I can hold my own. I promise you that."

There was something he wasn't saying, but Jian wouldn't press. He knew better than anyone that some secrets were better left hidden.

"There are three parts of the dao you must use to your advantage." He slid his hand close to the sharper edge. "When this side is sharpened properly, it will cut through our Kou enemies. They have adopted our weapons, so on the other side of that is the fact it will also cut through us. The weapons we practice with can injure, so we must be careful, but they will not cause lasting harm."

He tapped the blunt wooden side of her dao. "This edge seems useless, does it not?"

Minglan nodded. "I don't need a lesson in daos, Commander. It does not matter to me that one edge of my dao cannot draw blood. It can still do damage enough."

"Trust me, Minglan, this is important information."

"Fight me," he demanded. "Enough talk."

The bluntness made Jian take a step back. Only Luca spoke to him this way. But he didn't reprimand the boy. His ego would be good in battle.

Planting his feet, Jian shifted his weight as he readied his dao. Minglan lifted his weapon, as if ready to take whatever came his way. No fear shone in his eyes, only determination.

Jian stalked toward him, cutting his dao through the air. Minglan lifted his to meet the attack and stumbled back under the weight. He fell to his butt before scrambling back to his feet and turned to meet another attack.

Again and again Jian went after him. Minglan fumbled his responses, but he never stopped. He never slowed or showed any signs of frustration.

"Are you ready to learn?" Jian asked. "Never let your confidence keep you from learning important lessons."

"No." Minglan ducked out of the way of Jian's dao and scrambled back on agile feet. "Come again."

Jian obliged. This time, Minglan met him swing for swing, using speed in place of his non-existent strength.

Minglan advanced, forcing Jian back until he hit the wooden fence of the horse pen. Still, Minglan came, cutting his dao through space with a skill only trained warriors possessed.

As the camp stirred behind them, Jian and Minglan slowed their duel. Minglan's chest heaved from the exertion. After staying up the entire night training on the course in the dark and then spending the next hour fighting his commander, the boy should have collapsed where he stood. Yet, he seemed determined to defy his own body and prove he was more than Jian thought he was.

A few soldiers exited the tents and approached to watch them.

In a moment of distraction, Jian examined the delicate features of the boy. Maybe that was why he seemed younger than he was. Few men who worked the fields in Piao had unblemished skin and callous free hands.

Minglan steeled his gaze, all meekness replaced by a quiet strength.

Jian lowered his dao and Minglan followed suit. "Where did you learn to fight?"

"My father. Have I proven myself enough now, Commander? Am I worthy of being in your army?" He clenched his jaw, waiting for a response. "I don't have your strength. I won't match up against the taller men completing your course with ease. But I will work harder than anyone you've ever seen. When I stumble, I will rise again. You can't promise I'll survive this, but that's okay. I've already promised myself."

Without being dismissed, Minglan turned on his heel and marched away, leaving a bewildered commander staring after him.

# CHAPTER 10

Hua

"Huan," Chen called as she passed him.

She shook her head, unable to speak after what she'd said to the commander. If she was being honest, he scared her, but she refused to let him see that. Instead of being tired from her lack of sleep, adrenaline raced through her body.

She didn't know what had gotten into her.

Chen followed her into their now empty tent. The rest of their tent-mates stood outside waiting for the commander's morning assessment.

"Huan," Chen said again.

She turned on him. "What do you want?" She barely knew this man and hadn't come here to make friends.

"Sorry." He grabbed her arm. "But what were you doing with the commander?"

"How is that any of your business?" Everything seemed to come easy to the other men in their unit. They made it through the course without falling on their faces. They all grew up playing sword-fighting games with their friends and never had to hide it. Unlike her. It wasn't a proper game for women. She used to watch the village boys play, wishing she could join them, but Hua had to be satisfied with training in secret.

Sitting on the edge of her cot, Hua lifted her pant leg to check the scab over her wound. Red seeped through the corners as the scab came loose.

Chen was speaking, but she barely heard him.

"Are you even listening?" he asked.

She sighed. "What did you say?"

"You need to be careful with Commander Li."

She dropped her pant leg and looked up. "Why? He's our commanding officer. We have to follow him."

Chen held out a hand to help her from the bed. She took it and pulled herself up, trying to ignore the slight ache as she walked.

"There's a rumor going around camp." Chen brushed dark hair away from his face. "Don't you listen to camp talk? He's dangerous, reckless. The commander of the Piao forces shouldn't be training new recruits while his generals plan the war. They say he's here because he got a lot of his men killed."

Hua pictured the sadness she'd sensed in the general. Could it be true? She brushed her hair back into a top-knot and left the tent, unable to look at Chen. Something in her wanted to trust Commander Li, wanted to follow him.

But what if it was a mistake?

Something caught her eye around the corner of the tent, and Hua lifted her gaze to find May beckoning to her from the door of her own tent. Checking to make sure no one followed her, Hua slipped into the tent. Cots lined the walls, but instead of training uniforms and armor littering the space, women's robes and sashes sat folded on the beds.

"They're all off preparing breakfast." May turned to face her, a grin splitting her serious face.

"Why are you smiling?" Hua hugged her arms in front of her chest.

"I saw your fight with the commander this morning."

"Oh." Hua's cheeks heated. She'd never liked showing off with her skill. Her father was a great teacher, but along with her talent with a blade and bow, he'd instilled in her a need to hide it.

"Oh? That's all you're going to say? My husband used to tell me Jian Li was one of the best daomen in the entire Piaoen army." She laughed. "What will he say when he learns a woman tested him?" She clapped her hands together, making Hua jump.

"Nothing. He will say nothing," she hissed. "He won't find out."

May's smile dropped. "Someone had to teach that man a lesson. He's so arrogant."

Lifting her eyes, Hua studied May. She'd lost her husband in service to the commander. Was he one of the men who died because their leader was dangerous?

May sighed. "You find him attractive, don't you?"

"What? No!" She wouldn't tell the other woman how often the thought crossed her mind. "I am betrothed. I have no right to find other men attractive."

"It's so hard not to though. Many here blame him for things not under his control, but my husband was loyal to him, as am I. If you…"

"I don't have time for this girlish conversation. I am a soldier, not some camp follower searching for a man to bed."

May laughed, the airy sound seeming so out of place in a military camp. "Yet, I didn't hear a denial. It's okay, Hua, all of your secrets are safe with me."

Hua rolled her eyes and turned back to the door. "That's not a secret because it isn't true." She left before May could pull her further into her talk of attractive men and husbands. She was no better than the girls in the Zhouchang village who held nothing but scorn for the farmer's daughter.

Only, May spoke without malice in her voice.

Hua didn't want to notice how the commander's eyes burned with a deep-seated anger that scorched anything it touched. She wanted to ignore the way his gruff persona hid the man underneath, the one who wanted to teach and protect.

His personality was rough, hard, unlike the man

she was set to marry. Luca was the opposite of Jian, yet his gaze didn't cause the hair on her arms to stand on end. She didn't yearn to spar with him.

The men formed a line through the center of camp as they had each morning, awaiting their commander's approval. It trained them to always be prepared, to always portray a soldier of Piao proudly. Not a thing could be out of place.

Hua stepped up beside the silent Zhao Shi. He didn't spare her a glance as his keen eyes followed the commander down the line of men. Chen joined her at her other side, looking at her out of the corner of his eye.

Was Commander Li really dangerous?

When the commander got to them, he scanned them from head to toe, finding nothing out of place, before moving on.

When he finally yelled "Dismissed" Hua felt an odd sense of relief. She hadn't wanted him to find fault in her. She wanted to make him proud—no matter what her comrades claimed about him.

She joined Chen and Yan as they scooped rice porridge into their bowls and then sat nearby, talking incessantly.

She let their constant chatter relax her.

"What about you, Minglan?" Chen nudged her.

"Huh?" She stuck her spoon in her mouth.

"What do you miss most about home?"

Hua thought for a long moment. Her parents' and grandmother's faces flashed through her mind. Sure, she missed them, but they hadn't been her constant companions. "My brother and sister."

"Your sister need a husband?" Yan snorted.

Hua lifted her eyes to find the commander watching nearby. "My sister died before I left for the war."

Yan shut up immediately.

"But my little brother, Ru is waiting for me back home. He's only four and probably doesn't understand why I'm gone."

Yan rested a hand on her shoulder. "Same age as my son."

"You have a son?"

He nodded. "His mother died having him. He's a good boy. I hope I get to see him again."

Hua shared a smile with him. They all had people they'd left behind.

Chen spoke up. "I married the love of my life only a few months before the recruitment notices came. We needed the money, so here I am."

Yan shook his head. "Life, men. Life."

"Speaking of loves." Chen elbowed Hua and tilted his head to where May watched them as she scoured a pot.

She waggled her eyebrows to the approaching commander and sent Hua a wink. Hua's cheeks burned, and she stared down into her bowl.

Chen laughed. "Most of the men in this camp have been trying to get May to give them the time of day for weeks." He shook his head. "Minglan comes in and a week later he's already got her begging for it."

Hua's forehead scrunched. "Begging for what?" She flicked her eyes from Chen to Yan who wore a matching smirk. Then to Zhao who only shook his head.

Chen laughed and threw an arm around her shoulders, jostling her. "You're a laugh, Huan. Begging for what?" He descended into a fit of laughter.

"I don't understand." She shrugged off his arm and took a bite of food.

Zhao, taking mercy on her, was the one who answered. "Affections. She wants your affections."

"Affections?" She still didn't know what they meant. Her eyes widened as the meaning became clear. They thought May wanted a physical relationship with her.

A woman's voice sounded in front of them. "Sex, Huan." They hadn't seen May approach. She leaned down, nudging Chen out of the way and brought her lips to Hua's ear. "They're saying I want you in my bed." Pressing a kiss to Hua's cheek, she straightened. With one final wink, she sauntered back to her duties.

The men sat frozen, watching her go.

Finally, Yan spoke. "If you don't go after her, Huan, I will."

What was May thinking stirring up gossip? Was it her way of helping Hua keep her identity hidden?

Hua pasted a satisfied smirk on her face. "These things take time, men. Mielie she may be, but is any woman worth more than breakfast?" She grinned in jest, using the old term for pretty her mother taught her and hoping this was truly how they spoke of women.

Chen and Yan howled in laughter. Zhao muttered under his breath. "Yes, some are worth everything."

She barely caught the words, but they stuck in her mind like a thick cloud of sadness. Zhao would never get to see the woman he loved again. He'd gone to prison for her and now had to fight a war he might not survive.

All for a love Hua wasn't sure she believed in.

She'd always considered herself someone incapable of falling in love. There were bigger things in life. Her eyes drifted to Commander Li sitting on a bench across the clearing. Only Luca spoke to him, but many of the men sent cutting looks their way.

The chatter faded from her mind as she watched him, her heart aching for how he must feel surrounded by men who didn't trust him. He was the leader of all the Piao forces, yet the only men under his command were those no longer loyal to him or new trainees.

Without second-guessing herself, she stood and walked toward him, dropping onto the bench at his right.

"What are you doing, Minglan?" he grunted.

"Eating." She dug back into her porridge.

"Watch it, boy." He refused to look at her. "Don't think for a moment there's any room for a soldier to be friends with their commander."

"And don't for a moment think I even want to be your friend."

He did his best to hold back his smile, but Hua saw the edges of his lips tug up. He didn't say anything else, but he also didn't tell her to leave.

Each day, Hua's normally inexhaustible stores of energy ebbed away bit by bit.

And Commander Li knew it. The bastard. His scowl lessened as she stretched, and for him, that was the equivalent of a grin.

She tugged on the edges of her robe, making sure everything was in place. It hung past her waist before the breeches peeked out below.

Letting her guard down now and accidentally revealing her gender would have consequences she wasn't ready to face.

She ran through the course like she'd done too many times by now before sitting on the ground, trying to catch her breath and give her aching legs a rest.

Commander Li's shadow fell over her, blocking the sun. Looking up, she spoke before he could. "I'm okay. Please don't send me away again." Though, the thought of her cot sounded pretty damn good. She forced heavy eyelids wide.

He pursed his lips. "General Kai," he barked.

Luca appeared at his side. "Sir?"

"Get Minglan some water. I don't want him collapsing on my course."

"You're not going to make me lay down?" she asked, not used to being treated in such a way. At home, her parents and grandmother controlled everything she did. It was what it meant to be an unmarried woman. One day, that honor would be her husband's.

Commander Li studied her for a moment as Luca ran off. "Minglan, you are a soldier. I am not your keeper. You choose how to treat your body. If that means training late into the night as I know you've been doing, that's up to you." He turned away to watch the next runner.

Hua couldn't figure the commander out. Sometimes cracks formed in his hard exterior, allowing the light inside him to seep through.

Luca returned and knelt down beside her, handing over a water skin. "You okay?" He dropped his voice.

She took a long drink. "Yeah. Just winded. Thanks for the water."

"I wouldn't fetch it for anyone else." He shook his head. "And Jian apparently knows that. What are you trying to prove, Hua? You're not getting enough sleep. I can see it. All this extra training won't mean anything if you die from exhaustion."

She handed him back the water skin. "I'm fine. Really."

She'd come to an understanding with Luca. He wouldn't interfere in anything she did no matter how much he wanted to. She appreciated it more than he'd ever know. If they both made it out of this, a marriage to him wouldn't be nearly as bad as she once imagined.

"What's this rumor about you and one of the camp women?" Luca's eyebrows arched.

Hua couldn't look at him. "Umm… it's nothing. She's shown me some favor, and I guess that means she wants to bed me."

His lips curved into a grin. "Well, as your betrothed,

I don't think I'm allowed to approve, but I'm not going to tell you not to… bed her."

Hua shoved him, and he fell back on his butt. "It isn't like that. She's just having fun."

Luca grabbed her arm. "You told her, didn't you? It isn't only your career on the line here. How could you let anyone else know your secret?"

She ripped her arm out of his hand. "For your information, she guessed." She dropped her voice to a low hiss. "I didn't tell her. So, you can stop the over-protective future husband act now. I am not your property, Luca. Even after we wed, I won't just bow down to your every demand. If you want a wife who obeys you, find one of the village girls to fill that role."

He ran a hand through his hair and scanned their surroundings to make sure everyone else was still busy with the course. "You're right. I'm sorry."

"I have a feeling you'll be telling me those words a lot in our life together."

"I'm sorry?"

"No, 'you're right.'" She smirked and got to her feet, leaving him chuckling behind her.

Commander Li yelled commands to the men on the course, his jaw tense as it always was when dealing with his soldiers. Hua noticed that about him. Even when the men joked around, Jian never joined in the camaraderie. It was almost as if he was scared. Of what though?

He ran long fingers along the side of his face, his keen eyes tracking Chen as he darted across the field.

Feeling Luca's eyes on her, Hua turned to him. He

flicked his gaze between her and Commander Li before lifting a brow.

Hua shifted away from his overbearing stare and focused on the words now coming out of the commander's mouth.

"Go eat your evening meal. We are done for the day. Rest tonight. Our time on this course is done. We have very few days left to train. You must learn the skills that will keep you alive."

Whispers wound through the tent that night as versions of the story made their way from lips to ears. Commander Li intentionally gave his men up to the Kou general. No wait, he knew there was a trap but figured some would survive and the sacrifices were worth it. He didn't value the lives of his men. He wanted to get to General Altan no matter the cost.

And the best?

He was going to lead them all to their deaths.

Hua tried to fall asleep, but Chen and Yan's words bounced around her skull. She didn't know if she could believe the things they said of the commander with the hard but sad eyes. If she mentioned that to them, they'd call her a girl—which was exactly what she was despite their thinking otherwise. She wasn't immune to the broad-shouldered commander. She'd seen through his harsh commands and brutal criticisms.

Maybe there was some truth to the stories of his

men dying, but there had to be more, something to put the doubt behind the general's bravado.

As voices dropped off, loud snores took their places. With a sigh, Hua pulled herself from the bed and draped an overcoat over her shoulders before sliding her feet into her boots and stepping out into the night.

The stars here reminded her of home, and she liked to imagine her grandmother pointing out the constellations to Ru as she'd done when Hua was a child.

It seemed like another lifetime when she'd been the girl speaking to her grandmother of life and love. One topic they'd never covered? War.

The rumor around camp the day before was that a messenger came to inform the commander of a lost battle near the mouth of the Liudong River. How long would it be before Hua found herself facing hordes of Kou warriors who'd been training for war their entire lives?

She sucked in a breath, reminding herself why she was here. For her family.

A small fire flickered next to one of the sentries and as she neared, Hua recognized Luca's lanky frame.

"Couldn't sleep?" He didn't look at her as he scanned the darkness.

"No, sir."

Luca chuckled. "Please don't 'sir' me. It makes me feel like Jian."

Hua laughed. "But you're my superior."

"In battle, there will be no such thing as rank and superiority. In the beginning, the commander will issue orders, but chaos always overcomes, and every warrior becomes master of their own fates."

"Oh." She kicked her toe against the ground and followed his gaze, peering through the dark toward where a few lanterns winked in the distant town. During the day, they could see it stretching for miles, a high wall surrounding the homes. Only the outer farms sat exposed. In the night, everything seemed smaller.

"Want to sit?" Luca flicked his eyes to her. "Come on, soldier Minglan, keep an old soldier company."

"Old soldier," she scoffed. Luca, like Jian, probably had a few years on her, but not enough to be considered old. The other men her father considered suitable for her to wed were even older. Luca was probably the best of the group.

She lowered herself beside him, not wanting to return to the tent of snoring men. They sat in silence for a few moments, before Hua shifted. She'd never been one to hold back, always speaking with honesty, always seeking truth. So, why did her question struggle to come out? "Can I ask you something?"

Luca only shrugged.

"There are… rumors in camp about what happened with Jian before."

"Before," he repeated with a shake of his head. "You want to know about the mountain battle." He rubbed the back of his neck. "What are they saying about it?"

Luca didn't bother with titles when speaking of the commander, but that didn't surprise Hua. They seemed like friends, like they trusted one another.

"Some say he betrayed his men for a chance to fight General Altan."

He blew out a breath, his jaw twitching. "I can imagine who is spreading the rumors." He sent a scathing look to the other sentry who sat too far away to hear them. "Jian lost the trust of his men, that much is true. I'm sorry, Hua, but this isn't a story I'm prepared to tell."

"Why?"

"Because it doesn't belong to me." He met her gaze. "Just… be careful what you believe. Jian has many secrets, but he will always choose duty and honor over his own desires. He's a good man."

Warmth spread through Hua at this declaration. The commander spoken of in hushed terms hadn't reconciled with the one she watched every day, and Luca's words only confirmed her suspicions.

Her fellow soldiers were full of shit.

Her shoulders relaxed, and she stared into the flames.

Luca bit his lip, studying her profile. "Some secrets are more dangerous than others."

She nodded, knowing the exact secret he meant. Hers.

"Can I ask you another question?"

He huffed out a laugh. "I honestly don't think I could stop you."

"Why didn't you send me home? When I showed up here, why did you keep my identity a secret from your friend, your commander?"

He was quiet for a long moment. "Did your baba ever tell you about my mother?"

She shook her head.

A rush of air left him, and he looked away. The firelight flickered across his profile. "She died when I was a child."

"Was it the Kou?"

"No. She was ill for a long time. But I don't think it matters how someone dies, only that they're gone, in their next life. The emptiness they leave behind is the same. I would have fought any force that stood between me and saving her. The only thing that saved me was my friendships with Jian and his brother."

"I'm not really sure that answered my question."

He sighed. "I searched for someone to blame, to turn my grief into anger, but there was no one. You lost your sister, but it isn't just life that took her from you. There is someone to blame. And you deserve a chance to fill the emptiness."

"Do you think it can ever be filled?"

"Probably not." He rubbed his eyes. "You need to be careful, Hua. I see the way you meet Jian's eyes as if you've never heard the word fear. It's highly amusing, but I don't want to be around when he learns the only person in his unit who isn't scared to death of him is a woman."

"I thought you said he was a good man. Yet, he frightens you."

Luca chuckled, running a hand over the top of his head. "Yes, I love Jian as if he were my own brother, but I'm also not a fool."

# CHAPTER 11

Jian

Jian was a fool.

He'd thought normal was something he could have after his mission in Koulland, but maybe normal had never been a possibility for the bastard brother of the emperor. His secret parentage was like a weight around his neck. If his men found out the truth, they'd never look at him the same way. The mother he'd never known betrayed the emperor she was sworn to serve as consort.

And Jian was the product of that betrayal. He didn't know who his father was.

Was he an officer like Jian himself? Was he a good

man before losing his life? Jian liked to think he was. He had to have known what would happen if anyone found out he was in love with a consort. As Jian lay in bed, he imagined a great love story resulting in his birth.

A smile tilted his lips. There was very little good in his life, but he could pretend there was when he thought of parents who'd died to have him.

First light filtered into the tent, and he rolled from his cot. Soon, they'd be on the move. There were conflicting orders coming from his generals. Some thought the great battle would take place in the Shan mountains. Others wanted the army congregated around Dasha to protect the emperor at all costs.

Jian wasn't sure which he agreed with. On one hand, Bo needed protection. But a defensive strategy was what got Piao in the mess it was in with Kou attacking border towns. It was time to go to them.

And he had the final say.

Moving to the small desk in his tent, Jian sat and picked up the quill, dipping it in ink before starting a letter to his brother. He wrote of trivial things. Training regimens. Stories of his men. He left out their relative incompetence. Bo didn't need to worry.

He found himself writing about one soldier in particular. There was something that drew him to Minglan. Maybe it was loneliness, and he was in need of a friend—despite what he'd said to Minglan about soldiers being friends with their commanders. Other than Luca and Minglan, none of his men spoke to him outside training.

Maybe it was the fact that Minglan appeared those weeks ago with a small frame not fit for soldiering, but enough skill to make up for it. He'd been true to his word. He worked harder than anyone else.

Jian lifted his head as he heard footsteps outside his door.

"Commander?" Minglan's voice called. "Are you awake?"

He cleared his throat. "Come in."

Minglan pushed aside the flap and stepped inside, his feminine eyes dancing around the space before finally landing on Jian. They widened, and Jian felt a flush creep up his neck. Minglan's gaze made him feel exposed, and he reached into the chest beside his desk for a robe to pull on over his bare abdomen.

"What do you want, Minglan?" His voice came out harsher than he'd intended. He didn't like feeling uncomfortable.

The boy didn't even flinch, and that annoyed Jian more. Why didn't he fear him as everyone else did?

"I'd like a sparring partner."

Jian sighed. "Tell me, Minglan. Do you ever sleep?"

Minglan shrugged. "I sleep enough. Rest won't prepare me for battle." Fire blazed in his eyes as he spoke of battle. "I'd ask General Kai for help, but he had watch last night."

"What about any of the other men in this camp who don't have a commander's duties to attend to."

Minglan didn't seem deterred by his reluctance. "Honestly, sir, they're all just bumbling idiots. They can't teach me like you can."

Jian realized in that moment he didn't want Minglan going to anyone else for training. A commander didn't typically work with soldiers one on one, but Jian felt a responsibility for Minglan he'd never felt for anyone else. He remembered almost promising the boy he'd make it home when all this was done.

Jian pulled on his boots, laced them up, and stood. "Come on, kid. I'll help you, but we won't be sparring today." He tied a belt around his waist to tighten the woolen robe he wore. He had better quality clothing, robes of silk with wide sleeves fit for a relative of the emperor. But he didn't dare wear anything of such quality around his men.

A grin split Minglan's face. "Then what would you like me to do, sir?"

He flicked his eyes to Minglan's slim fingers. "We will be on horseback, Minglan. Our unit will be positioned in front of units of archers in the attack. The dao will be our weapon, but you are already more skilled than half my seasoned soldiers."

Minglan glanced down at himself, a frown forming on his lips. "That doesn't mean I don't need to practice."

"I want to see how you do with a different weapon." He'd try to get Minglan moved to a different unit for the battle, one that wouldn't be in the middle of the slaughter. "When you arrived, you had a bow strapped to your saddle. Have you used it?"

He hesitated for a moment. "Um... once or twice, sir."

"Good, that's a start. I can at least teach you the basics."

He retrieved a bow and a bundle of arrows before marching toward the trees. Archery wasn't a priority, so he'd had no targets set up. They'd have to make do. Gray morning light broke free of the dark clouds and filtered through the bare trees, illuminating their path in a golden glow.

Excitement lit in Minglan's eyes, and the sense of recognition was so strong in Jian he couldn't look away.

They stopped in a circle of trees. Minglan turned, taking in every sight as if each amazed him. He was a mix of contradictions. Innocent, yet daring. Excited, yet cautious.

And so damn endearing even Jian felt his hard exterior crumbling.

"The woods remind me of home." Minglan smiled.

"I thought you lived on a farm."

He nodded. "The northern pastures backed up to the woods separating our land from the village. I spent a lot of time among the trees."

Jian didn't have that. A place that felt like home. He'd never felt more adrift than he did while standing in front of Huan Minglan. *See, Luca? I can remember their given names.*

Shaking off the feeling, Jian set the arrows on the ground, pulling one from the bundle. "You say you've shot an arrow before, but I'm guessing it wasn't in a high-pressure life or death situation."

"You'd actually be surprised."

He imagined a lot about Minglan would surprise him. "Take this." He handed him the bow followed by the arrow. "I want to see your stance."

Minglan lifted it, holding his elbow so high, Jian laughed. "You're going to end up hurting yourself more than your enemy if you hold it like that." He gripped Minglan's arm and lowered it before sliding his hand along the man's arm and covering his hand.

Minglan went impossibly still.

"Breathe, soldier."

Minglan sucked in air and let it out in a long stream.

"Okay," Jian said softly. "Take an arrow and rest it against the bow, pulling it back with the string."

Without warning, Minglan whipped around to say something, but the words died on his lips as the arrow stabbed Jian in the chest. Minglan's jaw dropped open. "I'm so sorry." He jumped back. "I was just..."

"Minglan," Jian growled. "You have a weapon in your hands." He rubbed the point of contact on his chest. "You must be aware of it at all times."

Minglan ducked his head. "Yes, I know. I just..."

Jian's brow creased.

Minglan sighed and turned around. In one swift movement, he lifted the bow and released the arrow. It cut through the air before hitting the center of a far tree. Minglan turned back with a sheepish expression.

Jian only stared at the arrow. A perfect shot. "Minglan, how is it possible you just did that?"

He lifted one shoulder in a shrug. "I... When I told you I spent a lot of time in the woods... I was hunting."

"Who taught you to shoot like that?"

He issued a nervous laugh. "My nainai."

"Your grandmother?" His jaw fell open.

Minglan's jaw hardened. "She believes a woman can do anything a man can do, just in a different way. That her purpose was more than marriage and babies."

If he were honest with himself, he'd never considered what a woman's purpose was before. "She sounds different."

"Well, she is different. My father was either off with the army or busy in the fields. He trained me with the dao but didn't have time for the bow. My mother didn't have much time for children. So, Nainai took it upon herself to teach both me and my sister how to defend our land against animals. My sister never took much interest."

"I'd imagine not. Weapons aren't tools for women."

A dark expression crossed Minglan's face. "It wasn't because she was a woman. My grandmother took great pleasure in these tools that supposedly aren't for her. I am a..." She stopped speaking, his lips clamping shut.

"A what?"

He looked as if he'd caught him saying something he shouldn't. "Nothing. I'm nothing." He turned to walk away.

"Minglan!" Jian called after him. "You have not been dismissed."

He whirled around. "What do you want from me, Commander?"

Jian didn't know the answer to that question. What did he want? Why couldn't he let the soldier walk away? He knew the simple response. Hearing of Minglan's simple upbringing, living on a farm with family made him wish for something he'd never had.

Seeing the lack of fear in Minglan's eyes made him wish for something he could still obtain. All he wanted was someone who understood, someone who knew of his past and didn't judge him for it. Someone he could call a true friend. He needed more than Luca.

Sure, Minglan had secrets. He saw it in the boy's eyes. But Jian's likely dwarfed them. Maybe that was why he wanted to help Minglan. They both kept parts of themselves hidden.

Minglan stared at him, still waiting for an answer. So, Jian gave him the only one he could. "Find a dao. You and I both need a fight." He walked off toward his tent, retrieved his dao, and stepped outside to wait for Minglan to return.

As soon as he did, Jian led him to the practice arena they'd set up. It consisted of a wide-open circle surrounded by hay bales. Sounds of a waking camp drifted toward them, but Jian didn't stop.

This time, when they faced off, Jian didn't have any delusions about Minglan's lack of skill. They circled each other with light steps.

Jian turned, never losing sight of his opponent. When Minglan lunged, Jian batted his dao away easily.

"You can do better," he said.

"I was testing you."

Jian grinned at that.

Minglan jumped forward again. Jian ducked away

from his dao but grabbed his arm and pulled him close. "What are you hiding from me, Minglan?"

Minglan jerked his knee up, slamming it into Jian's thigh. Jian released him with a curse, and Minglan widened the gap between them.

"What are you hiding from all of us, Commander?" Minglan asked. He stepped closer. "Why did you lead your men into a trap?"

The blunt edges of their daos slammed together. As quick as Minglan was, he was no match for Jian's pure strength.

Jian didn't answer the question. Instead, he circled Minglan, waiting for the boy to strike again. Minglan didn't disappoint. He ran at Jian, arcing his dao through the air. Jian met the blow with his own weapon, and both crashed to the ground. Minglan didn't stop. He barreled into Jian, sending them both sprawling to the dirt.

Minglan landed on top of Jian and rolled off, breathing heavily. His eyes were black orbs as he stared down at Jian. "Did you kill them, Commander? Your own men. Are they dead because of you?"

Jian laid his head back, his eyes focusing on the gray sky above. A raindrop hit his face. As more rain began to fall, he finally met Minglan's gaze. "Yes." It was the truth. His men died because of his vendetta against Batukhan Altan. "They're dead because of me."

Minglan ran a hand over the top of his head and closed his eyes as the rain soaked his robe. When he opened them again, there was something in their depths Jian hadn't seen since the battle, even in Luca.

Understanding.

"I don't believe you." Minglan turned away from him. "This is war, Commander. People die. That is Samsura—our circle of life and death. It is suffering. It is pain. But we are not the cause. One day, when we reach Nirvana, maybe we'll understand there was nothing more we could have done." He looked back over his shoulder. "I don't know what happened to your men. But I do know if I were one of them, I wouldn't want you to claim my death as your failing."

He walked away, his boots leaving prints in the mud as he passed by.

Jian lay on the ground a few minutes longer. Minglan's words sounded like something Bo would have told him. There was something different about the kid, about Minglan. Maybe he'd been wrong. Minglan looked young, but he wasn't a kid at all. Maybe he was the most enlightened of them all.

Jian had never given Samsura much thought. He didn't know if he believed in Buddhist reincarnation. Religion didn't speak to him as it did Bo or Minglan. Yet, the soldier's words made more sense than any he'd heard on the subject. One day, he liked to believe his cycle of suffering would end.

He lifted his head, watching Minglan in the distance. He didn't enter his tent to escape the rain. Instead, he stood with his head tilted back, letting the water run through his hair.

Picking himself up off the ground, Jian went to prepare for a wet day of training.

"That's it!" Jian called as he saw Minglan disappear into the trees to complete the course. He'd told them they were done on the course, but his heart wasn't in fighting today. Training in the mud would be good for the men, struggling through adversity.

The other men took their turns, but Jian only watched the edge of the woods for Minglan's small frame to come barreling toward him. The boy had become something of a project, and Jian was determined to turn him from a skilled fighter into a true warrior.

He had the mind of one, that was for sure. Each time Minglan met the commander's eyes, refusing to look away, the young man's strength burned through, a strength he seemed to want to hide around the others.

Soldier Chen clapped Minglan on the back. "You've improved."

Minglan shrugged him off, but Jian didn't miss the flash of annoyance as he did. He'd spent too much time studying the budding friendships, noting how most of the men treated Minglan like he would never be quite as capable as the others around them. If Jian was being honest, it was one of the reasons he woke early each morning to spar with Minglan.

He wanted the kid to prove them wrong.

The funny thing was none of the other trainees would be able to best Minglan in a fight. Jian truly believed that.

"Chen," Jian barked. "You're up."

Chen's brow creased. "I already did my reps for the day. I thought we were moving on to weapons training."

"Are you disobeying your commander, soldier?" He crossed his arms.

Chen didn't argue, instead sending an exasperated look Minglan's way before taking off for the first wall.

Minglan sat on the ground next to his water skin.

"You okay?" He stopped in front of him.

Minglan looked to Jian as if the question surprised him. When assigned to this post, Jian promised himself he wouldn't get close to any of his soldiers. He'd made that mistake before. His old unit had been a sort of family. When it was ripped away, it hurt. In war, there could be no friendships.

Yet, since the night he'd found the boy running the course in the dark, Jian found himself seeking Minglan out. Something about him and his open, honest face made the hard commander want to talk until all of his problems sat between them. But he couldn't. He constantly had to remind himself they were commander and soldier, not friends.

As much as he might want them, Jian Li didn't get to have friends.

He'd even distanced himself from Luca. Tearing his eyes from Minglan, he found his second in command watching him. "I distinctly remember assigning you to writing correspondences today." They were sending messengers summoning any unit of the army that could be spared to convene here outside Kanyuan to prepare a march through the mountains during the summer months.

To Luca's credit, he didn't back down under the harsh stare. "I need to speak with you."

Jian nodded, leaving Minglan where he sat as he followed Luca a safe distance from their men. "What is it?"

"Batukhan Altan was seen in Kanyuan."

Jian pivoted on his heel without thinking as the words overtook everything in his mind. Altan was here. He'd crossed the border… for what? What did he want this time?

"His men," Jian said, knowing Luca followed him though he did not make a sound. "Have they been seen?"

"No. Hanan only said he saw Altan… alone."

Jian stopped walking and turned to his friend. "Alone?" He shook his head. It made no sense. General Altan never went anywhere without Kou warriors at his back. Even in Koulland, he had many enemies that would see him dead. Altan should be crossing the northern passes with his men, preparing for the battle they all knew was coming. Kanyuan wasn't supposed to be a factor. "Is Hanan still here?"

Luca gestured to Jian's tent. "I told him to wait for you."

Jian nodded before pushing inside to greet the mountain of a man. Hanan stood with his head ducked so as not to hit the top of the canvas. Thick, dark hair escaped under his rusted helmet. As one of the

Kanyuan town guards, the Piao insignia stood out on the lightweight armor he wore over his robes.

"Commander." He stuck out his hand for Jian to shake rather than the more formal salute or bows other men afforded Jian.

Jian grasped his hand. "Hanan, it's been a long time."

The big man grinned, his grizzled face brightening. "It wouldn't be so long if you came into town for a drink every now and then."

Jian released him. "Some of us have work to do."

Hanan only shook his head at that.

"So, Altan. Is he still in town?"

"As far as we can tell, he already came and went. My regiments have been preparing to leave the city for some time now. We're due to join you and the rest of the Piao forces here within the next two weeks. General Kai is using my messengers to summon the generals stationed in the Liudong valley."

Jian's mind was still on Altan. "Do you know what he was doing here?"

"We believe he was meeting someone but haven't been able to learn their identity."

"Hanan, put all your resources into this. We must find out what the general was doing on this side of the border."

Hanan bowed and turned on his heel to gather his men for the ride back to the village. Jian left Luca to finish running the men through their training exercises and entered his tent.

Digging beneath his thin mattress, he retrieved the most precious gift he'd ever been given. He'd never told anyone of his final night with Qara. How she'd seemed sad, like she'd known what was coming for her. There was an old legend in Koulland of the gift of sight being passed down through the Altan family line. He hadn't believed it.

Until that night.

His hand gripped the smooth jade as he pulled the dragon statue free. He sought it every time he wanted to feel close to Qara. To be caught with a dragon likeness could mean a death not even his brother could save him from. The fear and worship in Piao was too strong to allow anyone with a hint of the creature inside them to live.

Some days, he wished he was of the dragon blood, even though it meant risking discovery and death. Only then would he have any chance of being a Nagi and letting the dragon inside him save his people from what was coming. But he wasn't descended from the ancient lines, and he had no beast waiting to break free.

He'd seen the bloodshed in Dasha and then again in the mountain pass. And it was only the beginning. His messengers would reach each general in Piao, and within weeks, they'd arrive here for the march into the mountains, a march many wouldn't return from.

If they lost, what would happen to the people of Piao?

He felt the grooves of the dragon scales carved into the jade and closed his eyes. "One day, Jian Li, you will know why I give this to you," she'd whispered as they crossed the snowy mountains in their escape. "I won't be there to guide you. When the dragon comes, protect it. Protect her."

Moments later, Qara was taken from him. Jian hadn't been allowed to witness her execution, but General Altan made sure he heard about it.

When her brother came for her, she'd looked as if she expected it.

All these years later and he still couldn't get that image out of his mind. He'd never forgotten her words, but as time passed, they seemed like a scared girl's delusions. The dragons left Piao centuries ago. They hadn't protected the country in the civil war or in any of their battles with border nations.

Many people thought them dead and their magic gone, yet each emperor hunted down those suspected of having dragon blood, of being descended from the last dragon keepers. They feared those with the potential power to usurp them. In the past, the dragon inhabited keepers worked alongside the emperors until the war that saw the last of them die at the hands of their so-called allies.

Dragon blood was royal, and for an emperor to have absolute power, they couldn't have any question about their right to rule being asked.

A throat cleared behind him, and he turned to face Minglan. "You cannot enter your commander's tent without announcing yourself."

Minglan didn't even flinch. "I did announce myself. Many times." He leaned forward to look over Jian's shoulder. "Is that a dragon?" The boy's face lit up in excitement, and Jian quickly stuffed the jade back under his cot.

"Speak of this to no one."

Minglan didn't seem to have heard him. "I haven't seen a dragon statue up close. I didn't know they were allowed outside the emperor's temple." He nudged Jian out of the way.

Jian should have stopped him. He shouldn't allow a soldier to know his secrets, but there was a wonder on the young man's face he couldn't wipe away.

Almost as if in a trance, Minglan pulled the statue free and held it in front of him. His pupils dilated as he leaned forward, examining it closely. "This is wonderful." His hand ran the length of the dragon's back. "Beautiful. Strong. Graceful." As if snapping back to reality, Minglan shoved the statue at Jian. "But they're gone. There's no use wishing a beast can save us. We have to save ourselves."

He ran from the tent, leaving Jian to watch after him.

Jian should have been worried about people learning of the dragon statue he possessed. He should have feared for his position.

But, Buddha help him, he trusted that soldier.

And he didn't know why.

# CHAPTER 12

Hua

Hua had to get away from Commander Li.

Why did he have a dragon in his tent?

What did it mean?

He risked his life to keep it, but why?

Piao was not a harsh place to live unless one was a dragon suspect. The young emperor was kind to his people. Neighbors cared for each other. Families got by farming and raising animals. There was war, but the country still thrived.

No one of the dragon blood had been executed since the new emperor took his throne. It was almost enough to make the people of Piao feel safe.

Almost.

But Hua hadn't felt safe since the day her sister was killed. She'd spent the months since learning her family's secrets and walking the edge of a dangerous line.

And now, she lived in the middle of the Piao army, men surrounding her on all sides. If they learned she was a woman, they'd send her home in disgrace.

But if it came out she was dragon blooded… she'd never see her home again.

Did the commander know? Was it all a test? The moment she saw the statue, it drew her in until she had to touch it, to feel the scales. It heated in her hands like it had a life of its own.

But that was impossible, wasn't it?

Since returning from the festival in Dasha where an arrow should have pierced her skin, everything she'd thought she'd known didn't seem true anymore. What did impossible even mean anymore?

Statues didn't emit heat. Arrows pierced skin. Ink didn't disappear into flesh.

Yet, it all happened.

Her breath came in short gasps, and she shoved the statue away from her mind. She just wanted it to all go away, for life to return to normal. Well, normal for a girl pretending to be a man and preparing to march off to war.

She needed to get back to training. Only that made sense to her. Holding a dao in her hands would calm her, make her feel as if her deception still had a purpose.

Her entire body slammed into someone else, and

she fell back onto her butt. Someone fell onto her, and it took her a moment to realize it was May.

"I'm so sorry." May scrambled off and gathered the linens she'd been carrying.

Hua lifted her eyes, noticing the soldiers watching them as if it was all great entertainment. She laughed before clapping a hand over her mouth to stop the feminine sound that came out.

May matched her grin. "Come with me." She held a hand out, helping Hua to her feet.

Aware of the eyes following them, Hua followed May around the back of a tent. May turned to her, all hint of a smile gone. "You looked kind of freaked out before you ran into me. I thought you could use a minute away from the prying eyes."

Hua released a sigh. May didn't know how right she was. Seeing the dragon in the commander's possession shook her, but it wasn't only that. She'd been in camp for months now. Months of pretending to be something she wasn't. Months of not letting anyone see the girl underneath.

Sucking in a deep breath, Hua closed her eyes.

"Are you okay?" May put a hand on her arm. Hua opened her eyes at May's kindness. True to her word, the woman kept the secret. Not only that, she befriended Hua and helped her.

"I need to ask you a question." Hua met her gaze.

"Okay," May drew the word out.

"It's about the commander."

She ran a hand over her braid and gnawed on her lower lip. "And my husband."

Hua nodded.

Blowing out a breath, May turned away. "You want to know if the rumors are true. If Commander Li is the dangerous man they claim he is." She went quiet for a long moment. "He led his unit into battle against General Altan's forces. That much is true. It was a battle they shouldn't have been in, but the commander couldn't have known it was a trap. The Kou forces overwhelmed them from on high. The men who returned spoke of blame, as if it was the commander's fault, but I've known Jian Li for many years. My husband trusted him with his life. He is a good man, an honorable man. No matter what he tries to make everyone else believe."

Hua rubbed her eyes. Could she tell May about the dragon statue he possessed? That he was breaking the law? No, she trusted the woman with her own secrets, but that wasn't hers to reveal.

"Why, Hua?" May stepped closer and dropped her voice. "Why do you need to know?"

Hua had no answer to that question. She didn't know the reason she was drawn to an angry, rough man, one who only saw her as a boy.

"I have to go." Before Hua could round the tent, footsteps sounded on the other side. "I can't be caught talking to you." Panic rushed through Hua. Soldiers didn't mix with camp workers. They had no reason to talk, and others would know there was something she wasn't telling them.

May gripped her hand and pulled her back toward her. Before Hua could protest, she kissed her.

Hua stood frozen, her lips pressed to May's, until a throat cleared behind them. They broke apart. Hua's cheeks flamed ten shades of red when she turned to find both Commander Li and Luca staring at them. The commander's jaw clenched, but Luca's eyes danced with glee.

"Minglan," Commander Li barked. "This is not how I expect my soldiers to behave. May, return to your duties." May sent Hua an apologetic look before practically running back into the center of camp.

"Commander," Luca spoke up. "You were on your way to deal with a situation. Let me handle Minglan."

Commander Li glanced between them for a moment before turning on his heel and marching away.

Luca crossed his arms and bit back a smile. "What is the meaning of this?"

Hua blew a piece of hair out of her face and grimaced. "I didn't want to be caught talking with her in private."

"But you can be caught kissing her?"

"Don't laugh at me. You know it's much less of a risk. At least no one will question my manhood this way."

He shook his head with a laugh. "All right, boy, come with me. I was going to seek you out later anyway." As they passed the training area, Luca picked up a quiver full of arrows. "Grab a bow."

She retrieved a bow before following him into the trees away from camp. Running to match his steps, she didn't speak until they no longer heard the sounds of men training and cooks preparing supper.

"Where are you taking me?"

Luca glanced back at her. "I want to see this archery skill Jian has been telling me about."

"He talks about me?"

"Why wouldn't he, Hua? You're small, but you're fiercer than half the larger men. You have more talent with a dao than any of the other new recruits, and I've heard you can shoot a target twice as far away."

"Are you saying I'm impressive, Luca?" A grin spread across her face. "That you're glad we're getting married?"

He laughed at that. "Maybe if you weren't going around kissing beautiful women. Or if I actually thought you'd end up marrying me. You're too strong-willed to allow your family to choose your future, Hua. And as my letter told you, I love another. I'd never ask you to honor the agreement. Not now."

"Why not now? You agreed to it before."

"I agreed to it because you needed my family's protection. I'm not so sure you do now."

"Protection?" She stopped moving and stared at his back. His muscles contracted as he sighed and rubbed a hand over his face.

Finally, he turned to face her. "You weren't supposed to be here, Hua. I was never supposed to have to give you the answers you seek."

"Because I'm just a woman who won't understand?" She grunted in frustration and pulled an arrow free as she lifted her bow. Drawing her arm back, she fired.

The arrow sailed close to Luca's head before hitting a tree behind him. "Please, tell me how I should be at home away from the danger. How I should be dreaming of the day my life is tied to yours so you can offer this *protection* you speak of." She knocked another arrow. "I obviously need a strong soldier to keep me safe." The second arrow hit the same spot as the first.

"Hua, stop."

"Don't call me Hua. That is not my name, not here. I am Huan Minglan, a soldier in his Imperial Majesty's army. Just as you are. I'm standing at the edge of a military camp, Luca. The time for protection is finished. Now, I need honesty. Why did my father choose you?"

He blew out a breath and stared at the two arrows sticking out of the soft bark. "I grew up in the emperor's court with the princes. My father was the captain of the guard when I was young. Jian, Bo, and I were constant companions."

"Bo?" Hua took a step back. "The emperor?"

Luca nodded. "He..." He sighed. "I tell you this in confidence because my father trusts yours with his life. Our families are connected." He rubbed his face. "Commander Li is the emperor's brother."

Hua's eyes widened. "He's a prince?" Was that why he had a dragon statue? Had she walked into a prince's tent without permission?

Luca shook his head. "No. He was the son of Bo's mother, but not his father. He should be nothing to the royal family, but Bo loves him. That is why he's in command here. He has the emperor's trust."

"How does this relate to you and me?"

"My father always kept me close to the royal family in hopes it would protect me after my grandfather was killed by the late emperor Wei."

"Killed?" She swallowed heavily.

"For having the dragon blood."

It couldn't be. Hua bent at the waist to rest her hands on her knees and catch her breath. Hair fell loose from her knot, and she pushed it away. "My… My grandfather…"

"I know." Luca's voice softened. "They were executed together."

She knew the story. Her father moved the family under the new name of Minglan after the execution of her grandfather.

"You're…" She met Luca's eyes.

He nodded. "I've known I had the blood for many years. That is why your father and mine decided to tie our families. So we could protect each other should the need arise."

"Do you see the stars?" She needed to know there was someone out there like her, that she wasn't alone.

"The stars?" Luca's brow scrunched. "What do you mean?"

"The dragon in the sky. Does it hang above you each night?"

"There's no dragon constellation." He gave her a strange look. "Hua, having the blood doesn't make us different. It only means we're descended from the last dragon keepers. But the dragons abandoned us long ago, so we never have to worry about them living inside us. We can live normally as long as no one learns of our secret."

Normal? She straightened and stumbled away from him. What was normal? The stars rearranged themselves into a dragon, and she was the only one who saw it. The image on her arm… She yanked her sleeve up and shoved her arm at Luca. "Look at the mark." Her eyes traced the red lines of the dragon drawn by her grandmother.

Luca grabbed her arm and turned it over. "I see nothing but dirty skin." His lips drew down. "I don't like how little you get to bathe here, Hua. A woman needs more. Tomorrow, I'll take you to the stream myself."

"I don't care about a stupid bath," she yelled. She cared that for a moment she'd thought she wasn't alone. Luca Kai might have the dragon blood, but he wasn't like her.

She felt it, something clawing at her skin, trying to get out. It twisted her anger, magnifying it.

Red-hot ire seethed through her, and she ripped her arm away from Luca. "You say you've known about this for years? Do you want to know when I found out?"

He didn't respond.

"Go on. Ask me."

"When did you find out?" His voice was cautious.

"Days before leaving my home to fight a war I'm not legally allowed to be in. No one prepared me. They told me I was going to marry a man I didn't know, but they didn't say why it was you.

No, can't tell Hua Minglan the truth about anything."

"I'm telling you the truth now."

"It's a little late, isn't it?" Her nostrils flared as she glared at him. It wasn't his fault, she knew that. Her father spent years training her for some kind of war, but it wasn't a battle with the Kou he prepared her for. He'd known one day she'd need to fight for her life, possibly against her own people.

She turned to walk away from Luca when Zhao's lumbering frame ran toward them. "General Kai," he called.

The worry on Luca's face slipped away as he became the general again. "Soldier, what is it?"

"The commander sent me to find you. General Hanan… he's…"

"What happened?" Luca snapped.

"His horse was found wandering the countryside between our camp and Kanyuan. The scouts searched the surrounding hills and found his body. Killed by arrows, sir. In the back like…"

"He'd been trying to get away." Luca finished the sentence and started back toward camp.

Hua didn't know the general they spoke of, only that he'd led the garrison in the border village, keeping the Kou from crossing into Piao by way of their gates.

Smoke rose above the treetops. "Zhao, how long have you been searching for us?" Hua looked sideways at him.

Zhao's eyes widened as he looked up. "Not long. They… It's happening so quickly…."

Luca picked up speed, and Hua gripped her bow as she ran behind him. By the time they reached the edge of camp, she was out of breath.

Still, there was no time. Fire raged through the lines of tents as far as they could see. Soldiers scrambled to put out the flames.

The ground shook as horses thundered up the road from Kanyuan. Luca cursed.

Tattoos stretched up their thick necks as the sun beat down on the tanned skin of the enemy warriors. No one was ready for them. They cut paths through the camp, dividing Jian's forces.

Zhao gripped his dao, but Luca had no weapon.

Hua darted into the open, dodging an arrow flying through the air. She had to make it to the training ground for a dao.

A burning sensation pulsed along her skin, and she bit back a scream as pain pierced her heart. But she couldn't stop. Not when the enemy was at their doorstep. Footsteps sounded behind her, and she whirled around with her bow raised and an arrow nocked.

Zhao threw his hands up, and she lowered it. "Come on."

The fire hadn't reached the training pens where the men normally practiced with weapons yet. The daos here weren't as good as the ones kept in their tents. Both edges were blunted for training. But they could do a lot of damage with enough force.

Hua threw a weapon to Zhao, and he held it in his free hand with his sharpened dao in the other. He crossed them in front of his chest, looking every bit the warrior she wished she could be.

They'd lost Luca, and there seemed to be no battle plan in the camp, only a mad scramble for safety.

"You and me, Huan." Zhao met her eyes, giving her the knowing look she'd grown used to from him. "You ready?"

She nodded. She'd come here for this, to fight, to protect Piao. Somehow, the Kou were on their land, and they couldn't be allowed to stay.

Forming up beside Zhao, she surveyed the destruction. Her hand squeezed around the hilt of her dao until it hurt, but the pain was good. It distracted her from the pounding in her skull. Ice replaced the heat, prickling along her skin and making her hairs stand on end.

A man thundered toward them, but Zhao cut him down before he could get the first swing of his dao in.

"Huan, duck!" Zhao yelled.

She lunged out of the way as a spear soared through the space she'd occupied only moments before. *Calm down, Hua. This is what you've trained for.* Saying the words to herself was no use. Words didn't matter. Actions did.

She flicked her eyes from the spear sticking up from the ground to a man battling a soldier nearby. Chaos surrounded them as Piao soldiers fought for their lives. Her father never trained her to fight with a spear, but she reached for it anyway. Closing one eye, she drew her arm back and sent it sailing.

The tip lodged in the chest of a Kou warrior and he stumbled back, blood gurgling past his lips.

Every step Hua took felt like a struggle, as if her feet were stuck in mud.

The fight swirled around her, and she lost sight of Zhao. Stumbling forward, she searched for Chen and Yan, but her friends were either fighting in another part of camp or dead.

She refused to believe they were dead. Her foot snagged on a body lying still on the ground, and she stared down into the face of Healer Sasha, his mouth still open as if forming a scream.

A spear protruded from his chest.

Hua tore her eyes away. May. She had to find May and tell her about her father. But there was no time.

A man in lacquered leather armor rode toward her, his horse's hooves thundering across the clearing, and she readied her dull blade. As he turned his dark eyes on her, all she saw was an arrow sailing through the central square of Dasha as it shattered her heart before even reaching its final destination. She could practically hear Luna's body hit the ground as the moment froze in time, and the rest of the world ceased to matter.

Hua's eyes flashed red as the horse bore down upon her. She stepped to the side and met the attacker's dao with her own, sending a loud thwack ripping through the air.

The rider swung again, but Hua ducked and slapped the blunted blade against the rump of the horse, sending it running.

Heima, she had to get to Heima. The last connection to her family was somewhere in that camp among the chaos and blood, her last connection to Luna. Heima would help her find May.

Every part of her wanted to see the light fade from the eyes of each Kou warrior she ran past. Were they there when her world stopped? Did they participate in the attack on Piao's heart, its soul?

Hua's arm seared with pain and she pushed her sleeve back as she ran, glancing down at the red dragon etched into her skin. Luca hadn't seen it, but that didn't mean it wasn't there.

The stars. The dreams. It all made sense; the dragons spoke to her. They called to her, pulling forth her anger, her need for vengeance. She pushed Hua Minglan—the girl who'd been happy running through her father's fields, the one who'd just wanted to keep her family safe—to the back of her mind. There was no room for pretty fantasies of safety.

Not when the Kou were in Piao.

She couldn't be the girl dressing up as a soldier and just hoping not to get caught. No, she had to become something else, something more.

A woman's scream had her jerking to a halt. May. She tried to find the source of the sound, whirling to face a line of burning tents. Her eyes locked on her friend's terrified face. May knelt on the ground over a body—her mother? Two Kou warriors advanced on her.

Hua sprinted toward them, leaping over felled warriors. As one of the warriors brought his dao down over May's head, Hua lunged, blocking the attack with her own weapon. She kicked her foot out, forcing the attacker back.

May's cries echoed behind her, but she couldn't comfort her friend, not when faced with two men twice her size.

The first one attacked, forcing Hua to meet his every swipe of the blade. She lost sight of the second as she ducked, ramming her dao up into the man's chest, using all her strength to drive it through his leather armor.

An eerie silence followed, not one that results from a lack of sound. The battle raged around her still, sending cries into the night. No, what Hua no longer heard was May.

She pivoted on her heel just in time to see the blade draw across her throat. Losing people never hurt any less. Hua screamed in agony as the grief tore through her already broken heart. She ran at the man, lifting her dao and slicing him across the throat before he could react. May's killer died just as she did, with his life pouring from his throat. He collapsed next to the lifeless May, the girl who'd protected Hua and been her confidante. Only hours ago, they'd had whispered conversations.

And now she was gone.

A horse neighed nearby, and Hua took off, wanting to save at least one friend when she couldn't save May. She'd grieve her later. Now was a time for revenge.

Fire licked up the broken fence around the horse pens. Most of the beasts ran from the fight, but there was one who stood her ground as the flames crept closer.

"Heima." Hua breathed out a sigh. She ran forward, the heat of the fire matching the burning beneath her skin.

Heima stepped away from her.

"It's okay, girl, it's me."

After a moment, the horse dropped her head, allowing Hua to near. Hua gripped her charred mane and patted the side of her neck as she looked back toward the fighting. "They've come for us, Heima. And we weren't ready for them." They'd arrogantly thought they had time, that they would get to choose when and where the fight would happen.

The other units hadn't even had time to join them.

She glanced back down at the dragon on her arm, her grandmother's dragon. A glow emanated from beneath her skin. Heima tapped her nose against the dragon.

"Can you see it, girl?" Hua met Heima's deep amber eyes. There wasn't time for any more questions. Only a battle for the truth.

Leading Heima to a length of fence that hadn't yet caught fire, she stepped onto the cracked wood and hauled herself onto the horse's back. Tucking the dao underneath her butt, she fingered the bow. There were only a few arrows left. She needed to make them count.

Nudging Heima into a gallop, she had the sudden urge to turn her around and ride from this place, to forget her revenge and her duty to Piao. The old Hua was supposed to be at home by her brother's side.

But she wasn't that girl anymore. There was no other option but to ride into the melee. Heima ran past two warriors who'd set their sights on her and the soldier she carried.

A large Kou man had Chen pinned down near the flaming tents. Chen held no weapon, and the man standing over him raised his dao. Chen closed his eyes.

Acting quickly, Hua nocked an arrow and let it sail. It struck the man in the back of his head, and he fell forward onto Chen.

Chen's eyes popped open in panic.

"Get up!" Hua screamed. "Come on, you big idiot." She looked over her shoulder to where another enemy soldier ran toward Chen. Chen pushed the felled man off him and took his dao. He met Hua's eyes in thanks.

Hua kicked her heels into Heima. All throughout the camp, men died, her comrades. She didn't know most of them, but their shared uniform bonded them.

She doubled over as pain shot through her stomach. Something tried to claw its way out.

A cry left her lips as she slid from Heima's back, landing on her side. Her shoulder slammed into the dirt, but she barely felt the impact through the pain already searing through her.

Heima stood protectively over her. Hua pushed to her knees and crawled to where her bow and dao had fallen. She managed to aim the bow and ready an arrow, loosing it as a wiry man with a long, dark braid ran for her.

It struck him in the stomach, but he didn't stop. Blood poured from his wound, and still, he ran. She let a second arrow fly. It hit his leg. He stumbled forward, still coming after her.

The third arrow pierced his eye. His jaw fell open as blood poured free, and he crumpled where he stood.

Hua took a shuddering breath. What was happening to her? She'd heard the legends and seen the signs, but a part of her still didn't want to believe something writhed inside of her with the force of a beast she could not control.

A dragon trying to join the fight, and she held it back with all the strength she possessed.

Out of the corner of her eye, she saw Yan Sun fighting off a warrior trying to get to a dueling pair behind him.

There he was. Commander Li faced off against a lean-muscled man in black leather armor. His hair was tied into a tail hanging down his back. The sharp angles of his face were striking, even with the blood spatters coating his cheeks.

It wasn't a face one forgot.

Luca appeared, pulling on her arm to help her up. "Hua, are you hurt?"

She shook her head. The pain was real, but there was no wound. She gained her footing.

"Altan," Luca cursed.

Hua looked at the man fighting the commander again. General Altan? This was the man responsible for all the death, all the grief.

Red blurred the edges of her vision until all she saw was his face. Luna would be alive if it wasn't for him.

Heat built in the back of her throat, pushing up into her mouth. She released a puff of air, her mind going blank when steam left her mouth.

Luca didn't seem to notice. He ran toward the commander, slicing his dao across the back of Yan's attacker on his way.

An arrow tore through the air, ripping into Luca's side. He cried out and dropped his dao.

More warriors closed in on them. Chen joined Hua as she ran for Yan. Zhao fought his way through to them. Suddenly it was them in a sea of warriors.

Hua saw the plan develop as a nearby Kou warrior raised his bow. If they killed Commander Li, this war would be near a finish for them.

Hua's heart pounded as she saw the realization dawn on Commander Li's face. Jian Li was young for a commander, much too young to have his life cut short.

He was too good, too noble, despite what others said.

She thought of the jade dragon in his tent. It was probably gone now, but it gave her insight into the man. He had pain in his past.

Luca's words came back to her.

The emperor's brother.

*I'm scared of him because I'm not a fool.*

Hua wasn't scared of Commander Li, but she was terrified of watching him move on to the next life.

When she started running again, Luna wasn't her only thought. This wasn't for her revenge. She pushed away the anger and the pain of whatever lived inside her.

An arrow left the safety of a bowstring behind, carving an arc through the air. Hua barreled into the commander, knocking him away from Altan. She braced for the arrow to rip through her, blocking out all sound.

"I'm sorry, Luna." She couldn't get her revenge.

But the pain never came. The sounds of the fight crashed around her, and she realized she was still on top of the man she'd saved.

"Minglan." The commander's eyes widened.

She rolled off him and twisted around, retrieving Commander Li's discarded weapon.

"How did you do that?" General Altan tilted his head to the side.

"Do what?" She lunged for him, hoping to take advantage of his momentary distraction.

He grinned as he jumped away from her. "You don't even know the arrow hit you. Well, curious man or not, I'll enjoy killing you before getting back to Jian."

His smug smile hit every single one of her nerves, drawing out the anger she'd suppressed. Fire rose up in her, and she lunged for Altan.

He sidestepped her, but she wasn't ready to quit. "My sister is dead because of you."

His smile dropped. "For that, I am dearly sorry. I too have lost a sister."

"I don't want your apologies," she growled. "I want your life."

General Altan laughed. "Where are you finding these soldiers, Jian?"

Commander Li rolled to his feet and tried to step around her while he shook his head, a wince of pain crossing his features.

He'd had his chance. This was her fight now.

She lunged again, and the general's laughter faded away, replaced by anger. That was okay. It still couldn't match hers.

"Minglan, get out of the way," Jian yelled as he tried to push her away from Altan.

"Not a chance!" The being inside her amplified every feeling, turning it into pain and fire, calling for blood and destruction.

It matched her own desires.

She locked into her battle with General Altan, all the while keeping an image of Luna in her mind.

Every lesson her father taught her over the years was now muscle memory. Each move came without thought, each reaction without consideration.

"I want you to see my true face before you die." Hua narrowed her eyes as she reached behind her and pulled the tie in her hair free. If fell around her face. "You see, I've never been told I look like her. Like my sister. But there is a family resemblance. Luna Minglan. Do not forget that name. I am no ordinary warrior. I've been training to fight since I was just a girl. Are you ready to die, General?"

He lunged at her with a roar, but she ducked his dao and sliced hers into his side. He froze, staring down at the small wound.

Pressing a hand to his side, he stumbled back. This was her chance to finish it, her chance to end this war.

But the pain inside her intensified until blackness overtook her vision. The dao slid free of her weakening fingers as her muscles convulsed like they were trying to rearrange themselves. The bones in her back cracked, and she fell to her knees.

She heard the call to retreat moments before her face hit the dirt, and she sank into herself, trapped in her own mind.

# CHAPTER 13

Jian

"Altan!" Jian screamed. He wanted to go after him, to finish what they'd started, but the famed general only grinned as he grabbed a torch from one of his men. The Kou closed in around them.

"Commander," Zhao's strained voice cut through the smoke-filled air. "Minglan's barely breathing."

Jian tore his gaze from the man he'd spent years trying to find and settled them on Minglan's unmoving form. The soldier saved his life, but it wasn't the arrow that downed him ... her? Not this time.

Jian didn't understand any of it, but in that

moment, his mind flashed back to another battle and a girl no arrow could hurt.

*Like my sister. Luna Minglan. Remember that name. I am no ordinary warrior. I've been training to fight since I was just a girl.*

Was it possible? Huan Minglan was the girl he'd saved at the dragon festival. He couldn't reconcile that girl with the soldier he'd trained.

Altan's men forced Jian to his feet. This was it. The end. He hadn't been able to save his men. Minglan was probably dead. Luca wouldn't have long without treatment. Hands clamped on Zhao's arms, forcing him away from Minglan. He struggled, but there were too many of them.

Altan looked down on Minglan. "Shame such bravery had to be rewarded with death." He shook his head. "I could have used a soldier like this." He nudged Minglan with the toe of his boot.

"Don't touch her." Jian struggled against the men restraining him. Minglan was the toughest soldier he'd ever taught. Her womanhood didn't change that. She couldn't be gone. This war needed her. Her courage, her loyalty. It was too good for this world.

Altan stepped toward Jian, tilting to the side as he tried to stay upright. "Did you know we burned her? Qara. She was dead already, of course, but we couldn't let her spirit move on to the next life, not after her betrayal."

"Bastard," Jian grunted. Qara had been good in a way few people were. She didn't deserve to die by her brother's hand. Just like Minglan.

"Ah, that's where you're wrong, Jian. The bastard is you. And you, my old friend, will burn the same way she did. Only, you will feel every lick of the flames. I have men with me who'd like to tear you limb from limb, but we're short on time. We have to go prepare the defenses of our new border town." He grinned. "Kanyuan will suit our purposes nicely."

"The people will never welcome you."

"Average people grow tired of war more quickly than those who make it their life, Jian. They don't want us to continue attacking their farms and battering at the gates. In fact, once that soldier Hanan was out of the way, they threw open their gates for us."

"Liar."

"Yes, but not about this." He leaned closer. "I will control all of Piao one day. But you won't be around to see it. You won't witness your brother bowing at my feet."

"Your sister would be ashamed of you."

"Yes, I suspect she would. And that's why she's dead." He bent to press a finger to Minglan's neck before stepping back and motioning to his men. "Put them in the tent." He pointed behind him. "Not the girl." His eyes settled on Minglan. "She's dead already."

Jian stopped struggling as the words sank into him. The one soldier who hadn't feared him, the one who'd looked him in the eye… she was gone.

Altan laughed. "You didn't know this was no ordinary soldier, did you?" He shook his head. "I'm disappointed in you, Jian. Your instincts have failed you once again. Goodbye, old friend. May we meet under better circumstances in the next life."

They dragged Luca in first, leaving a trail of blood in the dirt. Zhao, Chen, and Yan put up more of a fight.

Jian knew it was useless. He kept his gaze on Minglan and his—her—serene face.

Did the deceptions matter when they'd soon both be dead?

Inside the tent, the Kou shoved him to the ground beside Luca. He leaned toward his greatest friend, noticing the paleness of his face. "Hold on, Luca. Please, just hold on."

"I-it's no use, J-jian." His voice shook. "T-there's no saving us now."

Heat enveloped them as flames engulfed the canvas overhead. The five men huddled together, waiting for the pain the fire would bring.

Was this what Qara meant? Dragons were fire and blood. Had she seen his death in the flames?

Smoke suffocated the air, choking all breath from their lungs. Luca removed his hand from where it pressed against his wound, letting the blood run free.

"No," Jian choked out the word, lunging to put pressure on his friend's side.

"Let me die, Jian," Luca wheezed. "It's the end for all of us."

Jian shook his head, refusing to believe it. Outside the tent, many of his men now moved on to their next lives. Most of them were novices, coming to the mountains outside Kanyuan to train for the war. They hadn't expected the war to come to them. Women who only wanted to serve the army in any way they could, now lay beside the fallen warriors, equal in death.

The experienced leaders in other parts of Piao would hear of this and know Jian failed. His brother trusted him, and he wasn't good enough. He never anticipated a village, tired of raids, would surrender to their foes, or a town guard, anxious to join what they saw as the winning side.

Across Piao, people would tell stories of his end, less heroic than weak.

"Bo was wrong to think I was ready." Jian looked away from the last of his men cowering in the smoke. Outside the tent, a girl he hadn't known was among them, laying still, her life stolen in the blink of an eye.

No weapon killed her. No Kou warrior. Jian didn't understand it, but then, none of this made sense.

"No." Luca coughed. "Bo knew what he was doing. He l-loves you."

And that love was going to destroy him. An emperor wasn't supposed to get attached. A harem was just a tool to provide the emperor with many heirs. Princes and princesses weren't raised to love each other. Bo was different. Jian never questioned his brother's love.

"He loves you too."

The ghost of a smile spread across Luca's sweat-soaked face. "I want t-to s-see him one last time."

"Me too, Luca. Me too."

Luca's eyes slid closed, and Jian didn't try to rouse him. If they were all going to die, he wanted his friend to go easy. He lifted his hand off the wound. "Most people never get to have a friend like you, Luca Kai."

A bead of sweat dripped into Jian's eye, and he wiped it away as he looked around at the other men.

Each breath came harder than the one before, but Jian wanted to remember the last moments of this life, so he kept his eyes open.

His mind grew cloudy, and he thought he'd imagined it. A dao appeared through the flames, slicing a line down the canvas.

Then she appeared.

How could he have missed it?

Minglan was fierce in a way none of his male soldiers were. His hazy thoughts didn't let relief come over him. He only noticed the fire in her gaze matching the flames trying to kill them.

"Go," he tried to say. "Save yourself." If Altan was still out there, she had to run, to tell others what happened here.

But she didn't seem to hear him as she cut the slit wider and dropped her dao. The sleeves of her robe had been singed away, revealing toned arms and black ink slithering along her skin in the form of a dragon.

"Commander." It took him a moment to realize she was shouting at him. "We have to go."

Zhao stumbled to his feet and took Luca under the arms, dragging him from the burning tent. Chen and Yan followed in a torrent of coughs.

Minglan held a hand down to Jian. He looked into her swirling red eyes for a moment before clasping her wrist and pulling himself to his feet. On weak legs, he stumbled from the flames seconds before the tent collapsed.

"Minglan," Jian barked once he found his voice.

The end of her robes flamed. Jian tried to stamp them out, but she pushed him away. "Hand me the dao." Zhao picked it up and threw it to her.

She gripped her robes, and the flames kissed her hand. She didn't so much as flinch when she sliced the bottom of her robe away, leaving her only in a short tunic and pants, not suitable attire for anyone in Piao —man or woman.

Yet, proprieties no longer mattered as the group looked around at each other knowing they'd just defeated death.

Jian searched the surrounding ruins of the camp, eyes stinging from smoke, but the Kou were gone.

Chen hovered over the body of two women, huddled together in death. "They're all gone." His words echoed the whispers in each of their minds.

Looking to Minglan, Jian wiped soot from his face, before crouching beside Luca. "He needs a healer." They'd have to deal with revelations about Minglan once they were safe.

Minglan joined him. "Give me your shirt."

"What?"

"Your shirt. Now."

Jian shrugged it over his head and handed it to her. "I'm guessing your name isn't Huan."

She used the doa to cut the shirt down the middle. "We need to wrap this around him until we can find someone to help."

Jian helped her tip Luca onto his side so they could wrap the cloth around his middle. Luca groaned, letting them know he was still alive.

Neither of them mentioned Healer Sasha, who had been one of the many to die in the attack.

"One of the emperor's brothers has an estate a few hours from here." Jian sighed. Going to Prince Dequan for help wouldn't be his first choice if he had any other. He was the oldest son of the old empress and—as she claimed—the rightful emperor. "He will want to know the Kou took a village so close to his lands. We can send messengers to my generals from there." Generals who were coming here with their men and possibly walking right into Altan's trap.

Minglan nodded as she stood. She made a sound with her tongue and a horse appeared. "Heima will carry him. We need to leave." Jian should have been surprised her horse stayed around the chaos and came when she called, but it was the least of Minglan's curiosities.

None of the men asked why she was suddenly the one giving orders. They'd seen her walk through flames to save them.

What Jian didn't know was what it all meant. Why was she there? How had an arrow failed to pierce her skin?

As if reading his mind, Minglan answered a question he hadn't asked. "There will be time for answers, Commander. Luca needs us right now."

He nodded in agreement, noting her use of his friend's name rather than title. She hovered over Luca with a familiarity that didn't normally exist between soldier and general.

Had he known?

With the help of Zhao, they managed to get Luca onto the horse's back.

Minglan rubbed the beast's nose. "It's okay, Heima. The fighting is done for now." Her voice didn't only calm the horse. Jian glanced at each man, noticing how their posture relaxed at her words.

They'd all just found out their friend, their comrade was a woman pretending to be a man, and they didn't look at her with any less trust in their eyes.

Because they all knew.

Whoever this girl was, they were alive because of her.

# Chapter 14

Hua

Hua met Prince Dequan's gaze as he stared out at the bedraggled soldiers, not letting them past the threshold of his high gates.

She'd seen too much to be intimidated by someone like him. His shining ebony hair was pulled back from his sharp features. He had the same father as the emperor, but none of the kindness she'd seen in the younger Bo's eyes during their single encounter.

"Jian." The prince crossed his arms. "Why are you here?" He surveyed their charred, bloodstained clothing.

Jian led Heima forward. "The Kou now hold Kanyuan."

Prince Dequan cursed. "You were camped near the village to protect the border."

Hua scowled. No one could have foreseen the village guard killing their leader and joining the enemy. They didn't think people of Piao would welcome Kou into their town.

"We have a lot to discuss." Jian rubbed his chin. "You know I wouldn't be here if I had a choice. Luca needs your healer. We don't have time to waste. And you and I need to talk. My men need rest and sustenance." He shot Hua a look. Was he telling her not to reveal her status as a woman?

If it had been up to her, she wouldn't have even told Jian.

The prince sighed and gestured to his men. "Your people will be taken care of. Come with me." Jian spared them one final look before following the prince.

Hua wanted to protest, to tell Jian he too needed to see the healer, but he didn't give her a chance before walking away.

Servants descended on Hua and the others. Two men helped Luca down and carried him inside, disappearing down a long hall.

The pitch-black night held an eery silence even as the estate bustled around them. It wasn't until Hua sat in the great hall with a bowl of stew in front of her that the events of the evening fully hit her.

The death.

The blood.

Flashes of the fight ran through her mind. She'd saved Jian, but what happened after that? The agony she'd endured had no source. It made no sense.

Something tried to claw its way out of her. She glanced at the image on her arm. Had she imagined it turning black as it had when her grandmother drew it? Before the ink sank into her skin, leaving behind a faint red line.

Zhao slid onto the wooden bench beside her, setting his bowl on the table. "Huan..."

"That's not my name." And they all knew now. Tears came unbidden to her eyes. None of it felt real. When she'd left her family for the army, she'd known she'd see battle. But she hadn't imagined a scene like that, a slaughter. All the men she'd trained alongside for months. The healer who patched her up when she needed it.

May.

She blinked away the tears as she thought of her friend's smiling face or the way she'd loved to drive the men crazy by showing Hua favor.

In the grand scheme of things, losing Kanyuan would hurt much worse than losing a small part of the army.

But to her... it ripped her open. She rested her elbows on the table and buried her face in her hands.

Chen sat across from her. "Um, don't cry... whatever your name is."

She lifted her face. "Whatever my name is?"

He shrugged. "I won't call you by your last name.

Not after all we've just been through. And Huan obviously was a lie."

"Hua." She choked back a sob. "My name is Hua. I'm the second daughter of General Fa Minglan of the Piao civil wars. My sister died in the attack on Dasha."

Zhao put a hand on her shoulder. "Is that why you came? Why you pretended to be a man?"

She nodded. "Luna... she deserved better. She was one of the emperor's consorts. That was supposed to give her the life she deserved. I want to defeat the enemy who took that from her."

Yan and Chen nodded as if they understood, as if they too had lost people to the Kou.

Zhao met her gaze. "The emperor released me from prison to fight his war, to win my freedom. But that isn't why I agreed. I grew up in a border town East of Kanyuan. Our industry was goats, so the mountains suited us. Until raiders came across the mountain pass from Koulland. My entire village was destroyed. The few of us who survived sought work in Dasha. I became a guardsman, but I never forgot the attack."

Hua reached for the tough man's hand, sliding her palm against his calloused skin.

Three serving girls appeared, looking as if they'd been roused from their beds. "Rooms in the guard's quarters have been made up for you." The one who spoke wrinkled her nose. "Wash bins are there for your use. When you are ready, someone will show you the way."

"A bath and a bed?" Chen stood. "If only it would wipe away memories of this night."

Yan and Zhao stood to join him, looking at Hua expectantly.

She eyed the youngest of the serving girls. "Can you show me the way to the healer?"

The girl nodded without a word. Despite the exhaustion weighing her down, Hua waved goodbye to her friends and followed the girl down a dark hall, lit only by small torches along the stone walls.

Her feet echoed against the tiled floor in time with her heart echoing in the empty chasm inside her.

The girl left Hua outside a heavy wooden door. She knocked, but no one came. So, she knocked again.

Finally, a young woman opened the door. Her wide smile gave Hua confidence.

"Can I help you?" she asked.

"I was hoping to see my friend. He came in with the soldiers an hour or so ago."

She nodded. "Yes, yes. Come in, dear. I'm the prince's healer." Her accent marked her as a foreigner.

"You're not from Piao." She was past the point of caring if that sounded rude in her tired state.

The woman only nodded. "I grew up in Koulland, but don't hold that against me. I was more their prisoner than anything else."

She kept talking, but Hua's eyes settled on Luca, and she didn't hear anything else. His naked torso shone bright with sweat, but no more blood ran from his wound. Hua rushed forward to examine her friend. If he died… He was a true friend, and she'd had so few of those in her life other than her sister.

He protected her and kept her secrets. She couldn't lose him too. Not after May.

"Luca," Hua whispered.

The healer sat on a cot along the far wall, her red robes hanging over her legs. "He hasn't woken yet. I stopped the bleeding and sewed the wound shut. Now, it's up to him."

"Do you mind if I stay here with him?"

"No. He'll need a friendly face when he wakes." She was quiet for a moment.

Hua leaned forward, dropping her voice so the woman couldn't hear her. "You need to wake up, Luca. I can't do this without you. It's supposed to be you and me. You were right, we were never going to love each other the way man and wife should, but maybe there's another way. Maybe we were meant to find each other, to protect each other."

Her hand found Luca's, and she squeezed, wishing she could feel him squeeze back. The only sound in the room was his ragged breath. As long as Hua heard that, she knew he was still alive.

She didn't know how much time passed. Minutes. Or hours. Morning would come soon, and they'd have to figure out what to do.

The healer stood and crossed the room to feel Luca's flushed skin. "We need to get some tonic into him." She went to a table littered with vials and began opening them and mixing them in a stone bowl before pouring hot water from a kettle into it.

She let it cool for a few moments. "We need to sit

him up." Together, they managed to prop Luca up. Hua crawled behind him to hold him in position.

The healer gripped his jaw and forced his mouth open as she tilted the bowl against it. Her fingers massaged his throat, making him swallow.

Luca coughed and sputtered, but still didn't wake.

"That's enough." The healer set the bowl aside and returned to her position across the small room. Hua didn't move out from behind Luca. Instead, she let his body relax against her.

The healer's scrutinizing eyes watched Hua, burning into her.

Finally, Hua met her gaze in challenge.

The healer smiled. "I never in my life thought I'd get to meet you, Hua Minglan."

Hua froze. "How do you know my name?"

"I know much more about you." She got up and approached once more. Hua shrank away from her, but the woman reached for her arm as if she could see the image that was invisible to everyone else.

"You were attacked this very night, were you not?"

Hua nodded.

"I can feel it writhing within you."

"You can?" Hua leaned toward her, desperate for someone to understand, to tell her she wasn't losing her mind.

She nodded. "But you cannot be told these things. You must learn them for yourself."

"How do you know me?" For the first time, Hua knew she was in the presence of someone who could give her the answers she sought.

"Oh dear, I've seen you."

"Seen me?"

She nodded. "I have the sight. It's unreliable, so I did not know if you truly existed. I merely wished it so."

"Who are you?"

"My name is Qara Altan."

# CHAPTER 15

Jian

Jian collapsed into a high-backed wooden chair in Dequan's sitting room. He needed sleep. His lungs needed to heal after breathing in so much smoke.

Yet, here he was facing off against a prince who'd never been fond of him.

"Excuse my lack of food and drink." Dequan walked toward the door. "I wasn't expecting visitors in the middle of the night." He spoke to a servant for a moment before returning. "I'm having something brought to you. You look as if you've been trampled by a stampede of horses."

"I guess it beats looking like I was trapped in a flaming tent preparing to face my death."

Dequan's eyebrows drew together. "Okay, Jian, let's start with this. You and I are not family. We've never seen eye to eye on anything."

Jian shook his head. "My loyalty to Bo is why you despise me; you can admit it."

"Contrary to what you believe, I too am loyal to my brother. Even more so, I'm loyal to Piao. You said we've lost Kanyuan. There has obviously been a battle. We need to put our animosity aside for the good of our country."

"You're right." Jian sighed. "I'm sorry. It's been one of the longest nights of my life." Only two nights came close. When he lost Qara it broke his heart. Leading his men to their deaths in the mountains broke his spirit.

But this, the attack on his camp… it broke his hope.

And a man without hope was nothing.

To his surprise, Dequan stepped forward and placed a hand on his shoulder. He didn't say anything and for a moment, silence stretched between them. A knock on the door broke whatever spell they'd been under.

Dequan answered it himself. Jian knew the man well. If this were daytime when servants bustled about, he'd never touch a door or a tray of food. He thanked the servant and carried the tray over, setting it on the table beside Jian's chair.

Jian's stomach rumbled, but he couldn't muster the energy to lift the bowl. Instead, he leaned his head back.

Dequan took a seat across from him. "I know all you want to do right now is find a bed. I can't imagine what you've been through in the last few hours, but if the Kou are now on my doorstep, this can't wait."

"You're right. There's so much to do, but first thing's first. Bo isn't here so the eldest prince has to suffice." Jian pushed himself from the chair and down on one knee in front of Dequan. It wasn't a position he'd ever wanted to be in: disgrace. As a member of the royal family, Dequan was one of the few men with authority over a commander. Only the emperor could overrule the orders of one of the princes.

"Dequan Wei, I hereby relinquish my command of the Piao army. I no longer hold my title and rank. I am not fit to serve this country any longer."

Dequan studied him as he rubbed the back of his neck. "Get off your knees, Jian."

Jian obeyed, letting himself fall into the chair once more.

"I accept your resignation." Dequan sighed. "Though, Bo will hate me for doing so. You were always his favorite pet."

"Because he trusted me when he shouldn't have."

"Jian, have you ever acted against Bo's wishes?"

"Of course not."

"Have you ever willingly led men to their deaths?"

"I-"

"No." Dequan eyed him. "I know the stories of your first battle in this war. You made a mistake that got your men killed, but you did not do so willingly. Leaders make mistakes, Jian. It is how they respond to them that determines how they will be remembered."

"I wasn't prepared for this. I didn't foresee the Kou taking Kanyuan so easily or attacking a camp full of newly trained soldiers."

"And neither did anyone else." He closed his eyes for a moment. "Tell me. Everything."

Jian didn't hold back. He told Dequan everything he knew about Kanyuan and General Altan's presence there before the attack. He spoke of finding Hanan's body and knowing what it could mean.

Then the attack. Every gruesome detail spilled forth until Jian held nothing more inside of him save for the secrets belonging to someone else.

He said nothing of a girl unable to be pierced by an arrow or burned by flames.

Dequan tapped his chin. "Messengers must be sent to intercept the generals traveling with their men to the plains outside Kanyuan. They will convene here instead. My brother will select a new commander, but until we can get word from him, General Yang will take command. I'll send someone I trust to Dasha. We must begin preparing to retake Kanyuan." He stood. "As for you, Jian Li, you will serve this army until we recover the border village. You must stay here until the rest of the army arrives. Once our task is complete, once we attack and fully enter this war, I don't want to see you again. Return to Dasha, to the emperor's side, or find some far-off hovel to hide in. I never agreed with the decision to give you command, and it looks like I was right."

Jian didn't have the energy to argue. Dequan was right. He'd given up his command and could no longer serve once Kanyuan was saved. "What about Luca? He needs to heal."

"Luca will not share in your disgrace. Do not fret, Jian, my healer is taking good care of him. She is quite talented."

"I thought the healer at this estate was Master Jing-Sheng?"

"No, that poor old man caught a sickness and died. Not long after, my men captured a woman at the border, and she had the healing touch."

"Your healer is a prisoner?"

"Not anymore. She won her freedom long ago by giving us insight into Koulland." He met Jian's eyes, his irises gleaming with pride. "She is quite the prize. A relative of General Altan himself."

Jian couldn't breathe. He felt like the smoke returned, choking the air from his lungs. A relative of Altan's. The only relative of Batukhan Altan's he'd ever heard of died by her brother's hand.

Jian's hand shook as he reached for the cup of water next to the food he didn't eat. "N-name." He took a sip. "What's her name?"

"Qara Altan." Dequan stood and clapped his hands together. "Now, if you'll excuse me, I must rouse my messengers before I can find my own bed once more. Do not wake me again."

He left Jian staring into space. *Qara?* It couldn't be.

A servant appeared in the doorway. "Can I show you to your room?"

He managed to shake his head as he clasped his hands together. "The healer's quarters. I need to go there now."

Each step felt more surreal than the one before it. He stopped in front of a heavy wooden door, a door that might separate him from the woman he'd thought about every day for years.

He knocked, knowing there was a good chance he'd wake her. But it didn't stop him.

When no one came to the door, he gripped the handle and pushed, finding it unlocked. The first thing he saw in the small room was Minglan with her back against the wall and Luca cradled in her lap. Her head lolled forward, resting on top of his as she slept.

An unfamiliar anger ripped through him when he saw them. But it was nothing to the rage he experienced when he set eyes on the other sleeping woman across the room.

Qara's familiar face was relaxed in sleep, not knowing her past and her present were about to collide.

As if sensing him, her eyes slid open, the blue irises Jian saw in his dreams fixed on him. She shook herself awake and sat up, his name a whisper on her lips.

He flicked his eyes from Qara to Minglan before gesturing to the hallway.

Qara nodded and followed him. They'd barely

made it into the hall when he whirled around, pushed her up against the wall, and pressed his lips to hers.

"How is this possible?" he whispered against her lips. Instead of giving her a chance to respond, he kissed her again. He'd spent so long just wanting her back and chasing her brother to get his revenge. Now that she was here, he didn't know what to think of the way he'd spent the last few years of his life. Her kiss felt like home, but a home that no longer welcomed him, belonged to him. There was something missing in her response, a passion they'd had before. Instead, his lips felt cold, like they no longer knew the woman barely kissing him back, their bodies were no longer in sync.

She put a hand on his chest and pushed him away, her eyes shifting between his. "Jian, I never thought I'd see you again."

"I thought you were dead."

Sadness grew in the depth of her gaze. "I should be."

"How—" She put a finger to his lips, stopping his words.

"Shh, Jian." Glancing back over her shoulder, she moved him away from the open door. Her fingertips caressed his cheek before she took a step around him. "It's good to see you."

"Qara… I never thought I'd even speak your name out loud again."

She smiled, reaching a hand toward him before dropping it. "I wondered if we'd meet again."

"How long have you been in Piao? Why are you here in the prince's household? Did you escape your brother? Why didn't you come find me?" Each question spilled out before he could stop them.

Her smile fell. "Prince Dequan has been kind to me."

Jian had never known him to be kind.

"He recognizes the gifts I possess."

Not the healing skill. It would have been easy to find a replacement healer from one of the villages. Dequan wouldn't have kept his enemy's sister for that reason alone. His eyes widened. "The sight?"

"You never believed in it." There was no disappointment in her voice, only a statement of fact.

Jian had always been a simple man. He didn't believe what he hadn't seen. People couldn't predict the future. It was impossible to imagine a villager transforming into a dragon as the stories of old claimed.

But then he'd seen a girl at the festival shot with an arrow that didn't pierce her skin. Again, that same girl walked through fire. His eyes flicked to the door, catching a glimpse of the sleeping Minglan.

If she had some kind of power, wasn't it also possible Qara did as well?

"You left me, didn't you?" It made so much sense now. How she was still alive. Why her brother didn't kill her. She went back to him willingly.

Tears sprang to her eyes, and he wondered if she too was remembering their chase through the mountain pass, or the moment she pleaded with him to go. Had she bargained for his life? "Jian, there was no other way."

He turned away from her. "All this time, I believed Batukhan took away the woman who would always be by my side. I've hunted him and made choices that got my men killed. Was it all for nothing?"

She shook her head. "No, he's an evil man. I escaped him as soon as I could. I never thought you'd hold on to me so tightly."

He whirled around to face her again. "Why? I loved you, Qara. With everything I had. I risked my life to get you out of Koulland."

"I didn't have a choice."

"There is always a choice."

Tears streamed down her face as she shook her head. "It wasn't supposed to be me, don't you see that? I wasn't the one who needed you."

"What does that mean?" He ran a hand through his hair in agitation.

"It means you have a destiny greater than me."

"Your visions." His anger deflated, leaving him hollow inside. "You saw me. And I'm guessing you won't tell me what you saw."

Regret shone in her eyes. "There is someone else who will need you at their side now, Jian Li. You gave up your command, but that does not relinquish you from your duty to protect Piao."

"How do you know... you know what, never mind. Losing you broke me. I never recovered, and it shattered the pieces of me I would have given to this war. I don't have anything left to give Piao."

"You have the dragon."

"The jade statue you gave me? No, Qara. That was

lost when my entire training unit was slaughtered. Whatever protection you thought it would bring was a lie."

"A statue is not meant for protection, only thought. When the real dragon comes, it will need you."

"A real dragon?" A harsh laugh broke out of him. "Visions and dragons, the stuff of fairytales. There have been no dragons in centuries—if they ever truly lived at all. Now, they only exist as a symbol of power, a power that is on the brink of crashing down around us."

Qara sighed. "One day, Jian, you will have to believe in something. The future of Piao may depend on it."

"I promise you, I will only believe in dragons if I see one transform with my own eyes."

Her lips drew down as she pulled him into a hug. "I am happy to see you, old friend."

"Old friends. Is that all we were to each other?" He breathed in her jasmine scent.

"It is all the future allows for us." She pulled away and placed her palm on his chest over his heart. "I did not break this." One corner of her mouth curved up. "Because it will belong to someone far greater than I. And she might just save us all."

"Who?"

"I already told you." She winked. "The dragon."

Without another word, she turned and went back into her room. Jian stood in the doorway, contemplating her words as he watched his sleeping friends. There would be no fairytale dragon coming to their rescue. Qara was wrong.

He studied her as she bent over a table scattered with bottles of herbs, looking like she belonged. The life of a healer fit the quiet girl he'd known. He was a young man when he'd fallen in love with her, a young man who thought he needed to save her from the evil in her life.

But she'd saved herself.

Some of the cracks in his soul he'd carried around since losing her stitched back together. He loved that woman, but he felt no sorrow at the words she'd said to him. Old friends felt like a good description of them.

At least then, his disgrace wouldn't touch her too.

# CHAPTER 16

Hua

Hua waited until the commander left before opening her eyes. Early morning light filtered in through the small window looking out on the courtyard. A heavy weight rested on her and she looked down at Luca, realizing she'd stayed with him the entire night. If her father saw her, he'd be ashamed at how close she was to him—injured or not.

He wouldn't understand how she felt about him, not in a romantic sense, but more as the one person who could understand what it was like to live with a giant secret.

"His color is better this morning." Qara's voice

shocked Hua out of her own thoughts. Would she mention her conversation with Jian in the hall? Both thought Hua had been asleep, but she'd heard their whispered words.

Who was this woman?

And what was she to the enigmatic commander? The man Hua couldn't seem to figure out.

She hadn't spoken with Jian about the revelations of the night before. Not only was Hua's femininity revealed, but she walked through flames to get to her fellow soldiers and there was not a burn on her.

The ends of her hair were singed, but her skin remained unmarred. She ran a finger over the red lines of the dragon on her arm.

Qara's eyes followed the movement of Hua's finger. "Ah, the Nagi."

"What?" Hua lifted her gaze to meet Qara's.

"That is what the symbol represents."

"You can see it?"

Qara smiled and walked closer to lift Hua's arm for a better look. "There are legends in Koulland about the Nagi. They're dragons who can take an earthly form."

"I'm not a dragon." Hua pulled her arm away. "I'm a girl, a warrior. I'm only in this fight to avenge my sister's death."

Qara smiled. "And I'm only here because I was a prisoner. We all have the truths we tell the world, and the ones we know deep in our souls." She patted Hua's shoulder. "But you're right. You, dear, are nothing more than Hua Minglan, a girl who joined this war for many more reasons than simple revenge. The Nagi are more complicated."

She wanted to tell her about the arrows and the fire, but she couldn't trust a woman she just met. Qara may have answers, but was Hua ready for those answers?

"You're the sister of General Altan." Hua thought back to the conversation she'd overheard.

Qara showed no surprise that she knew. "I am."

"He's the reason my sister is dead."

She bowed her head. "I will carry each death he causes as a weight on my soul. I love my brother, but I am here because I cannot allow him to destroy another country."

"Another country?"

"Koulland was a land of tribes. We traded with each other and roamed the countryside freely. My brother… he formed alliances between the tribes, destroying those who did not join. Eventually, the tribes became one. We settled in villages, ceasing our nomadic way of life. That is why we now wage war with Piao. It is a settler's dream. But we were never meant to be settlers." Sadness coated her words, and Hua realized she still loved her brother.

Could she blame her? If this was Ru or Luna, would she ever stop caring for them?

"You and the commander…"

Qara smiled. "That is not my story to tell. Jian Li is a noble man. He will face much criticism and abandonment. I hope you will continue to believe in him."

Hua glanced down at Luca. He'd had such faith in

Jian even before Hua saw the good inside him. "I will always believe in him."

Qara blinked away the sadness in her eyes so quickly, Hua wondered if she'd imagined it.

She shifted Luca and slid out from behind him. "I must find a bath and some breakfast." Her stomach rumbled in agreement.

Qara pushed Luca's hair back out of his face. "I will take care of our friend here."

Hua didn't realize how tired she was until she made it into the hall. She'd slept only a few hours since the battle, and the smell of it still clung to her clothes.

With directions from a guard, she found the room she'd been given. The wooden tub had been filled with water the night before, and it now sat cold. Still, nothing had ever looked so good.

Stripping off her singed clothing, she left it scattered in her wake as she stumbled on unstable legs to the washtub.

Climbing in, she sank down, letting the cold water envelop her. On a low shelf next to the tub sat a bar of lye soap. Picking it up, she sniffed it, reveling in the slight flowery scent.

As she scrubbed the dirt and blood from her skin, images from the battle came back to her. Running through a flaming camp. Bodies hitting the dirt with crimson life seeping from their wounds.

General Altan.

The pain that had no reason. That was what she didn't understand. Why had she collapsed? She scrubbed faster and faster until her skin was raw.

Leaning back, she dipped below the water, letting it block out all sound. She should have known war would be like this. Part of her hoped for a grand adventure the day she left her family. All she got was months of training and a few hours of death.

Her lungs screamed for air, and she broke the surface of the water as someone pounded on her door. Reluctant to let anyone into the first solitude she'd experienced in so long, she emerged from the tub and dried herself as best she could. Being that the prince was told she was a man, there were no womanly items nearby.

The pounding persisted.

She deepened her voice. "One moment."

After squeezing her hair into the bath sheet, she pulled on the clean linen trousers, and a robe made of the same material. Its ill quality scratched her skin, but she guessed it was the best unwelcome guests could hope for.

She didn't bother to belt it, leaving it hanging off her frame like a sack. Her damp hair hung around her pale face. There was no looking glass in the room, but she was sure dark circles would tell any observer of her exhaustion.

With a sigh, she pulled open the heavy door. Chen and Yan stood on the threshold with grins stretched across their faces.

"You look rested." She pushed the hair out of her eyes.

"Some of us sleep after the exhilaration of a battle." Yan's smile fell as he took in her appearance.

"Exhilaration." She snorted.

Chen's dimple winked. "No wonder we didn't know your true identity. Women don't make that sound."

Much to her mother's dismay, she'd never cared what women were allowed to do or how they were allowed to act. She shrugged and turned back into her room. The two men followed her. Chen jumped onto her bed and made himself comfortable.

Yan went directly to the fire to stoke it to life.

"Yes, please do come in." Hua's mother would chastise her for such sarcasm, but she was too tired to think of that.

"Did you stay with General Kai all night long?" There was a second unasked question in Chen's eyes.

"Yes," she snapped. "In case you don't remember, he is injured."

"And the healer wasn't a good enough caretaker?"

"I don't know what you're implying." Hua folded her arms across her chest.

"Yes, you do." Chen winked.

She'd let them think what they wanted. There was nothing between her and Luca, but if she explained how they were truly connected, it would reveal Luca's knowledge of her deception.

"Don't you two have better things to do than bother me?" Not having another option in the cramped room, she sat on the end of the bed. Oh, if only her mother saw her now, sitting on a bed with a man who was not her husband.

Yan turned and studied her. "I can see it now."

"See what?"

"You were never like the other soldiers. Only a woman would fearlessly go up against the commander."

That brought a sad smile to her lips as she remembered her decision to match each glare with one of her own, to not allow him to speak with disrespect she didn't deserve. Those days were done now. They had to be.

"They're not going to let me continue on with the army." As soon she said it, she knew it was true.

The men's silence was all the answer she got, but it was enough.

This was it. The end of her adventure. As soon as Commander Li finished his business with the prince and recovered his strength, he'd send her home to her family.

A family shamed by her actions.

Would they ever look at her the same way?

Would she ever see her friends again? Chen, Yan, Zhao, Luca… even Commander Li. He was probably the hardest person to leave. She wanted to fight for him, to make him proud. How disappointed he must be in her now.

Zhao appeared in the doorway, a scowl on his face. "Chen, Yan, what are you doing bothering the lady Hua? She needs rest, and you fools need walloped with the dull side of a dao."

Chen rolled his eyes, but he jumped from the bed anyway.

Yan smiled at her. "He's right. Sleep, dearest, Hua." He gripped Chen's arm and forced him from the room.

Hua scooted farther onto the bed and leaned back against the hard pillows. "Don't call me lady," she mumbled.

Zhao shook his head. "It is what you are."

"It's not everything I am."

"No. I suspect not." He bowed his head. "Rest, warrior Hua. Soon, we will have to discover a way to conceal your identity once more."

Her head jerked up. "What?"

"You wish to continue fighting, do you not?"

"More than anything. They need to pay for the lives they took."

He nodded in approval. "Then we will make it so." He said it so simply, but nothing had ever been more complicated.

Zhao left, closing her door in the process.

Finally, some peace. She burrowed beneath the furs, and the moment she closed her eyes, the world faded away, replaced by one of fire.

At first, she thought she dreamed of the battle. But the training camp never materialized around her.

Instead, she looked down on a burning village, one she'd seen in her dreams before.

A thought entered her mind, but it did not belong to her.

*Destroy the enemies. Protect my people.*

It was a sentiment she agreed with, but seeing the flames reaching high into the sky struck fear into her heart.

Wings sprouted from her back, giant, muscled appendages. She leaped into the air with a giant flap, and her body twisted as she dove toward the wreckage below. The ground shook when she landed in the middle of the screaming chaos. Eyes lifted to her in fear.

She turned to survey the damage, finding one man pulling people from the wreckage. His eyes locked onto hers as he marched toward her, dao in one hand and halberd in the other.

The winged beast moved of its own accord, but Hua, trapped inside it, felt frozen in place. Because Jian Li, the man she'd have fought to the death for, now looked at her with nothing but contempt.

Hua woke with a start, Jian's harsh eyes seared into her mind. Her skin felt alive, as if something crawled beneath the surface, sending heat through her every cell. And now she knew what that something was. Qara gave her a name. Nagi. Dragons who can inhabit a human with dragon blood. She couldn't deny it any longer, but that didn't mean it was any easier to accept.

What now?

Kicking off the furs, she got to her feet and paced the length of the room. Moonlight poured in through the window. Had she slept most of the day, trapped in her nightmares?

A tray of food sat on the small table near the bed. Someone had been in here. Eyeing the bowl of broth and bread skeptically, she approached it. Despite the ache of hunger, her stomach roiled at the thought of food, the beast inside her causing a nausea to rise up.

Finding a leather strap where she'd left her filthy clothes, she tied her hair back into a knot. For all she knew, the commander could have already told the prince of her identity as a woman. But on the chance he hadn't, she couldn't risk being seen with her hair down.

Tying a belt loosely around her waist so her womanly bits were less obvious, she pulled on her leather boots. Dried blood coated the thin soles and splattered up the side.

She stared at it for a moment, trying to remember the faces of those who'd lost their lives in the attack. General Altan appeared in her mind. She'd never forget the mirth in his eyes as he slaughtered young soldiers.

Did he wear the same smile during the attack on Dasha? Would he have looked down on Luna lying lifeless on the ground with a grin?

As she stepped from her room, she considered checking on Luca, but that could wait. All she wanted to do was get outside where the starry sky could give her comfort as it always had.

The guards on night duty barely paid her any mind. To them, she was just a visiting soldier, one who couldn't carry a weapon within the estate except in the training yard.

She reached the courtyard and lifted her eyes to the sky, but it wasn't good enough. She needed to get closer. Searching her surroundings, she found a flat roofed tower at the west end of the fortress.

No guard manned the tower, and she realized why as soon as she walked inside and began climbing the spiral stone staircase. Rock crumbled along the walls. Beneath her feet, the stone was cracked and uncared for.

At the other end of the estate, more ornate towers served the watch. They had no use for this relic from a different age.

Hua's legs burned as she climbed to the top. If this tower followed the structural patterns of Piao fortresses she'd learned in her studies, it would open onto the roof where a pyre sat waiting to be lit to alert the nearest fortress of coming enemies.

The nearest fortress to Prince Dequan's was in Kanyuan, serving the village guard. The fact that they'd never lit their fires was proof enough which side they'd chosen.

Hua struggled to breathe by the time she made it to the top. A hatch sat partially open in the stone roof. The steps to it were intact, but only barely.

Hua climbed the stairs and gripped the handle, yanking down with all her strength. Dust and rock rained down around her as the hatch opened. She reached up, gripping the sides and pulled herself through.

The roof stretched before her, a white platform balanced against the black night. In the center, a black scorch mark showed where fires once blazed. Something about the spot called to her, as if it had a memory of the fire.

She bent to brush her fingers along the mark before walking to the edge. Being this high reminded her of sitting on the roof outside her loft with her grandmother, the one person who might have real answers for her.

Yet, she'd given none.

"Why did you want me to figure this out myself, Nainai?" The wind carried her words away as if taking them straight to the woman in question.

Hua sat with her legs hanging over the edge. From on high, the estate looked every bit like the fortress it was, meant to protect Piao against their enemies.

But it hadn't been able to this time.

Stone towers sat in every direction. Only a few guards manned the high walls at this time of night.

Lying back with her legs still hanging over the edge, Hua studied the stars above, finding the brightest one as she always did, believing it was Luna watching over her.

"I miss you." A tear slid down her cheek. "But I don't know if you'd recognize me anymore. I abandoned Mama and Ba. I told myself it was to save Ba, and that was part of it, but I needed to do something to stop this anger burning through me. I thought if I avenged you, I could become Hua Minglan again, a simple girl from a farm in Zhouchang." She wiped her eyes. "But I'm not sure I was ever meant to be her, Luna. Please don't be disappointed in me. I couldn't take that."

The only thing she used to want was to make her sister proud. Now, she wanted to bring her back to life.

Maybe both of those had been impossibilities.

"They know." She pushed out a breath. "What happens to me now, Luna? There are things I haven't told you, things I can barely grasp myself." She shifted her gaze to the dragon constellation.

Qara spoke of the Nagi but then said that was not what Hua was. *You're nothing more than Hua Minglan.* It didn't make sense. If she was only Hua, why did the dreams come to her? What about the pain and the heat?

Footsteps sounded on the stairs before Jian appeared through the hatch. He froze when he spotted her on the edge of the roof.

"Are you insane?" He swallowed thickly but didn't move to come near her. "Get away from the edge."

Hua didn't look at him. "No."

"No? You could fall?"

"Yes, I could. But I won't." She tilted her head to look back at him. Silver light illuminated his tall frame, but she couldn't make out the expression on his face.

"You're infuriating."

"Thank you." She took pride in irking the stoic commander.

He sighed and sat in the center of the roof, far from the edge. "You... you're a woman."

"I am."

"I can't speak to you when I fear you'll tumble off the edge at any moment. Come here." He paused. "Please."

She'd never heard him utter the word please in the months she'd known him. Taking pity on the man, she scooted back and turned to face him, expecting some look of disappointment or scorn. She'd deceived him for months and convinced his greatest friend to lie to him as well. But he only studied her with curiosity alight in his dark eyes.

"My name is Hua." She offered him a small smile. "Not Huan."

He nodded. "How…" He sucked in a breath. "You saved my life. Twice."

"It wasn't anything anyone else wouldn't have done."

He let out a tired sigh. "Hua, you walked through fire to save us."

Her lips tipped up at the sound of her real name coming from his mouth. Her smile dropped when she remembered the conversation she'd overheard with Qara. No matter how kind the commander was to her, his heart belonged to a much more worthy woman than Hua Minglan.

That thought came suddenly and unbidden to her mind. She jerked back, trying to put it back in the box in her mind it exploded out of. She didn't want to be the woman falling in love with the first strong, kind man she saw.

She hadn't joined the army for that.

After a beat of uncomfortable silence, he spoke again. "It was you. In Dasha. I didn't get a good look at you before you ran from me, but I can see it now. The arrow." He reached out and gripped her wrist, his touch burning its memory into her. "Why didn't it pierce you? And again in the battle."

She yanked her wrist away. "I don't know what you speak of."

She couldn't tell him. She couldn't tell anyone when it was still hard to explain even to herself.

"What about the tattoo?" He leaned forward and pushed her sleeve up.

She froze under his scrutiny.

"I saw an image on your skin when you walked through the fire."

Hua forced a smile as her thoughts became a jumble inside her brain. He was so close to the truths that could get her killed. Jian was the brother to the emperor. Bo Xu Wei may not have hunted down suspected dragon blooded citizens yet, but like his ancestors before him, there would come a time.

And he'd most likely use his brother to do it, the man he entrusted with the command of his army.

"The smoke was thick in that tent, Commander. There is no shame in admitting it caused you to see that which was not there."

He shook his head, denial in his eyes. But the words out of his mouth shocked her. "I am your commander no longer."

She pictured Jian running toward her in her dream with his weapon raised. He hadn't been leading the battle or issuing orders.

"What does that mean?" She dropped her voice. "Did they take your command because of the attack?"

He shook his head. "I relinquished it because…" He

sighed and didn't finish that sentence. "Hua, why did you betray me?"

"I would never betray you."

His expression turned pained. "Every day for months you looked into my eyes as Huan Minglan."

"What would you have done if I told you the truth?"

He shifted his eyes away from her.

"I didn't want to be a useless woman in your eyes—someone needing your protection. I have been training my entire life to protect myself. I am every bit the warrior the men I trained with are."

He rubbed his face, and for a moment, she thought he was going to argue with her. Instead, he chuckled to himself. "You are not the first stubborn woman who shunned her place."

"My place isn't at home knitting beside my mother, sir. I deserve to be by your side when we face our enemies. I've earned it."

"You have." He looked to the stars. "I cannot believe I'm going to say this. I don't want to go into battle without you. When I go after Altan, you should be with me."

Her breath hitched. "You mean..."

"Hua Minglan must stay hidden still. Huan will ride at my side. No one else can know the truth."

Without thinking, she lunged for him, wrapping her arms around his broad shoulders. He stiffened at her touch before his arms came up to hug her back.

"Thank you," she whispered. He'd given her another chance to fight for her sister, her people. May.

She ignored the elation of the beast brewing inside

her, a happiness that did not feel like her own. Whatever was happening to her, she had to deal with it.

Jian rested his chin on her shoulder, the movement bringing Hua back to her senses. She couldn't hug the commander—even if he no longer held that title. Jian wasn't hers to hold.

Pulling back from his embrace, she met his gaze. She'd never known anyone with so much intensity about them. Her breath hitched in her throat as she waited for him to move, to either pull her closer again or push her away.

His eyes shifted between hers in the dark. So close now, she could count the long lashes fluttering against his cheeks, adding a softness to his otherwise hard features, a beauty to his strength.

He reached up to brush a finger down her cheek to trace the path of her lips. She parted them, not wanting to break the moment. Her heart thundered in her chest, trying to burst free. For so long, she pretended to be a man and was treated as such. It normally didn't bother her because she preferred more masculine pursuits. But now, in this moment, she wanted him to see her, the real her. Someone who didn't have to act like a man to be strong, to be capable.

He was letting her fight as Huan, but would Hua ever get her war?

"Jian," she whispered. "I'm not Huan. I never was."

"I know." His lips curved up. "How could I not have seen it?" He sighed. "Hua."

"Say it again?"

"What?"

"My name." She closed her eyes. "Please, just say it again."

He chuckled, the sound vibrating through them both. "Hua Minglan, where did you come from?"

She lifted her face to the night sky. "The stars." The dragon image stretched across the dark. When she looked down again, Jian was even closer.

"I need to ask you a question."

She should have pulled away, but she couldn't make herself move. "Yes?"

"Luca." His eyes met hers. "He knew, didn't he?"

As if a bucket of ice-cold water splashed over them, Hua pulled away.

Jian didn't reach for her again. He sat back against his heels, letting her get to her feet.

"He did." She hugged her arms over her chest and turned away from him.

"What made you trust him? Why tell him and no one else?" She detected hurt in his words. His real question should have been why she'd chosen Luca over him.

There was no more room for lies between them. If they were going to get past all of this, they had to be honest.

"I didn't tell him." She could no longer hold his gaze, so she turned. "He already knew because we are betrothed."

Like a coward, she didn't look back at him, and all that followed her was the price of that honesty.

Silence.

# CHAPTER 17

Jian

*We are betrothed.*

Somehow, those worlds felt more like a betrayal to Jian than learning the soldier he'd trained was a woman.

If he hadn't seen the skill Hua possessed, he wasn't sure he'd have believed it. But why not? He'd seen women fight before. It was common in Koulland, and even Qara had the skill. Yet, part of him wanted to send Hua back to her family where she'd be safe from the coming battle.

Every other part of him wanted her fighting by his

side. He got the distinct impression she didn't need his protection.

No, she had Luca for that.

He'd avoided Hua in the days following their conversation on the rooftop, but he couldn't stop thinking about the fearless girl sitting on the edge. Hadn't she been living on the edge of a cliff for months now? If the wrong person found out her identity, she'd face great shame.

If anyone else found out she'd survived two arrows without a scratch... well, he wasn't sure what they'd do to her. That was why she hadn't told him.

Trust was a thing to be earned.

And he wanted more than anything to deserve hers.

He sat in Qara's room where three men rested on cots. Two of the guards were injured in training. The third, Luca, still hadn't woken.

Each morning, Jian woke, hoping it would be the day he spoke to his friend again. Bo should be there with them. It had always been the three of them against the world. But Bo was the emperor now. No matter how much he cared for Luca, he couldn't come.

Did he know of the betrothal? He would have to. Luca and Hua's fathers would send a sealed letter to the emperor to mark the arrangement in the records.

"My friend." Jian sat next to the bed, his large body resting awkwardly on the tiny wooden chair. "What a mess we've found ourselves in." In truth, it was a relief to relinquish his command. He'd never wanted it. Commander Yang would lead them to victory in Kanyuan. If he ever arrived.

Prince Dequan's scouts reported only yesterday that the Kou army had retreated into the mountains, leaving only a small force in the city.

Jian rubbed a hand across his face. He'd never have thought he'd need to rely on the bitter prince, a prince who didn't send his own men to join the army despite his proximity to the border. He knew what the dangers were.

Qara sat talking with one of the guards, her laughter drifting over the room like peels of the sweetest music. He watched her smile and speak with big gestures as she got more and more excited about whatever her words revealed.

That was the woman he'd known. She was a light in a world full of darkness. It was hard not to hold on to her, to what they once had. But she was right. He wasn't in love with her, not anymore. He'd changed in the years since his mission into Koulland, and he'd only taint her with his darkness.

If he was being honest with himself, he never expected to survive this war. But the war was almost over for him. After reclaiming Kanyuan, he wouldn't be allowed to lead his comrades in fighting for their home even if he wanted to. He'd given up his command before it could be taken from him.

Movement caught the corner of his gaze, and he looked down at Luca as his eyes fluttered open.

Jian couldn't bring himself to smile as relief crashed over him in an angry torrent. "You're awake."

Luca tried to say something, but the words ended in a cough.

Jian leaned closer to catch what he wanted to say.

"Still stating the obvious, I see."

Qara bustled over, a grin stretching across her face. "Luca Kai, welcome back." She pressed a palm to his forehead. "Your fever is gone. It's good to see some color in that handsome face of yours."

He flushed. "Who… where…"

Jian put a hand on his arm. "We're at Prince Dequan's fortress." He gestured to Qara. "Meet Qara Altan."

Luca's eyes widened, and he started coughing again. Qara tipped a cup against his lips.

Luca sputtered. "That's not water." He grimaced.

"Yellow wine." Qara set the cup aside. "It will relax your throat and hopefully end the coughing. You have slept for nearly a week, General. There are bound to be some difficulties."

"A week?" His eyes darted around the room. "But how did we get here? Altan… the battle. We were going to die, Jian."

Jian didn't want to reveal anything in front of Qara. Hua's peculiarities weren't his to speak of.

Qara sat on the end of his cot and patted his leg as if she'd known him for years. "The girl saved you."

"The girl?" Luca looked from Jian to Qara.

Jian sighed and dropped his voice so the other soldiers couldn't hear. He wasn't sure how Qara knew of Hua's heroics, but that didn't matter at the moment. "Hua."

"You know."

Jian nodded.

"I'm sorry I didn't tell you. I—"

"Was protecting your betrothed. I know that too."

Luca sighed. "An arrangement our fathers made."

"Qara, do you think we could have a moment?"

Qara hopped off the bed. "Just when all of this was getting good." She shook her head with a laugh and went to tend to one of the other soldiers.

Luca met Jian's eyes. "So, Qara, she's alive?"

His shoulders dropped. "I didn't know. When I first saw her again, I thought she was a ghost. But her return from the dead is a story for another day. There's a battle coming."

"Where?"

"Kanyuan. After the attack on our camp, the Kou took the village. We must recover it." Kanyuan was the gateway into the mountains. While they controlled it, the Kou had great access to Piao.

Luca's eyes hardened. "I will be there when you lead the attack, even if I have to crawl."

"I won't be leading the attack."

Luca opened his mouth to speak, but Jian cut him off. "I never wanted command, you know that. I only wanted to serve my brother. To protect him."

"And you can do that better as the commander."

"No," Jian snapped. All eyes in the room turned to him so he lowered his voice. "I failed him. I will not do that again."

"If I had the energy to argue with you, Jian, I would fight until you realized just how stupid you sound. But

I don't. So, instead, I must ask you this. What about Minglan?"

"What about her?"

"I know she deceived you and broke the laws of Piao. But she is a warrior just as much as you or I. She's worked hard and she wants to—"

"Luca."

"—fight alongside us. Isn't it her right as a citizen of Piao?"

"Luca."

"The Kou are more barbaric than us, and yet they recognize a woman's right to—"

"Stop." Jian laughed. His friend thought he'd send Minglan home, but he had no intention.

"Is the great Jian Li laughing?" A grin spread Luca's lips.

"No." Jian cleared his throat. "Absolutely not."

"I heard it," Qara called across the room. "Almost reminded me of the Jian I knew years ago."

Before he lost her. Before he had to escape Koulland and become the commander. Since then, he'd lost an entire unit of men in a mountain battle, and another right in their own camp.

No one would be the same person after that.

"I'm not sending her home. While it is in my power, she is a part of this army." Once this battle was over and he left the army, what would happen to her? He met his friend's gaze. "Protect her."

"What?"

"If I no longer can, promise me you'll protect her."

"Jian." He sighed. "She can take care of herself."

"Against our enemy, yes. But what about the traditions of Piao? Who will protect her against those?" Her betrothed.

Something akin to fear sparked in Luca's eyes. Jian wasn't sure what brought it forth, but it was gone so quickly he could have imagined it.

Somewhere deep in the fortress a horn blared. Moments later, a young man in shining armor ran in. "General Li, your presence is requested in the courtyard. Commander Yang has arrived."

As he followed the boy out, Jian looked back at Luca once more. "I'm glad you're still with us."

In the courtyard, the prince's men stood in formation, rows of soldiers stretched across the stone space.

Jian searched until he found the prince. With a confidence he no longer felt, he strode toward him and stopped at his side. Turning to face the open gates, his eyes widened. The new commander rode at the head of lines of men stretching as far as Jian could see. He shielded his eyes from the afternoon sun.

The main Piao fighting force kept camp in the Liudong valley with smaller forces spread throughout the kingdom. They'd ridden for weeks to get to the border.

Commander Yang slid from his horse when he reached them.

Jian bowed, but Prince Dequad didn't so much as dip his head. Commander Yang returned Jian's gesture before issuing a more pronounced bow for the prince.

"Your Highness. We are here to serve you in this time of need."

Dequan's jaw worked as he surveyed the men. "Have your men set up camp beyond the walls. I hope they brought their own supplies for we cannot feed so many." With that, he turned on his heel and walked toward the hall.

Jian stared after him, amazed by his rudeness. "He expects us to follow him, sir."

Commander Yang lifted an eyebrow. "Then he should have requested it. My men have ridden through rain and tired nights to get here. Their well-being is my greatest concern." He looked sideways at Jian. "They should still be your men, Commander."

"I am the commander no longer."

"Yes, the messengers did say that." He inclined his head. "I am sorry for your loss." Jian got the impression he didn't mean his title, but the men under his command who were no longer with them. He looked upon his sea of glinting armor. "I am sorry for all of us. A lot more of them will die by the time this is finished."

"You've been a soldier much longer than me. War is your business."

He sighed. "I grow weary of this business, Jian." He fixed his eyes on Jian. "A business where we are blamed for things beyond our control. Do you feel them? The men you've lost? Do they weigh on your soul?"

"Every moment."

"Then you have not failed. Losing, being beaten, is not a sign of weakness unless you decide not to get up again. If you stop fighting for what you believe in, well, then you will truly be a failure." He handed the reins of his horse off to a servant and put a hand on Jian's shoulder. "Come. Let's go speak with the impatient prince who knows nothing of the true cost of war."

Jian followed the commander inside. Commander Yang may not agree with Jian giving up his role, but as Jian watched Yang walk through the fortress with determination, seeing people scramble out of his way, he knew it was for the best.

A commander must make the tough choices. Jian freed himself from the yoke of rules and order. Now, he could fight. He could find Batukhan Altan and make him pay.

Dequan sat in his study, drumming his fingers on the oak table. Other generals took their places around the table. They'd arrived only yesterday with their own men, having received the messengers from Dequan when they were already traveling to convene with the other units outside Kanyuan.

General Yu scowled as his gaze connected with Jian's. Next to him, Generals Tian and Ze-Cheng wore matching frowns.

It was no secret they resented Jian since Bo named him commander. Not a day went by when Jian didn't wonder if they were right, if he only received the position because of his relationship to the emperor.

A few unfamiliar men joined them, generals unknown to Jian.

The door opened and Minglan's young face

appeared. Her eyes widened when she took in the assembled men. Jian was so focused on her, he hadn't seen the man practically hanging off her shoulder.

She grunted under the weight of Luca. None of the generals jumped up to help except Jian. He crossed the distance between them. "You shouldn't be here, General Kai." He always used formal titles in front of the rest of the military leadership.

"I'm okay." Luca winced as Minglan stumbled forward.

"I didn't want to bring him." Her eyes met Jian's. "But he insisted, and…" She shrugged.

Right. Luca was her betrothed, so she wanted to help him regardless of what was best for him. Jian swallowed his biting words and slid Luca's arm over his own shoulders. "I have him from here, soldier. You can go resume your training duties."

Hurt flashed in her eyes at his quick dismissal, but she gave him a short bow and left. Jian led Luca to the chair he'd vacated and helped his friend take a seat before sitting beside him.

Commander Yang surveyed the men around the table. "There will be others joining us, but I'm afraid we cannot wait for them." He nodded to Jian.

Jian leaned forward. "Seven days ago, the training camp outside Kanyuan was attacked. We said as much in our messages to each of you. Hanan Sema, the captain of the village guard was killed, and the citizens of Kanyuan allowed the Kou army to enter their city. It now belongs to them."

Angry muttering broke out among the generals.

"Kanyuan will never belong to them." General Yu pounded a fist on the table. "How could our commander let this happen? While you chose to busy yourself training novices, our greatest border defense was overrun."

Other generals nodded in agreement. It wasn't anything Jian hadn't thought about himself before. He'd failed them. He shouldn't have taken the training on himself, but he'd seen the new soldiers as the future of the military, as their only chance in the battles to come. And now they were all dead.

Well, not all of them. He glanced at the door Minglan had disappeared through. The other men continued to argue around him, their words rolling through his mind in a jumble. Unable to take it any longer, he slapped a palm on the table. The crack reverberated around the room. "Fighting will do us no good. Kanyuan was lost. Our new recruits, lost. But we are still here. The military might of Piao has not been diminished. The Kou cannot be allowed to remain in Kanyuan. While they hold the town, they can enter Piao without traversing the more dangerous mountain passes. So, if we're all quite done arguing and discussing my failures, might I suggest we figure out how we're going to reclaim our land?"

Commander Yang inclined his head toward Jian, approval glinting in his intelligent eyes. Jian waited for him to take over the meeting, to speak to the men who would listen to him. But he remained silent.

This was what Bo envisioned when he named Jian

the commander, him planning strategy and watching the harsh Piao generals fall at his feet.

He probably hadn't foreseen the failed battles or the distrust of his men.

But Jian wasn't the commander anymore. He was simply a soldier who knew the area around Kanyuan, a man who wanted to force the Kou back across the border.

"We have an opportunity that won't last for long. We've waited here at Prince Dequan's fortress, but we cannot afford more delay. His Highness' scouts have been watching the village and speaking with a source inside. The Kou left a small unit of men to guard the town, but the bulk of the army has returned to reinforce the mountain pass. We will not wait. Gentlemen…" Jian swept his eyes around the table. For once, there was no scorn on the faces he saw. Instead, he held their rapt attention. "It is time we take the fight to them."

Silence followed his words.

Commander Yang pushed his chair back and stood up to loom over the table and stare at the powerful men around it. "Do we have your support?"

His words broke the stunned silence, and the generals clamored to agree. Luca let out a whoop.

A call to fight was what they'd been waiting for since their capital was attacked, since the safety they'd been living in shattered into a million pieces.

The commander pounded on the table, bringing them all to attention. "In five days, I want to be standing in the middle of the Kanyuan central square. Jian Li, tell me how that is going to happen."

Jian thought by giving up his command, he relinquished the responsibility that went with it.

But if this was going to be his final battle as a warrior of Piao, he'd make sure he wouldn't fail again.

# CHAPTER 18

Hua

Hua shifted from foot to foot and swung her dao over her head as she advanced on Chen.

"I don't know how I didn't see it." He grinned. "You aren't like any man I've ever fought because you're a woman!" He cackled like it was the funniest thing in the world.

Yan joined his laughter. Sometimes Hua wondered if those two were the same person in different bodies.

She sidestepped Chen's advance. "You're swinging too wild. Use more control."

"I don't need your advice. I've been fighting with a dao since I was a child."

"She's right." Zhao didn't lift his eyes from where he sat sharpening his blade.

Zhao was the only one of her friends who didn't look at her differently now that they knew the truth. Chen and Yan treated her almost like a child. Jian could barely look at her.

But Zhao continued on with his stoic respect. He jumped to his feet and knocked Chen out of the way.

Hua grinned as he faced her. Zhao was always the bigger challenge. He fought with the skill of a lifelong soldier, having been trained as one. His face showed no expression as he steadied his dao.

"Attack me," he ordered.

"With pleasure." Hua lunged, the blunt edge of her dao crashing against his.

"You won't hurt me. Use the sharp edge."

She shrugged. If he insisted. Her smile dropped as he blocked her attack and advanced with one of his own. She ducked his blade and whirled around, bringing her dao down in a wide arc.

Together, they performed the dance they'd trained for, one they'd honed over the months at a camp that now ran with blood.

If Hua's father could see her now, if he knew how his training saved her life, maybe his pride would overcome his shame.

Sweat dripped into her eyes as the early summer heat bore down on them. With nothing else to do, they'd been sparring with each other for days as the generals locked themselves away in strategy meetings.

Commander Yang arrived three days ago, and still the soldiers didn't know how long they'd be here.

Hua finally felt like herself again, like the girl who'd arrived on the plains outside Kanyuan with a mission. She hadn't felt the darkness slithering underneath her skin since she dreamed of fire. But she knew the beast wasn't gone.

Zhao grunted as she drove her body into his, knocking him to the side. It was like moving a stone pillar. Pain snaked up her shoulder, but she didn't have time to dwell on it because he stepped toward her.

Ducking another swipe of his dao, she kicked her leg out, catching the back of Zhao's knee with her foot and yanking. Surprise flashed across his face as he went down, taking Hua with him. She landed on his chest and pushed herself up, angling her dao at his throat. Her lips curved up. "Any critiques for me, Zhao?"

Chen bit his fist and laughed. "Big bad Zhao taken down by a woman."

Hua brushed off his comment. The only way to silence people like him was by winning fights such as this. A man only had to be average to gain the respect of his peers, but a woman… well, she had to succeed beyond anyone's expectations.

Climbing off Zhao, she held her hand down to him. He clasped it and let her help him up before turning a scowl on Chen. "If you think Hua Minglan is merely a woman, then you're more of a fool than we already thought." He settled his eyes on Hua. "I don't care if you're a woman, I'd rather have you fighting at my side than the rest of these idiots."

She smiled. It wasn't often the big man spoke his mind.

Someone clapped nearby, and Hua froze. Commander Yang watched them with a smile on his face. Had he heard Chen and Zhao speaking?

The commander approached Hua, ignoring the others. "That was an impressive fight." His eyes flicked to Zhao. "It's not often I see someone your size defeat such a mountainous foe."

When Hua didn't speak, Zhao stepped in. "He was the best of us in training."

The commander looked at each of them in turn, his lips turning down. "You're the survivors from the attack on the training base?"

"Yes, sir." Chen stepped forward. "But we're only alive because of Huan." He gestured to Hua.

Hua looked at the man who hadn't had many kind things to say to her, a new appreciation in her eyes.

"It wasn't only me." She met the commander's curious gaze just like she used to force herself not to look away from Jian. It was a way to keep her own power. She chose not to be intimidated.

He nodded. "We will need soldiers such as you in the days to come." He nodded to each of them before striding away.

Hua released a breath.

"He's not as much of an ass as the old commander," Yan said.

Hua bristled at the description of Jian. He'd been

brutish and serious, but never mean. When he looked at her, there was nothing cruel in his gaze.

"Minglan!" someone called from across the courtyard.

She turned to find Luca waving her over. He'd recovered most of his strength since his injury, but still tired easily and had bandages across his abdomen that Qara had to change daily.

Hua waved goodbye to the rest of the men and joined Luca. "Do you need spoon-fed, General?"

He gave her an indulgent smile. "I'm not an invalid."

"You were." She grinned. Luca was easy to smile around. Even after his brush with death, he had a lightness about him. She used her smiles to force images from the battle out of her mind.

They hadn't spoken of the secrets revealed between them before the attack, but they both knew they now had to rely on each other, to protect each other.

"The commander is preparing to make a speech from atop the walls."

"Do you know what he's going to say?"

Luca grinned. "We're finally going after them."

"What?"

"The Kou. We'll no longer wait until they attack us. It's our turn for victory."

A mixture of fear and excitement bubbled up in Hua. Another battle was coming. She still had flashes of the last one in her mind. But that had been more of a slaughter than a proper battle.

This time, they'd damage the Kou, and they'd save Kanyuan in the process.

She leaned in closer. "There's a rumor the people of Kanyuan chose the Kou, that they allowed them access to the city."

Luca sighed. "Those villagers have suffered more than anyone in Piao. Koulland has been attacking their farms and their walls for years. They only want an end to the fighting."

"But we're bringing another fight to them. If they don't want to be saved, why are we risking it?"

"Kanyuan is too valuable a location for us to let it go. It is the easiest access point into Piao, and we can't afford for it to remain in enemy hands." He nudged her forward. "Come on." Luca walked slowly, gingerly, as they joined the rest of the soldiers waiting for the speech. Once the commander gave the orders, his words would travel among the soldiers camped outside the walls. By morning, they'd all know their next move.

Commander Yang walked down the steps of the complex, stopping near the wall connecting the gatehouse to the towers. He looked out on the assembled generals and the few soldiers living within the walls.

"Rest up, men, for tomorrow night we attack!"

A roar rose from the crowd.

Hua sucked in a breath.

The commander spoke for a few more minutes, but Hua barely heard any of it as the feeling she'd tried so hard to rid herself of writhed inside her, a beast preparing for war.

"I-I have to go."

"He's not finished," Luca called after her.

Hua didn't stop. She ran from courtyard, stumbling down the open-air halls. Her shoulder slammed into the wall as heat pulsed beneath her skin.

Pain shot through her as she pushed open a door and fell into the healer's quarters.

Qara shot to her feet in surprise and rushed toward her. "Hua, what's wrong?"

"What's happening?" Hua asked in a choked voice

Qara put a hand on her back and helped her to a nearby cot. "You feel it?"

"What do I feel?" Hua's head thrashed from side to side. "It's like it's trying to get out. I don't understand." She lifted her arm and found the image of the dragon, but it wasn't just a red mark on her skin. It looked as it had in battle, as it had when her grandmother first drew the design. Black ink swirled in the intricate pattern. "What does this mean? You said I'm not a Nagi. Why do I have their mark on me?"

Qara shut her door and returned to the bedside. She lifted Hua's arm and examined the image. "When I told you the Nagi are creatures of story, I did not tell you everything. I have seen things I don't want to believe in, but you have appeared as proof of the truth in my visions." She sighed. "This road will not be an easy one, Hua Minglan."

Hua clenched her teeth against a stab of pain. "What road?"

"That of the Nagi."

"But you said—"

"The Nagi were said to be dragons who could take human form to live in this world. But that is not the whole story. They were unable to fully live in this world, so the dragons found hosts, people they lived within. You are not Nagi, Hua, but the beast inside you is. Nagi only appear when Piao needs their protection."

Hua squeezed her eyes shut as her breathing stuttered. "Hosts. You mean the dragon blooded." She opened her eyes to find Qara's gaze still on her.

"For many years, the emperors of Piao have hunted those suspected descendants of the ancient Nagi lines. What you call the dragon blooded. Dragons are powerful creatures. In the legends, they ruled over all life. Power. Protection. Luck. The Nagi's very existence challenges an emperor's mandate from heaven."

"How do you know all of this? You're not even one of us." Hua scrambled from the bed as a bolt of pain shot through her. "You're one of them. A Kou. An Altan. Why should I believe anything you tell me? None of this is possible, none of it is real." She clenched her fists at her sides, digging her nails into her palms to prove this was real. If she could feel the pain, it was like this was really happening. The woman before her knew things she shouldn't, things that were forbidden.

Hua pushed out a breath to calm the chaos in her mind.

Qara studied her for a moment before tapping the side of her head. "Have you ever met a seer, Hua?"

Hua shook her head. Before Qara, she believed seers to be of the myths just like the Nagi.

"I know what has happened in the past, and I can

sense some of what the future holds. I do not know everything, but you're important."

"I'm not important. I'm just a girl." Even as she said the words, she didn't believe them, not anymore.

Qara smiled. "No one is only one thing. I too am a village girl. I'm also of Koulland and the sister of the man terrorizing this country. Do you believe there is nothing else to me?"

"No… I—"

"We all want safety, Hua, for Piao to continue on in peace. You're not alone in needing to see the direction before setting your feet onto the path. But you no longer have that luxury. Hua Minglan must become more. You must embrace every part of yourself."

A tear slipped down Hua's cheek. "What if I can't?"

Qara approached her and reached out to wipe away her tears. "The dragon is the smartest creature to have ever lived, much brighter than you or I. If one of them chose you, there was a reason. You may be able to fool a camp full of dimwitted men into thinking you're someone you're not, but don't for one moment think a dragon would fall for it." She put a hand over Hua's heart. "If a dragon does indeed live inside of you, it knows exactly who you are."

Hua dried her tears with the sleeve of her robe. The pain lessened to a dull throb almost as if the creature listened to their conversation.

Could it be true? Were the legends coming to life right inside her?

"I dream of fire," she whispered. "Fire and devastation."

Qara's lips turned down and sadness entered her gaze. "As do I. It is our future, I'm afraid."

Hua turned toward the door. "We leave tomorrow for battle. Soon, it will be our future no longer and instead become the present."

"Be careful, Hua. Dragons have no masters."

"What does that mean?" Hua looked back at her. "I don't know what I'm supposed to do."

Qara's expression saddened. "I'm afraid there is nothing for you to do. The dragon will do what it must."

Hua stepped into the hall with those words filling her mind. If a dragon had no master, what happened when they broke free?

Fear coiled in her stomach, twisting with the rage rising from the depths.

In Kanyuan, an enemy awaited.

What if another lurked inside her, waiting to be released?

# CHAPTER 19

Jian

The Piao military was an impressive force. Rows of men standing perfectly still waited for the order to move. At the front, horses led the way with spearman on their backs.

Foot soldiers stood behind them with archers at the rear. The sun set over their heads. Soon, only stars would guide them.

Jian nodded goodbye to Qara who'd come to wish him well before nudging his horse up beside Commander Yang. "We are ready to march."

The commander nodded. "We'll reach Kanyuan in the early hours of the morning."

"And catch them by surprise." It was a well-thought-out plan, one Jian took pride in.

"Once this battle is through, soldier, I would very much like you to remain in my service."

Jian couldn't go from commanding the army to only fighting in it. That wasn't the way he'd serve Bo. "I'm sorry, sir. I have already resigned my post. The prince sent a notice to the Imperial palace. It is done."

"Nothing is ever done. This battle will not win the war, Li."

Jian sighed. "No, this is still the beginning, I'm afraid. Which is why I shall return to Dasha where I can be of use protecting the emperor. There are men in my service, however, that would be of great use to you, should they survive the night."

"Men?" He looked sideways at Jian. "Is that all they are?"

Jian swallowed his next words as he caught the commander's eye. How did he know about Minglan? "They are all warriors."

"I suspect so. Yes, soldier Li, I will allow them all into my service."

Jian didn't miss the word *all.* Relief spread through him at the same time an irrefutable sadness sank in. After this battle, he'd leave them all behind. He'd leave Minglan, a soldier he'd trained over the last months—not like she'd needed much training.

"Will you ride into this battle at my side, Jian?"

Jian couldn't recall the Commander ever calling him by his real name, even when Jian was his superior.

But there was somewhere else he needed to be. "I'm sorry, Commander. I must ride with my men."

"I respect your loyalty. It is a rare quality in those who lead."

Jian ignored the eyes of the generals forming up around the commander as he rode toward the back, looking for a familiar face. Minglan sat atop her chestnut warhorse, Heima. She looked fierce in her lamellar armor, plates of iron punched together to create a protective body casing. The armor hung to her knees and a thick robe reached to her feet as they rested in the stirrups. In training, most soldiers chose to wear lacquered rawhide instead of iron.

As he watched, Minglan placed her helmet on her head and it tilted into her eyes. She pushed it back into place, revealing a hard look of courage, readiness.

She was breathtaking.

One of the generals shouted the order to move out, shocking Jian from his momentary stupor. As he rode up to his men—and woman—Luca grinned. "Thought you'd ride with better warriors than us."

Jian couldn't believe that such a short time ago, his best friend was fighting for his life. He wasn't at full strength, but he'd never have missed this fight. "There are no better warriors than you." He shifted his eyes from Luca to Minglan.

Chen, Yan, and Zhao rode behind them, one unit among a sea of strangers. They were in this together just like they'd been in that smoke-filled tent.

He formed up beside Minglan, and the six of them nudged their horses forward. Many days ago, they'd ridden this same route with a dying Luca and questions on their minds.

The questions hadn't gone away, but as Jian looked sideways at Minglan, they didn't seem to matter in that moment. Whatever secrets she held, they wouldn't affect them this night. There were no more betrayals or deceptions. Only warriors on their way to war.

"When I left home," Minglan started. "I knew I'd never see my family again. I followed down a path I thought would lead to my end."

"And now?" Jian asked. "Do you still think this will be the end for you?" He'd had the same thought as her before every battle, every mission. That was what bonded soldiers. Knowing their choices could result in death and continuing to make them.

Minglan didn't answer his question. "I've never been afraid of death." Her voice drifted away as if the words were meant for only herself. "There are much bigger things to fear."

"I'll protect you, Hua." He didn't know what made him say the words. "We'll protect each other."

"There are things you don't know." She looked away. "I very much doubt anyone can protect me now."

Jian met Luca's eyes in question, but his friend only shrugged. No matter what she said, Jian would fight for Minglan. He'd fight for all of them. He hadn't been able to protect anyone else, but it wasn't over yet.

# CHAPTER 20

Hua

The closer Hua rode to Kanyuan, the harder it became to ignore the tension in her body. It took every ounce of will to control her limbs, to fight off the beast trying to take over. What would happen when it came time to fight? If she couldn't use her speed and agility, she wouldn't last long.

She lifted her eyes to the sky, searching for Luna in the heavens.

It was gone.

The dragon in the stars, her companion every night for so many months, no longer shone above her. She squeezed her eyes shut and opened them again, but nothing.

A cart rumbled past her, pulled by two massive black steeds. No, not a cart. A battering ram on wooden wheels.

This was what it came to. Destroying the gates of one of their own villages.

"What's going to happen once we get inside?" Minglan asked.

Jian turned his head toward her. "Our hope is the villagers stay in their homes and let us handle the Kou stationed in the village. We must get to the mountain gate before the rest of the Kou army arrives."

"So, our entire plan rests on the villagers welcoming our army back? The same villagers who handed their town over to the Kou?"

"Out of fear, Minglan, not loyalty. Those people do not want the enemy in their streets any more than we do. Kanyuan is not our foe. They are sick of war, but they will have no other option but to choose a side."

With darkness as their cloak, the Piao forces waited in the fields outside the Kanyuan gates. Not a word was spoken as they held their collective breath.

Commander Yang lifted a hand and threw it forward, telling the foot soldiers to move in. Those on horseback stayed behind, far enough so even the light from the stars couldn't give away their position.

Armor creaking, the men on foot ran for the gate with no battle cry and little noise to tell of their presence. The first wave of them reached the high walls and pressed themselves up against the stone where no guard looking down could see them.

The horses pulling the battering ram followed, led by the brutish looking General Yu.

A horn sounded as the ram neared the gates, alerting the city to intruders. Hua sucked in a breath and looked to Jian, but no panic crossed his face.

"Part of the plan," he whispered.

A general Hua couldn't remember the name of yelled behind them. "Archers!"

Rows of soldiers ran past the horses, bows in hand. Behind them, others wielded crossbows. Everything was coordinated, calculated.

The attack on her camp had been chaos, nothing but a fight to survive. This… this was war.

In the distance, General Yu unhitched the horses from the battering ram and led them away. Men lined each side of the wheeled ram.

The first boom of the ram against the gates rent the air, and Hua clenched her reins tighter.

Arrows rained down on Piao foot soldiers at the gate. Every time one fell away, another took his place. They didn't give up.

Another boom shook Hua, vibrating through her body and awakening whatever lived within. "Not now," she whispered, thinking of how the pain nearly got her killed when she passed out at General Altan's feet.

"Minglan." Jian's voice swam in her mind, but she couldn't move.

"Minglan."

It wasn't until his tone softened she managed to meet his gaze. "Hua, there's no time to turn back now."

"I don't want to turn back." She pushed out a breath. "I want to kill them all." The words weren't her own, and the deep tone sounded foreign to her ears. She wished she could take back the words when she saw shock flicker across Jian's concerned face.

Her body craved the blood they'd soon be soaked in. Her hands wanted to destroy.

Her heart hardened against the people of Kanyuan, the ones who'd threatened the peace of Piao. They didn't deserve her mercy.

"We're going to destroy them all." Her voice was a low growl.

Jian's eyes narrowed. "We're going to save our people from the Kou."

Hua forced herself to nod.

The archers loosed arrow after arrow. They arced high up over the walls to the town behind them.

Up ahead, the gate splintered. It was never meant to hold off a siege. With one more boom of the battering ram, it burst inward.

The foot soldiers ran into the city, their daos ready.

The sight burned into Hua's mind, and no hint of fear remained. A slow smile spread across her face. This was what she was meant for.

She was only vaguely aware the thoughts weren't entirely her own, but instead of holding back the monster within, she embraced it, and the pain faded away.

Maybe that was the key. She had to become one

with the darker force. She saw the world before her through a hazy film of red. Heat snaked up her arms as she watched the first wave of attack. If everything went well, they'd recover the city within the hour.

Commander Yang guided his horse in front of the others and raised his voice. "Remember, the people of Kanyuan are not our enemy. Seek out the Kou inside those walls and destroy them." He raised his dao. "Charge!"

Hua leaned forward. "Come on, Heima. Let's show them what we can do."

Heima shot forward, matching her pace with Jian's charging steed. Warm night air whipped around Hua, heating as it touched her skin.

Chen, Yan, and Zhao reached the town before her, cutting their way past soldiers to leap over the shattered gate.

Luca and Hua formed up on either side of Jian, and together, the three of them entered the fray. Hua cut her way through the enemy with precision, never slowing. The Kou and the city guard fought back with ferocity, but they were no match for the Piao army.

A small bearded man sliced at Luca's horse. The beast reared up, throwing its rider. Luca landed on his back and got to his feet slowly as two Kou warriors circled him.

Without thinking about it, Hua slid from Heima's back and jumped in front of the still-weak Luca. She blocked an attack from the first man before jumping back to avoid a second attack. Behind her, Luca engaged their other foe.

The Kou were supposed to be the best trained fighters in the world, but Hua sensed every attack before it happened. Strength coursed through her, a power that was not her own.

Luca stumbled back into her, and she whirled around, slicing her dao through his attacker's stomach before returning to deliver a fatal blow to hers.

Around her, blood coated the cobblestones as bodies dropped. Kou, Piao soldiers, Kanyuan guards. They all died with alarming frequency.

Wiping a bead of sweat away with her sleeve, Hua surveyed the melee. Men crowded into the square beyond the broken gates so tightly they barely had room to move.

The houses lining the streets were closed up tightly, and she could only imagine the families huddled inside wondering if this night would be their last.

The sharp sting of a blade nicked her arm, and she turned to block a second attack, using the blunt edge of her dao to smack the Kou across the head. He crumpled to the ground.

A woman ran for Hua, dressed in the traditional Kou leathers.

Hua grinned.

The beast inside her readied itself, wanting this to end in blood.

Hua ducked the first attack before twisting on her heel and crashing her dao against the woman's.

They circled each other, both breathing heavily, both waiting for the other to make a move. Hua narrowed her eyes, seeing flames flicker across her vision.

*Enough of this.* She lunged forward and was thrown off balance as the woman shoved her to the side. Hua hit the cobblestones, and she lifted her eyes, daring the woman to make a move.

Before she could, the tip of a blade appeared through her chest. Surprise coated her features as her mouth fell open, and she collapsed, leaving the bloody blade behind. Jian looked down at her from the back of his horse.

He reached a hand down. "Come with me."

She didn't think twice as she gripped his hand and pulled herself onto the horse behind him. "I can't leave Heima." That was the only piece of her family she had.

"I saw her running back through the gates. She's long gone."

At least she escaped the fighting. Hua gripped Jian around the waist as he kicked the horse into a run. "Where are we going? The fight is back there?"

She didn't want to leave the battle, not until they'd killed every last one of their enemies. "We have to get to the mountain gate."

Right. The Kou army. They were stationed in the mountains. If there was any hope of holding Kanyuan, they had to close off the gate into Koulland.

Beyond the fight, the town was deserted as citizens took shelter. Jian's horse thundered through the streets with a few other riders behind them, Commander Yang leading the way.

The mountain gate rose before them, much larger

than the one that now lay broken on the other side of town. Steel reinforced the wood, a protectant against a battering ram. They'd been keeping the Kou out of the border town for many years.

Hua couldn't contain her anger at the people of Kanyuan for letting them in now. Blood would forever taint their streets, an unavoidable consequence of their actions.

Commander Yang and his men entered the deserted guard tower.

Jian slid down from his horse. "The guards must have been called to the fight."

There was an eerie quiet in this part of town when only moments ago she'd been surrounded by chaos and screaming.

She wanted to go back. To fight. To shed the blood of her enemies.

She jumped down from the horse and stepped inside the guard tower where Commander Yang and Jian turned a giant wheel. The gates groaned and quaked as they shut. A definitive thud boomed when the two gates met in the middle.

Jian wiped his face.

A horn sounded outside the gates, and he ran past Hua with the commander on his heels. They climbed the steps to the top of the wall. Hua followed behind them, freezing when she saw what lay on the other side.

A hoard of warriors roared and crashed halberds against shields.

"The Kou army." Jian's eyes widened.

At the front stood a man, unrecognizable from this distance, but Hua knew it was General Altan.

An arrow whirred past her head, and she ducked out of the way.

One of Commander Yang's men screamed as a crossbow bolt pierced his stomach and he fell from the top of the wall.

"Get to cover!" Commander Yang ordered.

Jian reached for Hua, but she stepped away from him, unable to take her eyes from Altan. Anger burned along her skin, and she couldn't move. Her will sank back into the recesses of her mind, giving way to something larger, darker, more powerful.

An arrow sailed for her, but it did not pierce her skin. Instead, it clattered to the top of the wall beneath her feet. A roar escaped her mouth as her eyes settled on the enemies below.

She looked back over her shoulder to where rows of houses stood, houses belonging to traitors of Piao. They'd opened their gates to the Kou. They deserved to die.

A crossbow bolt grazed her arm as it flew by, drawing a bead of blood. The sight of it sent a jolt through Hua as pain spread through her body. Her face contorted as muscles stretched and bones cracked.

"Hua!" Jian screamed. "We have to go."

She turned to him and cocked her head. An arrow sailed for him, but she stepped in its path. It didn't hurt her. When she spoke again, her voice was not her own. "Hua had her fight. Now it is finally my turn." A cruel smile curled her lips.

Jian tried to pull her after him, but she yanked her arm out of his grasp. "Get to safety."

The man wasn't her enemy, and if he stayed any longer, he'd die.

She couldn't recall his name as her mind already turned back to the task at hand. Dusty gray scales appeared along her skin, coating her in a layer of impenetrable armor.

The Nagi had finally returned to Piao, and it would defeat all who would destroy the peace.

With fire. And with blood.

# CHAPTER 21

Jian

Jian screamed as an arrow ripped into his arm. He refused to leave Hua, but he couldn't believe his eyes.

The girl he'd come to know and care about screamed in agony as scales poked through her skin.

Her body contorted revealing two large… wings?

Another arrow narrowly missed him, and he stumbled down the steps. Steel tipped arrows fell to the ground around him as he made a break for the guard tower where Commander Yang and a few others avoided the storm of arrows and crossbow bolts.

"Where's Minglan?" Commander Yang asked as soon as Jian caught his breath.

All Jian could do was stare at him as his mind tried to comprehend the answer. Where was Hua? What happened to her?

A roar ripped through the air, causing the soldiers to jump back from the door and press themselves against the stone walls.

Jian sat on the floor and used a dagger to cut cloth from his robe underneath his armor. He wrapped his fingers around the shaft of the arrow piercing his arm and pulled it free. Blood poured from the wound until he managed to tie the cloth around it. Red soaked through the makeshift bandage, but there was nothing to be done for it.

"Commander," one of his men yelled as he resumed his position at the door.

Commander Yang joined him, and a string of curses left his mouth. "Is that…" His voice held a note of awe.

Jian scooted on his knees to where they stood. A winged beast jumped into the air, flying high above the town. "A dragon."

"It's been hundreds of years since they protected us."

Hua. Was it her? If he hadn't seen it for himself, he'd never believed it. Qara's words came back to him. She'd seen this. She'd told him his destiny was to protect the dragon. He'd just never imagined something like… this.

"Hua," he whispered. Bold, courageous Hua. Was she still in there or had the beast stolen her mind?

They watched as the dragon circled back, its massive wings spread wide.

Kou warriors shot arrows at the beast but the dragon dodged them easily.

"What's it doing?" Commander Yang asked.

They didn't have to wait long for an answer. A stream of fire erupted from its mouth, blasting into a row of homes nearby.

Jian's eyes widened. "It's going to destroy the village."

"We need to get the people out of their homes."

Jian ran from the guard tower. No more arrows flew, but another horn sounded. Were the Kou retreating into the mountains?

Stone burst apart with the impact of the fire, and Jian ignored the stabbing pain in his arm as he ran. He burst into the nearest home where a woman cowered with her two young children. "You need to leave. Now!" He reached for the nearest kid and picked him up before running back outside. "Get to the front of the town and through the gates." Jian didn't know if the fight was still going on, but these people were safer there than being targeted by a dragon. He handed the woman her child and ran into the next home.

Family after family ran into the night as the dragon burned their homes. A giant flap of wings sounded overhead, and Jian peered up into the smooth underbelly of the beast. As if sensing him, the dragon looked down and opened its mouth. Orange flames built in the back of its throat before breaking free.

Jian didn't have time to run, but the flames didn't

touch him. Instead, the dragon drew a circle around him with dancing fire. Screams filled the night as ordinary people caught fire, flailing wildly before collapsing to the ground.

The smell of burning meat mixed with the smoke choked the air. A gust of wind blew in, giving Jian the opening he needed to leap through the line of fire. The impact sent a jarring pain through his injured arm.

Commander Yang caught up with him. "We need to get to the gates and sound the retreat. Where's Minglan?"

Jian lifted his eyes to the dark sky. She was somewhere up there. "No longer with us."

The commander clapped him on the shoulder. "I'm sorry. Come, we must get our people to safety."

Around them, the homes burned. There were no more families to pull to safety, because nowhere was safe.

Bodies littered the way to the broken gates, some killed by the fight, others charred beyond recognition.

The dragon circled overhead, leaving no street unmarred by its flames.

Jian had to get to her. He had to stop this. Glancing down, he saw the blood seeping through the cloth wrapped around his arm.

His fingers flexed, struggling to curve around the hilt of his dao. Switching the weapon to his stronger hand, he searched the skies. "Come on, Hua. Tell me where you are."

The night's veil hid the beast from view.

"Jian," Commander Yang ordered. "We must pull back from Kanyuan."

One of the remaining generals not lying dead in the square, put a horn to his lips. The sound reverberated through Jian. Men helped their wounded comrades as they scrambled past the splintered gates. Families cried for each other and ran to escape the wreckage.

In the middle of it all stood a little girl. Her faded blue sleeping robe hung to her ankles and bare feet peeked out from underneath.

Soldiers scrambled around her. The Kou inside the city were dead and their army fled back into the mountains, but they weren't the real danger. Not this time.

Jian sprinted for the girl, not stopping as he scooped her into his arms. Tears streamed down her face, streaking through the ash covering her skin. Dust rained down from the stone towers as they crumbled in the flames.

The girl let out a wail as Jian tripped over a body lying twisted on the ground. He righted himself and kept going. At the gate, the few remaining men on horseback in the city ushered people through.

"General!" Jian yelled for General Yu. The man never liked or respected him, but now was not the time for personal feelings.

General Yu didn't scowl. Instead, he looked just as lost as Jian felt. The majority of the Piao army hadn't entered the town yet. A small mercy.

Jian pointed to the girl, and General Yu nodded.

"Get her to safety," Jian yelled over a deafening crash of stone behind him.

General Yu pulled the girl onto his horse in front of him and took off toward the plains where the rest of the army had retreated.

Commander Yang yelled for their people to go. An injured soldier rode in front of him, his face white. Jian should have followed them.

He should have gotten himself to safety.

But Qara's words wouldn't release their hold. The dragon would need him. But maybe it wasn't the dragon who needed him at all. The girl he'd seen transform into the beast had to still be in there. The one who'd challenged him since the day she showed up as a man in his camp.

The one who loved her sister so much she went to war.

He had to save her.

The ground shook as the large dragon landed amid the chaos, its long neck stretching above them. Its head turned from right to left, as if surveying its path of destruction. At its back, the town burned. Soon, nothing would be left but ash.

The dragon stomped a foot, and Jian swore the earth shook.

As he stared into the giant amber eyes of the beast, he tried to see her, the girl inside. The dragon opened his mouth, revealing hundreds of pointed teeth. A glow built in its throat, and Jian started running.

For Hua, he couldn't let the beast destroy Piao.

As he ran, he retrieved a halberd from the ground, not breaking his stride.

He lifted the battle-ax over his head. The dragons were said to only target enemies of Piao.

Yet, he was a warrior fighting for that very country, and when the fire exploded past its lips, the dragon was no longer their protector. It could destroy them all.

# CHAPTER 22

Hua

It happened like the dream Hua remembered so clearly, and she was powerless to stop it. Locked in the mind of the dragon, she hammered against its defenses, trying to free herself.

Blood soaked through the bandage on Jian's arm, but it didn't stop him. He picked up a halberd and sprinted through the dust and debris.

The dragon didn't move. It didn't jump into the sky to look for more enemies. If it truly were a protector, it would have chased the army in the mountains.

But it hadn't. Instead, a city lay in ruins. It didn't matter to Hua that Kanyuan surrendered to the enemy, not when she'd watched families die under the weight of their own homes, mothers and children burned beyond recognition.

And Jian.

Heat corded along her skin, rising from the depths of her belly to pool in her throat. She wanted to cry, to shield her eyes as the beast set his eyes on the man she wanted to protect.

The man who'd earned her loyalty.

No matter what rank he held, Jian Li was her commander, her leader. She would have followed him straight into death if that was what it took.

Goodbye, Jian.

The stream of fire exploded forth, dousing the surrounding square in flames. The remaining Piao forces fled, and she hoped the dragon would let them be. He was meant to protect Piao, but all she felt from it was a desire to destroy.

The dragon rose to its full height, flexing its giant wings and let out a roar.

Hua searched the flames, expecting to find Jian's body. She never got to say goodbye to any of them. Chen, Yan, Zhao, Luca. Were they all dead because of her?

And now Jian, too.

As the flames receded from her vision, the sight before her took her breath. Jian stood unharmed in a circle of flames. The dragon hadn't killed him.

She caught sight of a group of Kou warriors moving together and stabbing their spears into every Piao body they found, making sure they were dead.

The dragon's eyes narrowed as it twisted around to swat them with its tail. They sprinted toward the gate even though the Piao army sat on the other side.

Two of the warriors ran for Jian, and the dragon stepped back, letting the flames protecting him die.

*Do something!* She screamed inside her mind. *Fight for him!*

Jian stumbled forward, struggling for breath. One arm hung limp at his side while the other tried to keep the dao raised.

They attacked at the same time, and all Hua could do was watch in horror as he tried to block them. She screamed, but no sound left the dragon's mouth.

*Please.*

What good was it to have a Nagi inside of her if she couldn't protect the people she cared about?

*You stupid beast! Help him.* Her thoughts strengthened. *They're going to kill him.*

Jian cried out as a dao slid between the scales of his armor, puncturing his side. He fell to his knees.

*Jian.* Hua tried to scream.

Tears slipped down her face, and she thought she'd imagined it. How could she feel them? Was the dragon crying?

Her thoughts pounded harder at the wall in her mind separating her from the dragon.

Jian looked up into the faces of the attackers before shifting his gaze to meet the dragon's eyes. No, not the dragon's. He looked straight through him to Hua, trapped on the inside.

*I'm sorry.* She was sorry for everything. All the

people who died, the devastation. It was all her, and she hadn't been able to stop it. *I'm so sorry, Jian.*

He nodded as if he knew. He rose up on his knees and took the hand he'd pressed to the wound at his side away. Blood seeped through the plates of armor. Jian's life faded before her eyes.

His gaze held a defeat she'd never seen in him. Anger raged through her, but this time the dragon couldn't claim the emotion.

Hua let it overcome her, vibrating through every cell. The dragon reared up on its legs, and a roar shook the night. Fire slid along its tongue, setting Hua's every nerve ending aflame. She let herself assume the dragon's shape. Instead of one controlling the other, they existed together.

She shook her head, and the Kou warriors screamed as they caught fire and ran toward the town gates. They didn't make it before they fell, their bodies twitching as their skin melted from their bones.

Smoke swirled in the air from every building, every person who'd burned alive. It twisted up toward the heavens as if to tell the stars what happened this night, as if to tell Luna.

But she wasn't up there watching over Hua. The brightest star Hua searched for every night didn't protect her. Luna was in her next life with no memory of the former, and the only person left to watch out for Hua was herself.

A wind pushed the smoke toward the plains rolling down from the mountains. Hua sucked in a breath as her chest heaved. Then she saw him.

Jian, untouched by her flames, hadn't been protected from everything. She was too late.

He lay on his side with his crimson blood seeping out and pooling in the cracks between stones in the once bustling border town.

His chest rose and fell with shallow breaths, and his eyes fluttered open, latching on to hers. Was he challenging her? Telling her it was okay to let him go?

How did he know she was still in there? He didn't stare as one would at a beast that destroyed an entire town.

His eyes softened, and his lips moved. She didn't hear his words, but his eyes drifted shut.

*No!* She pleaded with the dragon sharing her body. The dragon's face dampened with her tears. *I can't let him die.*

A rumble of approval sounded low in the dragon's throat. It reached out one foot, wrapping its long claws around Jian's limp body before jumping into the air with jarring force.

One quick circle of the town showed Hua what she'd allowed the beast to do, what she'd done. There was no coming back from this.

The beast slowly took control again, and she faded to the back of its mind, content to forget herself and the images that would haunt her for the rest of her life.

The dragon soared over the retreating Piao forces, skimming the skies above the fortress they'd left hours ago.

By the time it slowed, the sun rose on the horizon, highlighting the dragon against the pink skies. Hua drifted further and further away, only to come back to herself when they landed with great force in the middle of a cornfield. The dragon laid Jian on the ground as the pain seared through Hua once more.

Her entire body shook at the wings receding into her smooth, scale-free back. The cool morning air struck her naked skin, cooling the remaining heat as she stumbled back, her legs wobbling beneath her.

Breath exploded into her lungs, and she lifted her hand in amazement that she could do it once more.

Her knees slammed into the ground, and she pitched forward, every last bit of energy fading from her limbs.

She rolled onto her side next to Jian and reached for his hand, finding it ice-cold. His pulse beat weakly in his wrist.

She didn't know where the dragon brought them, but there was one thing she realized.

They were alive.

Her fingers thread through Jian's as flashes of his final moments in the battle came to her. In her dreams before the fight, she saw fire, she saw blood. Jian ran toward her carrying the weapon just as she'd known he would.

What she hadn't seen was the man she'd once hid her true name from saving her from herself. The most dangerous thing about Hua Minglan wasn't that she was a woman playing the part of a soldier.

Her greatest secret, the one that could end everything she knew, had been hidden even from her.

Hua harbored a beast inside her, one she couldn't

control. What if the Kou weren't going to destroy Piao? What if General Altan was only a distraction?

She tried to keep herself from falling into darkness, but her eyelids fluttered closed. As she fell into the black abyss, the screams of burning children filled her mind.

# Epilogue

Jian

Jian woke to sunlight streaming through an open window. A groan escaped his mouth as he tried to sit up and pain lanced through him. He managed to turn his head, taking in the simple wildflowers in a bronze vase on the wooden sill.

A fur blanket covered his bare torso. He lifted it to find a bandage wrapped around his midsection. Another wound around his arm.

It all came back to him. The battle. The dragon. Flying through the sky. It still didn't feel possible.

Hua?

He had to find Hua.

His eyes darted around the small room as he tried to figure out where he was. Stone walls closed in on him, leaving only enough room for the bed he woke in and a table in the corner beside it.

A clay cup of water sat on the table.

He tried to push himself up again, but his strength failed him, and he flopped back, eliciting another stab of pain.

Feet sounded against the floor like someone running outside the door moments before it opened and a tiny boy sprinted in.

"The soldier's awake!" He grinned, and all Jian could think about were the children who'd never smile again. The ones killed as the town of Kanyuan burned to ash.

The boy approached the bed slowly, pushing curly black hair out of his face. "You're in the emperor's army." He crossed his arms. "Why did we find you in the fields?"

"Boy," an older voice snapped as an ancient looking woman in a simple woolen robe and apron walked in. "Don't bother the man. He needs his rest."

The kid stuck out his bottom lip. "But, Nainai, I just wanted to know—"

"Hush, child. He doesn't need your questions."

"But what happened to—"

"Go. Your baba is heading into town."

The kid's face lit up. "And I can go?"

"If it gets you out from underfoot, away with you."

The injured soldier all but forgotten, the boy ran from the room.

Jian cleared his throat and tried to speak but no words came out.

The older woman moved to the side of the bed and reached for the water. She helped him lift his head and tilted the cup against his lips.

The lukewarm water slid down his throat, and he coughed. "Where… how…"

The woman offered him a kind smile and set the water back on the table. "I can answer the where, but we've been waiting for you to wake for the how." She looked over her shoulder at the door. "Don't mind Ru. He's an excitable child." Her eyes fixed on him again. "You're on a farm outside the village of Zhouchang. We found you collapsed in our field. Tell me, how did you and my granddaughter end up here?"

Granddaughter? "Hua." Alarm washed over him. "Is she okay?"

Her face fell. "We do not yet know. She hasn't woken up."

"Did you say she was your granddaughter?"

She nodded. "That girl is the light of my life. If she doesn't wake up… Please, young man, tell me what has happened."

"The dragon brought her home." The words were no more than a whisper on his lips. What did that mean? Why did the dragon fly here?

The woman's eyes widened and glistened with unshed tears. "Oh. I had hoped she'd have longer to prepare herself."

"You knew?" The words were an accusation, but he couldn't help the anger rolling through him. Hua wouldn't have wanted this, and he didn't believe she knew what was going to happen at that battle. If she had, she could have been ready. He could have helped her.

But how did one ready themselves to let a dragon take control of their mind and body?

The older woman buried her face in her hands. "My poor girl."

"Where is she?"

"In my room across the hall. We couldn't carry her up to her own bed." She lifted her eyes to his. "You saw it? The dragon?"

He nodded. "It destroyed an entire city."

She covered her mouth with her hand. "A city?"

"I don't know what it would have done if I hadn't been injured."

"What do you mean?"

He pictured those moments in his mind when he'd thought the Kou warriors were going to kill him. Or when the dragon burned everything around him, leaving him intact.

"She saved my life. Not the dragon. Hua. Somehow..."

"She controlled it," the woman whispered, her pupils dilating. "And then brought you both here. Oh my."

"How could you know what was coming and not warn Hua? She's the fiercest and strongest person I know. She could have found a way to prevent the destruction."

She put a hand on his shoulder. "You care about my

Hua." She smiled. "That will help her in the days to come."

Jian didn't deny it, not even to himself. He'd watched the dragon soar above Kanyuan, destroying at will, and his heart cracked thinking she was gone forever, replaced by a beast. Until she'd fought her way back to him.

Hua's grandmother heaved a sigh and turned back to the door. "I must check on Hua." She stopped with her hand on the doorframe. "This knowledge is dangerous." She hung her head. "If word gets out, people will come for her." She dropped her voice. "They'll all want her destroyed."

Her words caused more pain than any of his wounds because he recognized the truth in them. His own brother would destroy Hua if he ever found out about the dragon.

He met her grandmother's eyes. They were in this together. His need to protect Hua matched hers. Even after what happened in Kanyuan, he couldn't let anyone take her. "I disappeared from the battle with Hua. There is only one thing we must do."

Understanding sparked in her eyes and she nodded. "Everyone you knew must think you are dead. Jian, your old life is over now."

"My old life was over the day a girl walked through fire to save my life. Maybe the new one began when a dragon carried me away."

"That dragon… it's not Hua. We must remember that. We must make sure she knows it too." She offered him one more worried smile and left him to his thoughts.

Jian leaned his head back, picturing her the first day she'd arrived at camp, innocent and unblemished by the evil they'd see together.

If it was the last thing he did, he'd make sure that girl lived. He wouldn't let the dragon destroy her.

**Book Two, Dragon Rebellion, will be here in June!**

# ACKNOWLEDGMENTS

This book was the most difficult I've ever written for many reasons. Partly because the RESEARCH. Oh my gosh, the research. There were times I wanted to tear my hair out. I have never wanted to give up on a book so often.

And in the process, I wrote something I'm immensely proud of, in part because I didn't throw in the towel every time I worried I couldn't possibly do this beautiful culture justice.

But I can't take all the credit for keeping with this story. If it wasn't for my tribe, it would never have been published.

Melissa A. Craven, my editor, my sounding board, my friend. Thank you for telling me (nicely) I had gotten the architecture completely wrong despite my research and helping me fix it (along with telling me I wasn't allowed to quit).

Kimberly Readnour, Michelle Bryan, and Linda

Higgins (And Melissa again) thanks for giving me a retreat to rejuvenate my creativity when I felt it waning. We've been friends for a long time, and I don't know what I'd do without you ladies.

Caitlin, my lovely proof editor and new friend. I can't wait to see the stories you come up with.

I feel like a broken record with how often I thank Daqri of Covers by Combs, but you outdid yourself on this cover. I appreciate you always giving me your best.

Natalie Naudus, the audiobook narrator who brought Hua to life. I'm so thankful to have found you and your voice.

To the wonderful writers of past Mulan stories whether they turned it into plays, movies, novels. You've kept this ancient and beautiful tale alive.

My family never knows when I have a tough writing day because I don't talk about it, but they are able to ease my nerves anyway. Thanks for not getting too annoyed when I shrug off your questions because I'm too embarrassed to talk about my books. Thanks for keeping me eating and making sure I get plenty of water and sunlight just like a beloved plant.

To all the gracious ARC readers, supporters, and cheerleaders out there. You make this feel worth doing.

Thank YOU, the readers who picked up this book whatever your expectations were. You're wonderful, and I'm so thankful to have you along for the ride.

And finally, my creator. He bears my struggles with me and reminds me that I can keep going even on my worst days. He teaches me the gratitude I try to live every day of my life.

# ABOUT M. LYNN

M. Lynn is a USA Today bestselling author of love. Yes, love. Whether it be YA romance (Under Michelle MacQueen), NA romance, or fantasy romance, she loves to make readers swoon.

The great loves of her life to this point are two tiny blond creatures who call her "aunt" and proclaim her books to be "boring books" for their lack of pictures. Yet, somehow, she still manages to love them more than chocolate.

When she's not sharing her inexhaustible wisdom with her niece and nephew, Michelle is usually lounging in her ridiculously large bean bag chair creating worlds and characters that remind her to smile every day - even when a feisty five-year-old is telling her just how much she doesn't know.

*See more from Michelle MacQueen and sign up to receive updates and deals!*

www.michellelynnauthor.com

## ALSO BY M. LYNN

### The Hidden Warrior

**Dragon Rising**

**Dragon Rebellion**

### Fantasy and Fairytales

*Golden Curse*

*Golden Chains*

*Golden Crown*

*Glass Kingdom*

*Glass Princess*

*Noble Thief*

*Cursed Beauty*

### Legacy of Light

*A War for Magic*

*A War for Truth*

*A War for Love*

### Queens of the Fae

**Fae's Deception**

Fae's Defiance

Fae's Destruction

www.ingramcontent.com/pod-product-compliance
Lightning Source LLC
Chambersburg PA
CBHW030526310726
48979CB00010B/1816/J

* 9 7 8 1 9 7 0 0 5 2 7 0 1 *